TAKE ME THERE

TAKE ME THERE

CAROLEE DEAN

Simon Pulse

New York London Toronto Sydney

SIMON PULSE

An imprint of Simon & Schuster Children's Publishing Division
1230 Avenue of the Americas, New York, NY 10020
First Simon Pulse paperback edition July 2010
Copyright © 2010 by Carolee Dean
All rights reserved, including the right of reproduction
in whole or in part in any form.
SIMON PULSE and colophon are registered trademarks
of Simon & Schuster, Inc.
For information about special discounts for bulk purchases,
please contact Simon & Schuster Special Sales at 1-866-506-1949
or business@simonandschuster.com.
The Simon & Schuster Speakers Bureau can bring authors
to your live event. For more information or to book an event contact
the Simon & Schuster Speakers Bureau at 1-866-248-3049
or visit our website at www.simonspeakers.com.
Designed by Mike Rosamilia
The text of this book was set in Tyfa ITC.
Manufactured in the United States of America
2 4 6 8 10 9 7 5 3
Library of Congress Control Number 2009033514
ISBN 978-1-4169-8950-9
ISBN 978-1-4391-5743-5 (eBook)
Excerpts from The Mermaid, A Man Young and Old, and
Two Songs from a Play by W.B. Yeats.
Reprinted with the permission of Scribner, a Division of Simon &
Schuster, Inc., from THE COLLECTED WORKS OF W.B. YEATS,
VOLUME I: THE POEMS, REVISED edited by Richard J. Finneran.
Copyright © 1928 by The Macmillan Company; copyright
renewed © 1956 by Georgie Yeats. All rights reserved.

For Sal and Calle Treppiedi—
thanks for everything you do to promote poetry for teens;
and for the educators, lawmakers, and poets who try to make
the world a better place for the youth of today who will
become the leaders of tomorrow.

MY FATHER

I know two things about him.
He's locked away
down there in Texas,
I've heard my mother say.
She only talks about him
when she's full of wine.
His name is Dylan Dawson,
same as mine.

1

DARKEST PLACE I'VE EVER BEEN.

Middle of the California desert. No lights for miles. Another hour to Needles.

Wade watches the road behind us in the side mirror. Baby Face thumps her tail. Looks out the back window, growling at every shadow. The three of us need sleep, but we won't rest until we make it to Arizona.

I want to kill Wade. He is my best friend, but I want to rip off his head and leave his body on the highway for the vultures and wild dogs. I understand why he did what he did, but I had three months at a good job. I was turning myself around. I had a girl. I had a future.

Not anymore.

I remind myself how Wade saved my life in juvie. It's the only thing that stops me from leaving him on the side of the road.

We ride with the windows open because the air conditioner is busted. Still feels like we're traveling in an oven. Watch the temperature gauge. Radiator has a leak. Gallon jug of water in the backseat in case the engine overheats.

I strain my eyes to keep them focused on the white reflective lines so the Mustang won't fly off the blacktop. At least there's a full moon, but it makes my eyes play tricks on me. Every time I pass a cactus I think it's a man with a gun standing outside in the sand. A shining reflection becomes the glint of a badge ... or a barrel.

I remember the rage in Eight Ball's eyes. He'll come looking for us. Of that I'm sure. My only comfort is that he doesn't know where we're heading. I didn't tell anyone. Not even Jess or Mom. Better that way.

If they are lucky, they will forget about me.

I still have Jess's note in my back pocket. I don't know why she ever fell for a guy like me. What must she be thinking now? Will she hear about me on the news?

And my mother. How will she react when the police come looking for me? It almost killed her when I went to juvie last time.

I realize I'm pushing the gas and have to force my foot to relax.

Keep it slow. Don't draw attention. Remember to breathe.

I've got to put some highway behind us, but we can't afford to get pulled over. If a cop checks my license or registration, he'll notice the plates I lifted from the Volkswagen in San Bernardino.

Wade and I don't speak. There isn't much to say after what has happened.

I try to stick my head out the window, hoping for a blast of cool wind to revive me, keep me awake, but it doesn't help. All the air has gone out of the world. I cannot breathe. The night is an endless sea of desert and blackness. I clutch the steering wheel—my life preserver—though I'm not sure anything can save me now.

"You're goin' kinda fast." Wade mumbles the first words he's uttered in four hours.

I look at the speedometer and see I've edged past eighty. Ease my foot off the gas. Take a deep breath. Can't let my thoughts go wandering. Have to make it to Arizona. Then we can pull into a rest stop and grab a couple hours' sleep.

"I didn't think it would go down like it did." Wade looks at me.

I want to scream and tell him what an idiot he is, that as usual, he didn't *think* at all. But he already looks like a puppy expecting to get beat—slouching in his seat, head hanging, greasy blond bangs covering his eyes, trying to make himself small.

Wade has made an art out of trying not to be seen or heard. Something he learned from living with an alcoholic stepfather. Wade came to stay with me and Mom when he was fourteen, after his stepdad pushed him down a flight of stairs and broke three of his ribs. He is part of my family. The only brother I've ever known.

"Don't worry," I finally tell him. "It's all gonna work out." I know this is a blatant lie. We are both screwed, and only time will tell just how totally screwed we are, but Wade seems to take comfort in my words. Sits up a little taller. Smiles. "Want some corn nuts?" he asks, tilting the half-empty bag that is his dinner toward me.

"No thanks," I say, but Baby Face sticks her head into the front seat between us and licks his chin, eager for a snack. Wade gives her some food and scratches her ears.

"How long till we cross the border?" I ask him.

Wade wipes his hands on his jeans, turns on the overhead light, unfolds the map, and traces a long red line. "Little over an hour. From there Flagstaff's another two hundred miles and Albuquerque's three hundred more. Hey, look! The Grand Canyon is just north of Flagstaff. Wanna go?"

He's grinning like a little kid. It takes so little to make Wade happy. Sometimes I envy him. "We'll see," I say. I am *not* taking a detour to the Grand Canyon, but there's no reason to disappoint him just yet.

Wade turns back to the map. "We'll take I-40 all the way to Amarillo, then catch Highway 27 south through Lubbock. After that it's 87 to Fredericksburg, 290 to Brenham, then ten miles north to Quincy. You sure your grandma won't mind us staying with her?"

"I'm sure." I haven't seen my grandmother in over a decade. Can't expect her to shelter two guys on the run, but I don't want to worry Wade. I just hope Levida will tell me how to find my father.

Dylan Sr. has been a guest of the Texas Department of Corrections for eleven years, since I was six. I don't know where exactly. Don't even know what he did. Mom cries if I ask her too many questions, so I quit asking.

I wanted so badly to make her proud and not disappoint her the way my father had done, but some things aren't meant to be.

I *will* find my father. Then I will understand why I am the way I am. Why it is that no matter how hard I try to stay away from trouble, it always finds me.

THE GIRL WITH SEA GREEN EYES

Happiness is

S	I	M	N
W	M	I	G

in the ocean of her eyes.

2

HOW DO YOU KNOW WHERE A STORY BEGINS? I COULD START with the night I killed Two Tone, but even if I described how Eight Ball's gang came after us, ten against two, you still might shake your head like a tired judge who has heard too many pleas of innocence.

When it is so clear I'm anything but innocent.

I could start with what happened in juvie that made Wade the way he is and put me in debt to him for the rest of my life, or tell you how we never thought we'd do time for chopping cars, until we jacked a CD player out of a Honda one of Eight Ball's gang had used in a hit-and-run.

I could go back to the day I dropped out of school and my uncle Mitch said he could get me a job with his old friend Jake, who owned a car lot in East L.A., and how Jake taught Wade and me a way to make some quick, easy money.

I could explain how I first met Eight Ball and how before we knew it, Wade and I had become associates of the Baker Street Butchers (BSB).

I could go back even further to when I was six years old and my father went to prison and how after that I couldn't stay on the right side of anything.

I could even start with my father and tell you what led him to a life of crime, except for the fact that I don't know.

And back there somewhere there's probably another story about his father and his grandfather, what kind of men they were and what made them that way.

I could keep going back and back and back until I got all the way to Cain and Abel and Adam, but I won't bore you with the history of the world.

Instead I'll start with a girl named Jess.

I was twelve years old the first time I met Jessica Jameson. I'd gotten busted for lifting a pair of sunglasses from a grocery store when my mother decided to give up singing in nightclubs to become the assistant choir director at a church in Long Beach in an effort to give me a stable home life. Of course, she had to lie about her references, which wasn't a good start.

When I first heard Jess sing, I thought she was an angel. I actually believed I could become a good person if I was allowed to just sit and listen to her voice.

Jess got the lead role in a musical at Holy Faith called *The Starz of Bethlehem*. One Sunday afternoon, about an hour after rehearsal had ended, Mom and I were starting to leave when we spotted Jess sitting alone in the foyer. She jumped up when she saw us heading for the door. "Wait!" she called out to us. "Don't lock me inside."

"Oh, I didn't realize anybody was still here," Mom said.

"My mom just sent me a text. She had to show a house in

Paramount. She'll be here in fifteen minutes. I can wait outside." She started for the door.

Jess was always the last kid to get picked up. Usually long after the others had gone. My mother and I shared a look.

"I completely forgot," Mom said. "I can't leave. I haven't catalogued the new sheet music. Dylan, stay here with Jess while I run back to the office for a few minutes."

The relief in Jess's eyes was plain to see, and I silently thanked God for my mother.

While we waited, I entertained Jess by beat boxing and rapping my own lyrics for the Christmas musical.

Away in a manger, no crib to call home.
The boy is in danger and Mom's on the roam.
She has a hard time explaining the truth about Dad.
So don't ask no questions. Too much truth can be bad.

My singing was so awful Jess laughed her head off, and it sure felt good to make her smile. It was another hour before her mother finally pulled up in front of the church in her Volvo.

Mom never said a word about Jess or her parents, but she made it a point to have lots of cataloging to do when practice was over. Jess and I started hanging out every Wednesday and Sunday night, making up our own version of the Christmas story. Unfortunately, Mom's job didn't last long. She soon discovered how nosy church people can be.

We relocated to West Covina, and after a few more moves I found myself at Downey High School, where I met Wade the spring of my sophomore year. I was taking a nap in the theater one day while I ditched English, when I looked up and saw Jess on the stage. I had to pinch myself, because I figured either I was dreaming or else I'd died and gone to heaven—which given my history was probably not where I'd end up.

She was even prettier than I'd remembered her, with hair that glistened like fire when the stage lights hit it just right, and bright green eyes. She'd gotten the role of Maria in *West Side Story*. That April I went to every single rehearsal. Wade gave me shit when I bought the soundtrack and started singing along to all the songs, but I didn't care.

"Dude, there should be a law against people singing that bad."

"Bite me."

Day after day, I watched Jess in the theater and sitting at lunch with her rich friends. It was enough just to see her smile at them and pretend she was smiling at me. I don't ask girls out. I can't take the rejection and there's usually no need. The sorts of girls I date are happy to make the first move. And the second . . . and the third.

That was never going to happen with Jess. Girls like her don't go for troublemakers like me.

The final night of *West Side Story*, Jess finished singing "There's a Place for Us," and the entire audience gave her a standing ovation even though it was in the middle of the show. We were all thinking the same thing: how we were all going to be able to tell our friends, *I knew her when* . . .

Afterward I finally worked up the nerve to talk to her. She was standing outside waiting for a ride, holding a bouquet of roses, the stage makeup still coloring her cheeks. Kids all around her, pressing in like she was some kind of rock star.

"Jess," I said, but not too loud, so she could pretend to ignore me if she wanted. I wasn't sure if she'd even remember me. I'd changed a lot in three years and not for the better.

She turned around. Looked at me funny for a minute. "Dylan?"

"Yeah," I said, and then I looked away so that she could go back to talking to her friends if she didn't want to talk to me.

But she pushed past them and grabbed my hand. "Dylan! I haven't seen you in forever. Where have you been?"

I didn't think where I'd been was a topic for civil conversation, since I already had a file down at juvenile court, so I just said, "I go to Downey High now."

"Really? Do you have A lunch or B lunch?"

"B."

"Me too. I sit by the pizza window. Come find me. We'll catch up."

"Okay," I said, even though I knew I'd never fit in with her crowd.

"Wow, it's really good to see you." She looked excited, but I figured that was because of the play and all the attention she was getting.

"Jessica!" a voice yelled, and I looked up to see Jess's mother pulling up to the curb in a convertible Mercedes.

"I've got to go, but find me at lunch," Jess said. Then she got into the car.

"Who's *that*?" Jess's mother asked, looking at my long hair and baggy jeans.

"Mother, that's Dylan!" Jess said, looking back at me to see if I had heard the disapproval in her mother's voice, and I looked away—pretending that I hadn't.

The following Monday I stayed as far away from the pizza window as possible. I even avoided the theater and went to English for the first time in two months. Mrs. Bates, who was none too happy about me ditching her class, called on me to read out loud from *Great Expectations*.

I was fifteen years old and until that moment had been able through lying, sulking, avoiding, complaining, acting like a badass, and convincing my girlfriends to do my homework, to hide the fact that I couldn't read, at least not well enough to keep up with school. We'd never stayed in one place long enough for me to learn.

So I did the only reasonable thing I could think of. I threw the book on the floor and said, "This class is bullshit." Then I walked out of the room.

There was a wrought iron fence surrounding the school. The back gates were locked and the front was guarded by security, so I had to lay low until school was out. It was during that hour of watching the front gate and trying to avoid the campus police that I came to realize that a school is just another type of prison.

I decided getting a job would be a better use of my time. We were always short on money. Uncle Mitch got me the position with Jake. My uncle owns a used car lot in La Puerta, Texas, and he brings shipments of cars to Jake, who can sell them in California for higher prices.

Wade, who was already living with me and Mom, finished out the spring at Downey High and then started working with me at Jake's. He never went back to school, though, because by the time August came around, we were in juvie.

Wade got his GED while we were in jail. I have to give him credit for that. We got out in March, and I was sure I'd never see Jess again, but then she came into my life for the third time, and that's when I began to believe that maybe destiny didn't always have to be something bad.

3

IT WAS LATE JUNE AND ALREADY SO HOT THE NEWSCASTERS were talking about rolling blackouts and power shortages. Wade and I were working at Gomez & Sons, jobs our probation officer, Mr. Grey, had gotten for us, hoping we might put our knowledge of cars to some lawful use. I have a natural talent for tearing things apart and putting them back together, and Gomez was training me to be a mechanic. Wade, who only has a talent for tearing things apart, was still sweeping floors, cleaning toilets, changing tires, and doing a piss-poor job of it.

While Gomez was yelling at him for forgetting to tighten the lug nuts on a Taurus, I took the opportunity to slip out of my sweat-drenched work shirt and hang it next to the Allen wrenches to dry. I was wearing a white tank top underneath, but I knew Gomez would tell me to put the shirt back on if he saw me. He is a proud and meticulous man. Not a tool out of place or a dirty rag left dangling. Gomez used to be a rich man. Years ago he owned a ranch down in Guatemala, before the government took it and he came to the United States as a political exile.

"You want the tires to fall off out on Rosecrans Avenue? You want someone to get hurt? You want me to get sued?" Gomez asked Wade, pointing at the Taurus.

"No, sir," Wade said, hanging his head, the posture he assumed even when he wasn't in trouble.

"What am I going to do with you? And pull up those pants. You think our customers want to know the color of your underwear?"

"No, sir," Wade said, tightening his belt.

I could tell Gomez was nearing the end of his rope with Wade. I couldn't blame him. Wade was a constant screwup. But he needed the job. It was a condition of our probation. Besides, he tended to get into trouble when he had too much free time.

Lucky for my friend, a man came into the shop looking for Gomez. Baby Face, who I kept chained in a corner, instantly sprang to her feet and started growling. She's really a pushover, but she's half Rottweiler and looks fierce. Gomez doesn't mind having her around. He even posted a sign, WARNING: GUARD DOG, on the window out front. His shop is in south Downey, but it borders on Compton and break-ins are pretty regular.

"Is that an attack dog?" the man asked Gomez.

"Yep," he replied.

"Down," I told Baby Face. She sat, but kept her eyes locked on the well-tanned stranger, who took a step in the opposite direction.

"My Mercedes is making a strange noise," the man said.

Gomez forgot about Wade and turned to Kip, the head mechanic. They shared a smile. One of a mechanic's greatest joys is listening to people describe the "funny noises" their cars make. Gomez usually knew within five seconds what was wrong with an automobile, but he liked to have a little fun with people.

"Describe the noise," Gomez said.

The poor man was sputtering and coughing like a backfiring engine when all of a sudden Max from M & M Towing came walking in, followed by Jess, wearing a bathing suit covered by some kind of wrap knotted around her waist.

I nearly dropped the battery I was changing.

"Got a dead Beemer," said Max, pointing out the bay at the car on the tow truck.

"I'll take care of this one," I told Kip.

He looked at Jess and smiled. "I bet you will."

Jess pushed her bangs out of her blazing green eyes. They looked like they were on fire. "There was a wreck on Rosecrans Avenue, and traffic got detoured onto a side street. All of a sudden my car just stopped. Right in the middle of Compton! My cell phone went dead and I didn't know what to do. Thank goodness a cop stopped and helped me call for a tow."

I tried to picture Jess, dressed the way she was, waving down low riders in the middle of Gangstaville, California.

Max went outside and started backing the Beemer into an empty bay while I set down the battery. It could wait till later. "I'm supposed to meet some friends at Soak City over in Buena Park in half an hour," Jess said frantically. "What do you think is wrong with my car? It just died. Do you think this will take long? Can you fix it? Will it be expensive? Wait, are you laughing at me?"

A huge grin had spread across my face. I couldn't believe it. Here she was, Jessica Jameson, standing right in front of me. Eyes on fire. Hands waving. Beads of perspiration forming on her neck. "I'm not laughing," I said, trying to flatten my grin.

Recognition turned her eyes from flaming emerald to deep sea green. "Dylan?"

"Yeah," I said. I wanted to swim in those eyes.

"Dylan, what happened to you? I saw you that night outside the theater and then you just disappeared."

"Something came up. I had to quit Downey High."

"Me too. My family moved to Hermosa Beach last November."

Hermosa Beach was even farther away from my world than north Downey.

Jess narrowed her eyes and tilted her head, studying me. I could feel my heart pumping as she checked out my chest, and I wished I hadn't taken off the blue work shirt. Did she think I was a slob, or was she impressed with my build? I'm pretty muscular. You have to have a strong upper body to work on cars all day, though I didn't think that was the sort of thing that would impress a girl like Jess. I hoped she couldn't see how hard it was for me to breathe.

I put my arms behind my back, not wanting her to notice the crude tattoo on my right hand. Caught my reflection in the side mirror of a Lexus. God, I looked like one of those muscle dudes puffing out his chest on the cover of *Iron Man*. I quickly folded my arms in front of myself and tried to remember to breathe.

"Wow," she said. "Do you work out?"

"Just here in the garage," I said. "I like to bench-press the batteries." Stupid thing to say. How could I be so lame? Why didn't I ever know what to say to girls?

When she realized she was staring, Jess blushed and turned away. I don't know why, but I found her even more beautiful just then. I wasn't used to girls who blushed.

"You cut your hair," she said. "I almost didn't recognize you. I like it. You have nice eyes."

Baby Face barked at Mercedes man, who was making a grinding noise even though nobody was listening to him anymore. Jess turned around. "A Rottweiler," she said, walking over and scratching Baby Face behind the ears. My ferocious attack hound instantly starting wagging her tail and licking Jess. "He's beautiful," she said.

"She. Her name is Baby Face."

"Like the gangster?" Jess asked, and I felt like an idiot again. Why did I ever name my dog after a bank robber?

"Sort of." I shrugged.

Baby Face plopped herself down at Jess's feet and stuck her belly in the air, and Jess scratched her.

"Some guard dog," Mercedes Man remarked.

"Hey, quit that," I said to Jess. "We got reputations to uphold."

Jess stood up and smiled at me with the same crooked, one-sided grin I'd seen her use a hundred times, but this time it made me feel weak and helpless, because this time she was smiling at me. "What kind of reputations?"

"You don't wanna know." All of a sudden I was wishing I'd stuck with changing the battery and given Kip the Beemer. My palms were sweating something awful, and I was afraid that if Jess hung around while I worked on her car, I'd pull a Wade. That's what Kip called it when the mechanics screwed up. "You should probably wait up front while I take a look at your car. There's air conditioning and a soda machine."

"Okay," she said, and headed for the front of the shop.

"You have nice eyes," Wade said in a high-pitched girly voice, as soon as she was gone.

"Shut up!"

"Now that is a girl with class," said Gomez.

"How can you tell?" I asked. He'd seen her all of five minutes.

"Look how clean she keeps her car." Gomez smiled and pointed to the interior of the Beemer.

"What about my funny noise?" asked Mercedes Man.

"Quit using cheap gas. Things of value require special care." Gomez gave me a sideways glance. "And put on your shirt," he told me, "before I have a whole crowd of girls lined up in here buying tickets to look at your muscles."

"Yes, sir." I slipped on the blue shirt and got to work on the car.

Thirty minutes later I walked up front to find Jess reading a magazine. "All done," I said.

"That was fast."

"It was just a broken serpentine belt."

"How much will that cost?" She sounded worried, which surprised me.

"A hundred and thirty," I said, wishing I could just tear up her bill.

"That's all?"

"It was a quick job, and belts are cheap," I replied, relieved that she seemed happy.

"My car is due for its thirty-thousand-mile service. Do you do that?"

"Sure."

"What would that cost?"

"I don't know. Foreign car. Probably three hundred."

"That's all?"

"Could go a little higher if we ran into any problems."

"The dealership in Hermosa Beach said it would cost me at least seven hundred."

I shrugged, trying to stay cool, even though the desire to see her again was suddenly overwhelming.

"How long would it take?"

"Better part of a day. We're closed tomorrow, but if you bring your car back Monday morning, I could get on it first thing."

"I have a class in Hermosa Beach that starts at eight, but . . ."

I wanted to offer to pick up her car, drive her back to Hermosa Beach, take her to the moon.

"If I could save four hundred dollars, I could probably get a ride. . . . Okay, yeah. I'll bring it back Monday."

"It's a date then," I told her, before I realized what I was saying.

She smiled at me again, eyes shining. I thought about death by drowning and decided that when my time came, that's how I wanted to go.

4

WE STOP IN NEEDLES FOR GAS. IT'S THE LAST TOWN before we hit Arizona.

Wade takes Baby Face out for a walk so she can stretch her legs and do her business. Then he puts her back into the car and goes into the 7-Eleven to buy more corn nuts.

I put water in the radiator while the gas is pumping.

A cop car pulls in and slowly snakes its way around the station.

Hold my breath as I replace the radiator cap.

Lots of people must travel the desert at night. Too hot during the day. But where are they? The Mustang is the only car at the pumps.

Cop looks in my direction.

The numbers on the gas gauge move in slow motion.

The air is so hot and dry and still, it feels like time has stopped.

What's taking Wade so long?

I see him through the window flirting with the chubby girl working the counter.

Why won't the pump go faster?

The cruiser moves toward me in slow motion.

The girl at the counter laughs and tosses back her hair. *Come on, Wade. Hurry up. Let's get out of here!*

It takes all my self-control not to yank the nozzle out of the tank and jump in the Mustang.

Baby Face sticks her head out the window and growls.

"Easy, girl."

The cop rolls past us so slowly I can't tell if he's still moving.

I am hyperaware of the *chuk, chuk, chuk* of numbers rolling, time not passing fast enough.

Cop looks at me. Looks at the car. Looks at Baby Face.

I force myself to glance up and smile. Give a little wave.

Wonder if he's calling in the license plate number.

The cop moves on and pulls out of the station.

Snap! I jump at the sound. Realize it's just the pump clicking off.

Try to breathe. Finish with the gas. Get back in the car.

Collapse behind the wheel. Arms and legs shaking. Covered in sweat.

"I got her phone number," Wade says, slipping into the passenger seat and waving a piece of paper at me, smiling like he just won the California lottery.

"Whose phone number?" My voice is trembling, but Wade doesn't seem to notice.

"Amy," he says, reading the name scrawled on the paper in purple ink.

"Who?"

"The girl at the counter."

I look back through the window at the girl, who is waving

at Wade. She blows him a kiss through teeth covered in metal braces.

"Wade, we're never coming back here. Not in a hundred years."

"So?" he says, tracing the numbers with his fingertips.

I am tempted to bash in his head, but then I think of Jess and remember a time I would have been content just to hold her number in my hand.

"Let's get out of here," I tell him.

But Wade doesn't hear me. He's sniffing the paper.

"She smelled like cherries," he says as I drive off into the night.

MY MOTHER

Drink

away your yesterday.

Don't think

about tomorrow.

Escape a world

of sorrow

I cannot understand.

5

AFTER JESS LEFT THE GARAGE, I SPENT THE REST OF THAT
Saturday smiling and humming tunes from *West Side Story*.

When work was over, Wade told me he was going to get
some brews with Nathan, another guy from the shop. "Come
with us," he offered. "It's been a long week."

"Drinking is a violation of our probation," I reminded him.
Truth was, when we were forced to give up liquor and pot in
lockup, it scared me how hard it was. Once my head cleared,
I swore to never go back to the stuff, and I didn't, even when
Wade found some guys who were fermenting liquor out of fruit
they took from the commissary.

"We ain't gonna get caught," he said.

"That's what we said about working for Jake."

Wade rolled his eyes. "Do what you want. I'm goin' with
Nathan."

"Suit yourself." For someone who lived in constant fear of
returning to jail, he sure wasn't doing much to avoid it.

I put Baby Face in the backseat of the Mustang and was

relieved we were alone. On Saturdays I liked to relax by cranking up the stereo and cruising the coastline. When Wade came along, he always turned down the volume so he could talk.

I thought about going to Hermosa Beach, but decided against it. Instead I headed north on the 405 and took Santa Monica Boulevard. Finally ended up on the Pacific Coast Highway, playing the music so loud the speakers started rattling. Baby Face sat in the backseat with her head on my shoulder while I sang along to the music.

Mom let it slip once that my father's favorite song was "Dream On." Sometimes I played just that one song, over and over, singing along until my throat went dry, trying to imagine I was in my father's skin. Trying to figure out what kind of man he was.

But not on that night. I took out Aerosmith and exchanged it for *West Side Story* and "There's a Place for Us." I remembered Jess, standing up on stage singing that song, and how the whole auditorium went crazy with applause. And now she was back in my life. Okay, maybe I was just the guy who fixed her car, but that was enough.

By the time I turned around and headed home, the sun was setting over the ocean, a huge ball of fire sinking into the sea, leaving streaks of red and gold like a melting candle. I thought of Jess, how being near her made me feel like liquid wax, and from somewhere inside of me came words: *I know a girl with sea green eyes. . . . She melts the sun, swallows the sky. . . . Then breathes out stars to kiss the night.*

I didn't know where lines like that came from, but sometimes when I was alone, they just popped into my brain. Luckily, I wasn't alone much. It could be embarrassing, not to mention dangerous, if guys found out I had stuff like that in my head.

I turned up the music, trying to turn off whatever channel those words were coming from, and looked back out the window at the sun. I know they say you shouldn't do that. It will make you blind. But I've never been good at following rules. Besides, I was wondering if that was what the eye of God looked like and if he slept when the sun went down, 'cause it sure didn't seem like he was on the job a lot of the time.

When I finally got home, it was dark. I parked out front and went inside to find my mother in the living room, singing along to the CD player and dancing with a bottle in her hand.

She must have gotten the check from Uncle Mitch. It came once a month, and once a month she would splurge on a bottle of Crown Royal, play "Fly Me to the Moon," and wallow in self-pity.

He sent us a thousand bucks a month and then charged Mom six hundred to rent the house. I knew that was a steal in Southern California, even if the place was a cracker box, but I never understood why he didn't just send four hundred and call it a day. He said it was the principle of the thing. He'd bought the house hoping my mother would stay put for a while.

I walked into the kitchen with Baby Face and poured three cans of chili into a pot. Filled a dog bowl with Purina. Baby Face sat at my feet whimpering and wouldn't touch her bowl until I poured chili on her food.

"You're gonna spoil that dog."

Mom was standing in the doorway, holding the half-empty bottle of bourbon, wearing a summer dress, hair falling softly on her shoulders.

"Did you eat?" I set two bowls on the table. I knew she hadn't.

Mom put the bottle on the table, sat down, and covered her face with her hands. Started to cry. I grated cheese to go on top of her chili. "You'll feel better if you eat something."

"I was going to be an opera singer. Did I ever tell you that? I studied Mozart and Stravinsky at the University of Texas. I'm not just barroom trash, you know."

"Want some crackers?"

She didn't answer, so I sat down next to her and crumbled saltines into her bowl.

"Then I met your father."

I held my breath for a minute. I was well aware that Dylan Sr. was the source of her unhappiness, but she rarely talked about him.

"He promised me the moon. I believed he could deliver it. God, you should have seen him in college."

"He went to college?" I never pictured my father as being university material.

"He had this way of talking about dreams as if they really could come true. He said he was going to take me to New York City. Instead I ended up on his parents' pig farm in Quincy, Texas." Mom took another long drink from the bottle. "I was in the chorus of *Carmen* with the Houston opera when I was eighteen, and by the time I turned twenty I was three months pregnant, living in a single-wide trailer."

I knew it was just the liquor talking, but I couldn't help but think about how I'd helped ruin her life just by being born.

Mom set the bottle back on the table and I coaxed the spoon to her lips. She took a bite and then cried some more and blew her nose into her napkin.

"How about I read to you from Yeats? You always like that."

She dried her eyes on her napkin and tried to smile. "That would be nice."

I helped Mom back into the living room to the threadbare sofa. Then I took *Poetry Through the Ages* out of the stack of plastic milk crates she used as a bookshelf, found my reading glasses, pulled a chair up beside her, and pretended to read from the section of the book dedicated to William Butler Yeats.

My uncle Mitch has a saying, "Cozy up to the things that scare you. Snuggle up next to 'em and then bite off their damn heads." Uncle Mitch has a lot of sayings, most of which can't be repeated in civilized company. You have to sift through a lot of junk, but occasionally there's a gem of wisdom in the trash heap.

I took that one to heart and started cozying up to books. No one would think of accusing a guy of being illiterate when he's got himself a book of poetry. The reading glasses were another trick. I didn't need them, but they came in handy whenever somebody asked me to read something. I would just say I couldn't find my glasses.

"Do 'The Stolen Child' on page twenty-two," Mom told me.

I turned to page twenty-two, though I knew the poem by heart. I had for years. Mom never read me Dr. Seuss or *Hop on Pop*. When I was little she read me Yeats, Dickinson, Walt Whitman, and Robert Frost, over and over. So many times their words burned paths through my memory. We'd sit on the threadbare sofa of whatever dive we were living in, listening to the police sirens going by every few minutes. Mom always said we'd be rich as long as we had poetry.

"The key is in Yeats," she said. Mom told me that whenever she got drunk. I had no idea what it was supposed to mean. "Fourteen, thirty-eight, twenty-two. Remember those numbers." They were her three favorite poems; the pages were dog-eared with their numbers circled. She patted my hand and nodded her head to emphasize the point, as if this information might save my life someday.

"Okay, Ma," I told her, and then pretended to read from the book, about the fairies of Sleuth Wood who stole children away:

"Come away, O human child!
To the waters and the wild
With a faery, hand in hand,
For the world's more full of weeping than you can
    understand."

Mom squeezed my hand. "You're a good boy, Dylan. I know you've gotten into some trouble, but you have a good heart."

I closed the book and stood up. I couldn't listen to her talk about my "good heart" when she didn't know half the things I'd done. "You sleep now," I told her.

She nodded, and I turned the television on to the Shopping Network, Mom's favorite channel. Then I walked back into the kitchen. Saw the bottle of Crown Royal. Got real thirsty all of a sudden. Decided to pour the whiskey down the drain before it did any more damage.

There was a room at the end of the hallway that used to belong to me and Wade, but while we were in juvie it got taken over with Mom's boxes. When we came back home, we found she had moved all our stuff to the garage, which we had to convert into our current bedroom. I stepped inside the box room, Mom's shrine to order and organization. Testimony to her belief that life could be managed if things were only kept in their proper places.

On the right were all the boxes for the things Mom had

ordered from the Shopping Network—the slicer, the dicer, the blender, the indoor grill, even the fake fur coat, which didn't get much use in Southern California. If and when we moved again, everything would go back into its original container. There were even a few things, like the do-it-yourself car-waxing kit and the fondue machine, that Mom had never opened.

On the left side of the room were stacks of white file boxes, each one labeled with a thick black marker: RECEIPTS, TAX RETURNS, BABY PICTURES, etc.

I hate to admit it, but I liked the box room. Sometimes I would go in there and stand in the middle of the room, just looking at the words on the white boxes. I guess it made me feel good because I could read them. They didn't jump around, fighting with each other for space, like words on a page did.

I grabbed a box marked DYLAN from the top of one of the white rows, set it on the floor, and opened it. Inside were old art projects, report cards from a dozen different schools, a pair of booties, and, at the bottom, something I had hidden.

A map of Texas.

I opened the map, and the lines and words instantly started dancing. I tried to focus until I found Quincy in the bottom right-hand section. Wade had circled the name of the town for me in red ink one afternoon—when I couldn't find my glasses. Then I called information and got the number for my grandmother, Levida Dawson, and had Wade write it on the map so I wouldn't lose it.

Hadn't worked up the nerve to call her yet.

Maybe one day I would just go there and get some answers.

One day I was going to find out what had happened to make everything turn out so wrong.

THE ROAD TO HUNTSVILLE
by D.J. Dawson
University of Texas Press

Prologue

My name is D.J. Dawson—inmate #892. My home is a ten-by-six-foot cell at the Polunsky Unit just outside of Livingston, Texas. There is one metal bunk with a two-inch mattress in this cage I call my home. One stainless-steel sink and a stainless-steel toilet. A small table stacked with books, an electric typewriter, and a small transistor radio.

There is one window, three feet wide and six inches tall, but I can't see outside unless I stand on my bunk, and even then all I get is a view of the guard tower.

I spend twenty-three hours a day in this cell. I eat in this cell, sleep in this cell, shave in this cell, and crap in this cell. I get one hour a day of solitary recreation in a concrete yard surrounded by chain-link fence. I am not allowed to mix with the general prison population. I am not allowed a television or computer or e-mail.

Reading about how I live, you might assume I am some kind of psychopath, the sort of beast that must be locked away from society. But the truth is that I'm not that different from you. Not very different at all.

And that should scare the hell out of you.

6

I AM DREAMING.

It's the same old nightmare.

I try to force myself awake, but I can't.

Something moves me forward, toward the sound of screaming.

I hear fireworks and think it is the Fourth of July, but then I remember it's the middle of winter.

I reach a room with blue curtains, swaying in the breeze coming through a broken window.

The sound of ticking draws my attention to a clock above a door. The ticking gets louder, like the countdown of seconds until a bomb will detonate. Then a door on the clock flies open and a bird bursts through, squawking and screeching. The cackling of the bird mixes with the screams in the room until all I can do is cover my ears and close my eyes while I pray for it to stop.

I sit up, covered in sweat. Look around. Try to get my bearings.

I'm in the Mustang. Wade and Baby Face are curled up together in the backseat.

Look out the front window at a gas pump.

Remember we pulled into a truck stop outside of Kingman.

The memories of last night come back to me.

I think of Jess waiting for me.

No! Stop! She's better off without me, and I have to keep my head together so we can get to Texas. I must find my father. That's all I can think about right now.

I fill up the car, and then I get back on the highway heading east.

Craggy mountains ahead as far as the eye can see.

Before long the highway splits so that the westbound lanes are a good thirty yards away, across a field of juniper and turpentine weed.

No buildings but an occasional mobile home.

No cops. Nobody chasing us.

I let myself breathe and read the signs as I pass.

SPEED LIMIT 75

WATCH FOR ROCKS

NEXT SERVICES 22 MILES

DEER FARM 43 MILES

WATCH FOR ELK

They make me think of my mother's box room. There is distance between the signs, and I find them easy to read. The pleasure and pride I feel surprises me. Not like California, where words lurch out at you from billboards, flashing neon signs, and passing commuter buses. Out here there is enough space between the words.

Words are like people, I think. Put too many of them too close together and they cause trouble.

"Grand Canyon National Park—a hundred and three miles," says Wade, waking up and pointing to a sign. "I never seen the Grand Canyon. We gonna go?" he asks, and I realize this is the first time he's ever been out of Southern California.

"We'll see," I say, not wanting to disappoint him so early in the day.

All I can think about now is finding my father. I will see him and talk to him and know what kind of man he is. Then I will know if badness is in my blood, or if, by some miracle, it is something I can outrun.

7

JESS HAD SAID SHE'D BE BRINGING HER CAR IN EARLY ON
Monday, so I got to work by seven. By the time seven forty-five
came around I was edgy. At eight o'clock she still hadn't showed
up, and I was a lunatic. By eight fifteen I was wishing I still kept
a bottle of Jack Daniels in the trunk of the Mustang.

"Somebody piss on your parade?" Nathan asked me when
I jumped down his throat for asking me to hand him a lug
wrench.

I told him where he could put the lug wrench.

At nine fifteen Gomez left to go to the salvage yard. He
spent every Monday there, looking for cars he could buy cheap,
fix up, and turn for a profit. Five minutes after he left, I was surprised to see Baby Face looking out the front of the garage and
growling. A hopped-up Prelude Si was parking, and a black van
pulled in behind it. My grip around the wrench tightened when
I saw who got out of the car.

Eight Ball.

Eight Ball got his name and his tattoo—the number eight

inked on the back of his shining head—after beating a rival gang member to death with a pool cue. The guy had killed Eight Ball's older brother, Nine Iron, the former leader of the Baker Street Butchers.

After he beat the guy's face to a pulp, Eight Ball put his body on the pool table, tied his arms and legs together behind his back, and shoved an eight ball in his mouth so he'd look like a stuffed pig when his homies found him.

Eight Ball had been the leader of the BSB ever since.

His younger brother, Two Tone, got out of the Prelude, and two guys named Ajax and Spider got out of the van. Eight Ball looked around the exterior of the shop, checking things out—he was always checking things out. Then he walked through the front lobby and into the back of the shop.

"How did they know we were here?" I asked Wade. I didn't even carry a cell phone anymore. That's how paranoid I was that they would find us. I hadn't seen them since that night they brought in the car from the hit-and-run.

"How would I know?" Wade answered, a little too defensively.

"Gomez won't like this," Kip whispered behind me. "If he sees them here . . ."

"He won't see them here." Eight Ball would have been watching the shop. He had to know the old man's routine.

My whole body tensed as Eight Ball walked over and stood in front of the Range Rover. He folded his arms across his massive chest and stood there staring at me. He was wearing a satin tank top, satin workout pants, and more gold chains than I could count. Two Tone, his shadow, took the same pose.

"Break yo'self," Eight Ball told Kip and Nathan.

"What?" said Kip.

"Take a walk," Ajax translated.

Ajax and Spider, the only white guys in the BSB, wore nothing on their upper bodies but shirts of spider web tattoos. A web meant you'd been involved in a plot to kill somebody. Kip and Nathan took one look at their body art and disappeared out the back door.

The really creepy thing about Ajax and Spider was that when they covered up their tattoos, they looked almost respectable. They knew how to dress so they could mix in with a crowd and pick up unsuspecting beach girls—their favorite pastime.

Wade slouched his shoulders and started bopping his head, trying to look like a homie but resembling a plastic Chihuahua on a dashboard. "Wassup, bro?" he said to Eight Ball.

"Ain't nobody told you to talk," Eight Ball said. Then he turned to me. "Thought you might cruise by the hood when you got out."

"We're on probation."

"So's half the set. You been out for a while."

"Three months," I admitted.

"Some reason you been keepin' your distance?"

"Wade and I did our time. We didn't rat." We had stuck to our lame story about finding Ellen Carter's car on the side of the road, even after the DA showed us pictures of the old woman in a coma and I started making bargains with God. Even when she died and the lawyers threatened to charge us with accessory to murder. Wade and I had alibis for the night she got run over, so all we served was eight months in juvie for possession of a stolen vehicle.

Ellen Carter had been an innocent little old lady who ran a

florist shop in El Segundo. Not the type of person you'd expect
to jump out in front of a twenty-year-old Honda Civic, waving
her arms to try to stop a bunch of gangbangers from stealing
her car.

Eight Ball kept staring at me. I didn't understand. We
weren't members of the gang, just associates. Associates came
and went as the gang found them useful.

"We did our time," I repeated.

"Anybody ask you 'bout doin' your time?" yelled Two Tone,
puffing out his scrawny chest and trying to sound like his
brother.

"Don't act the man, Two Tone," Eight Ball reprimanded
him. A smile flickered across Ajax's face, and Two Tone
looked at the floor of the garage, trying to hide his embarrassment. Two Tone should have been second in command, but
Eight Ball wouldn't allow it. After watching his older brother
die, he refused to let the younger one do anything even slightly
dangerous. And so Two Tone was left painting stolen cars,
making fake IDs, and performing other meaningless jobs.

"Wade and Dylan, they been down for the crew," said Eight
Ball. "They kept their lips sewed. We 'preciate that, 'specially
Ajax, since he be the one who ran down the old lady." Eight
Ball threw Ajax a look of disapproval. Eight Ball was dangerous,
but he had a code, and I was pretty sure it didn't include killing
defenseless old women.

Ajax didn't live by any kind of code, which made him more
dangerous than any of the rest of them. "You got a tight little
place here," he said, looking around the garage. "Real clean.
Make for a nice chop shop."

"No!" I said, a little too forcefully. Gomez would die before he'd let the BSB invade what he had built.

"No?" said Eight Ball.

I felt perspiration trickling down my back and wondered if he was planning to kill me. "We're on probation. So are a couple of the other guys. We never know when the cops are gonna roll by." Cops had never come by to check on us, but it was possible.

"I don't think you 'preciate the situation," Eight Ball said, running a finger across the side of the Range Rover. "'Splain it to him, Ajax."

Ajax walked around Wade and me, circling us just like the DA had done. "You two done proved yourself to be stand-up—this time—and we appreciate that." He stopped in front of us. His arms were massive, and I considered how easy it would be for him to kill me with his bare hands. "But what about next time?" he asked me.

"We got a major operation to protect," Eight Ball explained.

"You kept your mouths shut," Ajax continued, "but all you were looking at was some weak-ass time in juvie."

Weak time! We almost got killed in juvie. All because of him. I bit my lip to keep the rage from pouring out.

"What happens next time?" asked Spider. "When you're lookin' at two to ten in County and the DA says 'plea bargain.' You suddenly remember you got the four-one-one on a hit-and-run in your back pocket."

"There won't be a next time," I said, thinking that if I played it cool maybe they wouldn't kill us, just beat the crap out of us to scare us into keeping quiet.

"There's always a next time," said Ajax. "Besides, we can offer you protection if you tatt up." He pointed to the BSB tattoo, and it suddenly dawned on me why they were here. They hadn't come to kill us. They wanted us to join their gang—which was worse.

"Protection?" Wade said, suddenly smiling. He'd talked about protection constantly when we were in juvie, especially after what happened to him. Kept wanting us to run with the white supremacists because he thought they'd watch our backs, even though he knew they were the ones who'd almost killed him. He rationalized that they were just trying to warn us what could happen if we didn't join the Brand. That's what they called themselves.

I saw what happened to their "soldiers." The grunts forced to do the dirty work. The ones most likely to get caught and have additional charges added to their sentence. One guy got sent up at sixteen to serve a year for breaking and entering, but he didn't get out till he was twenty-one because he kept getting re-offended for stuff the Aryans made him do.

Ajax was circling us again. "You get protection, and we know you gon keep your mouths shut. It's a mutually beneficial arrangement."

"No."

Spider got in my face. "What did you say?"

"Dylan, are you crazy?" whispered Wade. "I can't go back to jail. Come on. They can watch our backs."

I'd seen how they took care of people. I knew I was walking a dangerous line, but I also knew that if I didn't stand my ground right now they would own me forever.

"We're goin' legit. There won't be a next time," I said to Spider. "We did right by you, now you do right by us."

Spider's hand was instantly around my throat, closing off my airway so I couldn't breathe. I tried to cough, but nothing happened. Just as my head started to spin, Eight Ball put a hand on Spider's shoulder. "Kid's right. Let him go."

"What?" Spider said.

"Dylan knows he's dead if he talks. Let him go. They got our backs."

Spider loosed his grip on my throat and stormed out of the garage. "Go chill outside with Spider," Eight Ball told Ajax and Two Tone. They glared at him but did what he said. Ajax turned and gave me a look of warning before heading out.

"Go find somethin' to tear apart," Eight Ball ordered Wade. My friend looked at me and shook his head, as if to say, *I warned you*. Then he disappeared out the back door that Kip and Nathan had exited.

Eight Ball looked around at the shop. "This ain't just about rattin' or not rattin'. You got skills," he said. "I 'preciate you wantin' to go legit. Was a time I thought about doin' the same." He glanced out the window at his little brother. Then he locked his eyes on mine. "But the world ain't arranged that way. They say they want you to be different. But nobody gets out of the hood alive. Guys like us got two choices. Kill or be killed. You kick around my offer. It be the best one you ever gonna get. Think about it real hard."

He left, and I looked down at my tightened fist to realize I was still clutching the wrench. I thought about Eight Ball's words and wondered if they were true. Once you stepped a foot on the wrong path, was there no going back? Had the story of my life already been written? And if it had, then how would it end?

THE ROAD TO HUNTSVILLE
by D.J. Dawson

No story of my life would be complete without an explanation of small-town Texas football. In Quincy the whole town revolved around high school football. We knew other things were happening in the world, but come Friday night, they just weren't important.

On Friday nights in Quincy the stores closed their doors and hung up signs that said the owners had gone to the game. Afterward you could get anything you wanted—sex, drugs, booze. A boy could become a god, even if his father was a simple pig farmer.

Or so he was led to believe. And this belief was a dangerous thing, because there was a larger world out there. A world that had never heard of Quincy, Texas.

But there was one teacher who wouldn't make allowances. Her name was Betsy Jones, and she was a brand-new English literature graduate from the big city of Dallas who didn't understand the Quincy Code.

She and I and Coach Rogers, who also doubled as the school principal and the superintendent, sat down for a powwow after my first failed vocabulary test. Miss Jones suggested I stay after school for tutoring. Rogers reminded her of my all-consuming workout schedule and suggested it might be more effective if she modified her tests.

Miss Jones reminded him that her job was to educate me, and that she wouldn't be doing me any favors by letting me slip by. She said that my ability to read and write would long outlive my ability to play football.

She said she knew I could do the work if I only applied myself.

But she was wrong.

I was a high school senior, and I could pick up almost any book in the library and read it out loud, but if you asked me the simplest question about what I had read, I couldn't answer it.

There was nothing afternoon tutoring was going to solve.

I made it through most of that semester by cheating, lying, and keeping enough of my afternoon appointments with Miss Jones to get her off my back.

Until the week of the state championship.

On Monday she gave a pop quiz. On Tuesday she told me I had failed and that according to league rules I couldn't play in the big game. She said she understood how upset I was, but now I had to take her seriously and one day I would thank her.

I went to Coach Rogers in desperation and asked him what could be done.

By Wednesday morning we had a new instructor for senior English. Miss Jones and her stack of pop quizzes just went away.

That Saturday the Quincy Eagles won the state championship against the Doonville Bobcats. A scout from the University of Texas offered me a scholarship to play ball for the Longhorns.

I'd like to say that if I had known how soon my glory days of football would end, I would have made different choices, I would have traded the state championship for the chance at a real education. On the other hand, knowing how people grapple for what little happiness they can find, remembering what it felt like to bask in those stadium lights, I'm pretty sure I would have done things just the same.

8

WHEN WE GET TO THE MOUNTAIN TOWN OF FLAGSTAFF, there are pine trees lining both sides of the highway. A big change from the desert we crossed just last night.

"Grand Canyon, next three exits," Wade says, referring to the map. "It's only ninety miles to the north. We could be there in an hour and a half or less, depending on the roads."

"It's out of the way," I say.

"We don't have to stay long. I just wanna look at it."

"That's an extra three hours drive time, plus looking time."

"Five minutes. I just wanna be able to say I saw it."

"Wade, please."

He folds the map so hard it rips at one of the creases. "It's one of them seven natural wonders of the world. When are we ever gonna get another chance to see somethin' like that?"

"Wade, we're not on vacation."

"You think they're gonna come lookin' for us at the Grand Canyon?"

"Wade!" I say. "We killed somebody last night."

"No," he says quietly. "You killed somebody last night." He shoves the map into the glove box and stares out the window in silence.

THE ROAD

Life isn't a destination.
It's a journey.
But you gotta be
heading somewhere
or you're just a mouse
going round.
Even if
the place you wind up
isn't the place
you were bound.

9

IT WAS THREE O'CLOCK ON MONDAY, TIME FOR ME TO LEAVE and go see my tutor. Working on my GED was a condition of my probation.

It seemed obvious Jess wasn't bringing in her car, but I still had a hard time leaving. Part of me was relieved she hadn't come. I didn't know how to talk to a girl like Jess, and I would only embarrass myself by trying.

Part of me would have done anything to see her again.

I finally packed up, dropped Wade and Baby Face at home, and drove to the community center in north Downey where I was supposed to meet Miss Lane, my reading teacher. It had taken all my nerve to admit to Mr. Grey, my probation officer, that I'd never pass my GED if I couldn't read the test. He was the one who set me up with Miss Lane. Nobody else knew. I told Gomez I had to do community service work on Monday afternoons, and I told Wade I had a girl.

I sat at a little table across from Miss Lane with the copy of *Poetry Through the Ages* that Mom had given me on my sixteenth birthday, which I had spent in juvie.

Miss Lane and I had started with the alphabet, but that wasn't my problem. I understood letters and sounds and I could decipher most words. It was just that when too many of them got together, they started dancing across the page, and when they broke the rules they were supposed to follow, which it seemed they did most of the time, I got completely lost.

I liked poetry, though. More space between the words.

Miss Lane knew I'd memorized poems from my book, so we'd started using those. She made me a special bookmark with a window cut in the middle. That way I could only see a couple of words at a time and they would stay in their places. I was working on "The Stolen Child" and doing a piss-poor job of it.

"'Come away, O human child!/ To the'—"

"One word at a time," she reminded me. I hadn't really been looking, just rattling the verses off from memory. "Look at the first word. Just the first word. C-O-M-E, what does that spell?"

"Come away."

"You're not looking."

I snapped the book shut and slid it across the table. Then I crossed my arms and slumped in my chair like I used to do in school when I wanted the teachers to leave me alone. "This is stupid. We both got better ways to spend our time."

"Have you written any more poetry?"

"I don't *write*."

"Have you *created* any more poetry?"

I shrugged.

"Poetry started as an oral art, you know. Lots of poets never wrote down their verses. Homer created entire epics all in his head."

"I'm no Homer."

"Give me your notebook and I'll write down your new poem." She studied me and smiled. God, she was pretty—and persistent. "I know you have something new. I can see it in your eyes."

"It's personal."

"Excellent! That's the best kind." She reached across the table and grabbed the notebook from in front of me. It was a beautiful leather-bound journal with my name embossed in gold. The first nice thing I bought myself after I got my job with Mr. Gomez, to celebrate my new direction in life and the fact that Wade and I had survived eight months in juvie.

Miss Lane opened to an empty page. "Go on, tell me."

"It's embarrassing."

She held a pen toward me. "Fine, then you write it."

"I can't!"

"You mean you won't."

I could feel my face burning in anger. I remembered a bright red F– I got on a language arts assignment in sixth grade, the red writing all over the paper, and the boy who snatched it off my desk and waved it around the class, laughing, for everyone to see.

He wasn't laughing after I broke his nose.

Miss Lane thumbed through the twenty or so poems written in her hand. I'd come with at least one a week for the past three months. Mostly short, rhymey, and sappy, but I was proud of them.

"You haven't written anything," she said. "That was your homework assignment. One line. That was all I asked."

The leather journal was beautiful and perfect. There wasn't a single word in my handwriting. It wasn't right putting my chicken scratch next to her well-formed letters.

"I got it at home," I lied.

"Fine. Bring it next week. But this is the last thing I'm writing for you. From now on you do it yourself." She sat with pen poised.

"Whatever," I said, but she'd won again, so I figured the sooner I got it over with, the better. "I know a girl with sea green eyes. She melts the sun, swallows the sky, then breathes out stars to kiss the night so guys like me will have some light."

I felt like an idiot sitting there reciting a poem about one girl to another one. Besides, what had sounded clever in my head sounded stupid coming out of my mouth.

"Is there more?"

I took a deep breath and continued. "She doesn't know the things I've done, the places that I've been. But if a girl like that could love me . . ."

Miss Lane kept writing, and then looked up. I felt naked all of a sudden. The kind of naked you feel when you're showering in gym class and all the guys around you seem to have more equipment than you do. I wished I'd never bought the stupid notebook. Wished I didn't have words dancing around in my head, banging on my skull, looking for a way out.

"That's all," I lied.

"No, it's not. Don't be afraid to say how you feel, Dylan. Holding things inside is what gets people into trouble."

My mind flashed back to when I was a little kid and I wasn't allowed to talk about my father. When the pressure built too much, I'd start tearing things up. Like the time I was eight and stuck a firecracker inside the neck of my neighbor's Baywatch Barbie just so I could watch its head blow off. I thought about how words were building up inside of me the same way. How badly I needed to see what was in my head on the page, even if I could barely read it.

Maybe Miss Lane was right. I took a deep breath and continued. "She doesn't know the things I've done, the places that I've been. But if a girl like that could love me, I might be clean again."

I looked at my hands, rough and grease-stained, and knew Jess would never see me as anyone but the guy who fixed her car. Even so, every time I thought of her it seemed like the black stain covering my soul was fading.

When I looked up, Miss Lane was staring at me.

She pulled a thin paperback book out of her briefcase and slid it across the table to me. "It's called *Black Mesa Poems*, and it's by a poet from New Mexico named Jimmy Santiago Baca. He taught himself to read in prison."

"How?" I couldn't imagine anyone teaching himself to read, much less in prison.

"I don't know. I guess his passion finally outweighed his fear," she told me, and then she was gone, leaving me sitting alone with my journal and a book of poems I couldn't read.

THE ROAD TO HUNTSVILLE
by D.J. Dawson

When you are locked alone in a cell twenty-three
hours a day with no television or computer,
there isn't much to do to pass the time.

An inmate comes by with a cart full of books
every Tuesday, and for the first year, I just
watched him pass. The second year I started
checking out books. The third year, I actually
started reading them, mostly crime novels and
adventure stories, even a few trashy romance
novels. The fourth year they started making
sense. The fifth year I got interested in nonfiction.
The sixth year I tackled THE AUTOBIOGRAPHY
OF MALCOLM X. By the end of my seventh year
I had read everything in the prison library and
started making requests for books to be brought
in from outside.

The eighth year I started writing.

One of the first things I wrote was a letter of
apology to my old English teacher, Betsy Jones.
I asked my lawyer to try to find out where she
was so I could send it. As it turned out, she
wasn't hard to locate. She'd been appointed as
the director of special programs for the Texas
Education Agency.

She got my letter and surprised me by writing back. We started corresponding, and one
day she asked if she could come to the prison for

a visit. I was more than a little nervous, since I figured I was the one responsible for her losing her job back in Quincy, but she seemed to have done okay for herself despite that setback, so I agreed and told the warden to have her name added to my visitation list.

At that time, the only person who ever visited me was my lawyer, Buster Cartwright. The prospect of getting out of my cell, even for an extra hour or two, thrilled me. I can have visitors Mondays through Fridays and after five on Saturdays, but I'm not allowed any physical contact. I am separated from those who come to see me by a window of glass, and we must speak over a telephone to be able to hear each other.

Betsy Jones-McGinnis (she was married with two children by then) arrived on a Tuesday morning, and we talked for nearly two hours. I told her everything that had happened to me after I left Quincy High School, including the spinal injury I got while playing for the Texas Longhorns that ended my football career. How I'd lost my scholarship and flunked out of school. I was surprised how easy it was to talk to her, and also amazed by how good it felt to tell my story to someone besides my lawyer.

Betsy returned the following Tuesday and the one after that. She came every Tuesday for a full year. Somewhere along the way she encouraged me to start putting my story down on paper. She proofread my work and taught me the grammar rules I was just beginning to understand.

On one Tuesday visit Betsy leaned toward me, and even though a thick sheet of glass separated us, I could feel the heat of her eyes burning a hole through me. "Did you know that seventy-five to eighty percent of juvenile offenders can't read at grade level?"

"Really?" This was news to me.

"Your world becomes a much smaller place if you can't read. You have far fewer options. It's not the only factor, but it's a big one. If they want to know how big to build a prison, all they have to do is look at the illiteracy statistics."

It took a minute for her words to sink in, and once I understood, my entire body began to shake uncontrollably. "They knew I was coming."

"You or someone like you."

"You knew it too, all those years ago, back in Quincy. That's why you tried to help me. Because you knew I was coming here."

"Here or someplace like here."

I had never asked for help because I felt ashamed and alone. Suddenly I realized there were thousands just like me. "Why don't people know this? Why doesn't someone tell them?"

"Why don't you?"

It was then that I understood what I had to do. I had to find a way to warn you.

They have built you a house of steel, and they are waiting.

10

THE NEXT DAY GOMEZ WAS YELLING AT WADE AGAIN because the owner of a Tahoe had come in complaining that his oil drain plug hadn't been put in right and oil had leaked all over the floor of his garage.

I was working on a diesel extended cab. I hate diesel engines. The grease works itself into your hands worse than anything and won't come out, even if you scrub it and scrub it. I was in the back, trying to clean up, when Kip stuck his head into the bathroom.

"Looks like that Beemer's back."

I dropped the soap container and ran out to the lobby, where Mr. Gomez was writing up a ticket for Jess. She was wearing a cotton sundress. Her hair was pulled up in a pony-tail, making her long neck and bare, bronzed shoulders look even more beautiful than the day before. Even the dark circles under her eyes couldn't lessen her beauty. They worried me, though.

Jess was with two girls dripping in gold jewelry and wearing

miniskirts with tank tops that said THE JAVA HUT in glittery letters. They flashed their fake fingernails, trying to look classy, in
contrast to Jess, who was classy without trying. They glanced
around the shop in disgust, as if afraid something might jump
out at them and soil their expensive shoes.

"We'll try to get to it today, but we're kind of backed up,"
Gomez told Jess. "Give us a call around four and we'll let you
know where we're at."

Jess noticed me walking in behind Gomez. A huge grin
spread across her face, and she waved. I smiled and waved
back, feeling like a little kid, but then I remembered my grease-
covered hands and shoved them into my pockets, staining my
pants in the process.

"I'm sorry I didn't bring it in earlier," she said. "I had to wait
for a ride." She looked in the direction of a massive guy in a
muscle shirt who was walking toward her with sodas from the
drink machine. He had the build of someone who spent all his
free time pumping iron. When he saw Jess smiling at me, he set
the sodas on the counter and pulled her close, kissing her on
the cheek.

My heart twisted in my chest. From the way he was smirk-
ing at me, I could tell he was full of himself. The sort who likes
to check out his own butt in the mirrors at the gym. All the
same, I figured he was probably better for Jess than I was.

"Dylan, this is my boyfriend Jason. Jason, this is Dylan.
I told you about him. He and I were in school together at
Downey High."

Jason looked at my grease-covered pants and frowned at
Jess. "Together?"

"No, not *together*," Jess said, blushing and looking away.

"Jess told me you quit school to become a grease monkey," Jason smirked.

"That's not what I said!"

I felt the blood rush to my face. "I'd better get back to work," I told her.

"I really didn't say that."

"I think he's kinda cute," said one of the girls standing next to Jess.

"Reminds me of James Dean in that *Rebel* movie," said the other. "Better watch out, Jason. You might have a little competition."

"Yeah, well, nobody asked your opinion, Katie," Jason said with a coldness that warned he could be dangerous.

I walked back into the garage and started a radiator flush on an Escalade. I couldn't help but wonder what Jess had really said to her boyfriend about me. Had she told him about the loser she'd found to work on her car for cheap?

I didn't care. The idea of her talking about me at all meant she'd been thinking about me. That was enough.

More than I expected. At least that's what I tried to tell myself.

We were slammed with work that Tuesday, so it was four o'clock before I even started on the Beemer. By six o'clock all the other guys were cleaning up. I'd finished everything but the oil change and had just put Jess's car up on the lift when I heard Baby Face whimper and saw her wag her tail. I looked out front to see Jess getting out of the backseat of a Camry driven by Katie. Jess slammed the car door and ran into the lobby.

"Watch out or you're gonna pull a Wade," Kip said as he

pointed to the Beemer. In my distraction I'd forgotten to put
the oil drain container under her car, and a slick pool of motor
oil was forming on the floor. I was cleaning up the mess just as
Gomez walked into the back of the garage, followed by Jess.

"She asked if she could wait back here," Gomez informed
me with a smile. "I told her that was okay."

"Are you crazy?" I whispered to him. Gomez never let customers hang out in the back. He said it was a liability. "I can't
work with her watching me."

"Talk to her. Can't you see she's upset?"

Jess was pacing back and forth in front of the Beemer. Her
entire body was trembling, and the dark circles under her eyes
seemed to have grown darker.

Wade came out of the restroom, saw Jess, and smiled.
"Looks like you're gonna be awhile. I'll catch a ride home with
Nathan."

"Whatever," I told him, wanting to slap the grin off his face
before Jess saw it.

"I'll be up front if you need anything," said Gomez.

Jess and I were suddenly alone. The sort of moment a guy
like me would try to take advantage of if he didn't smell like
a men's locker room. "Want a soda?" I asked, looking for an
excuse to send her back to the lobby.

"What jerks!" she said, continuing to pace.

I dusted off a folding chair and set it down beside her car,
but she didn't seem to notice it. "Fight with your boyfriend?" I
asked.

"No, my alleged *friends* Katie and Alice. They've been riding
me ever since they found out my father gave me a credit card.
I'm only supposed to use it for emergencies, which I define as

my car breaking down and they define as a shoe sale at Dillard's. When I refused to take them shopping on my father's plastic, Katie told me I was selfish. I can't believe my parents made me go to a new school halfway through my junior year. You know how hard it is when your parents are moving all the time?"

"I got a pretty good idea."

"I tried to stay in touch with the old crowd from Downey High, but they started acting weird when we bought our new house. They say money changes you. It isn't true. It changes everybody around you." She got quiet. "I don't have any real friends," she said.

I wanted to ask, What about your boyfriend? But I didn't.

The oil had finished draining and I figured I should get back to work, but Jess sat down in the chair and started crying.

I had no idea what to do, so I got a clean cloth out of the rag bin and handed it to her. She wiped her eyes and blew her nose in the rag. "I don't know why I'm telling you all this."

Because I'm a nobody, I thought. I crouched down in front of her, so my eyes were level with hers. Then I took her beautiful silk hand in my rough-stained crude one and said, "I could be your friend." Probably the five lamest words that had ever come out of my mouth. Jess looked at me in surprise. "If you're really desperate, that is," I added, trying to pass it off as a joke. Then I let go of her hand and went back to work on her car, before I could embarrass myself any further.

I felt her warm breath and turned to see that Jess had come to stand right next to me. "I know this sounds crazy, because we haven't really seen each other much in the last four years and we've both gone in different directions, but I have a feeling I could tell you anything."

"That's because what I think doesn't matter." I wasn't trying to feel sorry for myself. Just stating what seemed obvious.

"Oh, yes it does. It matters a lot. What *everyone* thinks matters. That's the problem," she said. "And mostly what they think is that you should stay in your place. Be small and insignificant so you don't outshine them. But you're not like that, are you?"

"No."

"I didn't think so." She smiled for the first time that afternoon. Then she walked back out to the lobby, leaving me standing there, pouring oil on my boots, wondering what made her sound so lost and desperate, wishing I could wrap my arms around her and let her cry on my shoulder forever.

11

WADE AND I HIT RUSH HOUR IN ALBUQUERQUE, NEW MEXICO.
Besides a couple hours' sleep in Kingman and our lunch stop in Flagstaff, I've been driving twelve straight hours.

"We ain't goin' nowhere," Wade says, looking at the trail of cars standing still on I-40. "We should stop and eat."

"It's only five thirty."

"Ain't nothin' but little cow towns between here and Amarillo." He points at the map.

I merge into the right lane and creep at a snail's pace toward the exit for Rio Grande Boulevard, hoping this will make him happy so he'll stop sulking.

"Order a burrito for me and a hamburger for Baby Face while I take her out to stretch her legs," I say as I park in front of a Mexican restaurant called Little Anita's. At least I have a wallet full of money. I cashed my paycheck at the end of the month and still have most of the cash on me.

I take Baby Face out of the car, and she pees by some bushes in the parking lot. I put her back in the Mustang and go to a pay phone outside, pulling my map of Texas out of my back pocket. My hand shakes as I punch in the numbers under the name, Levida Dawson, written on the map, not sure what I will say when and if she answers. Don't even know if the number is still good.

"Hello," says a gravelly voice on the other end of the line.

"Hello."

"Who is this?" the voice demands. I'm pretty sure it's my grandmother, but she sounds like a man. A very angry one.

"I'm looking for Levida Dawson."

"What do you want?" The voice becomes shrill, and I'm sure it's a woman now.

What do I say, that I'm her long-lost grandson? "I'm trying to find D.J. Dawson."

"Are you a reporter? I told you people a hundred times, I got nothin' to say. Why can't you leave me alone?" She slams the receiver down so hard, the sound cracks through my ear all the way to my brain.

In the restaurant I find Wade sitting at a table with two plates covered in red chile sauce next to a hamburger in a Styrofoam box. "Did you talk to your grandma?" he asks.

"Yeah. She was so excited to hear we're coming, she was nearly speechless." I slip into the booth and take a bite out of a chile-smothered burrito that instantly sets my mouth on fire. I drain my glass of water and then grab the honey container and start squirting the stuff into my mouth. "Damn, what do they put in this stuff—battery acid?"

Wade smiles in amusement as I start drinking his water. "It's red chile. I asked for the hot stuff."

"Great."

Once I get past the first bite, the rest isn't so bad, though I worry what it will do to my insides later. As the food settles, an overwhelming exhaustion comes over me.

"Want to drive?" I ask Wade when we get out to the car.

"Sure," he says in surprise, and I toss him the keys.

"Stick to the speed limit and no detours."

"No detours."

Traffic on I-40 has thinned out a little, but not much. Wade weaves in and out of cars like a madman, and I know there is no hope of me sleeping until we get out on the open road. A nervous energy rises up in me, the kind that comes when you really need to sleep but you're so strung out on adrenaline you can't even close your eyes. The need to *do* something, anything, is overwhelming. Plus, the chile is starting to work its way through my gut.

I want to tell Wade to pull over and let me drive, but we're in the far left lane by this time and traffic has come to a halt again. That's when I think of the leather journal, sitting on the backseat next to Baby Face. I reach back and get it, open it up, and look at the first word scrawled there in my own hand: Jess.

I wrote it above the last poem Miss Lane put in my notebook. I think about what she said about keeping things inside. Think about the day I have just endured. Not even twenty-four hours have passed since our encounter with Eight Ball, and already we're two states away, our lives changed forever. I need to put the words on paper. I don't know why. I'm not sure how. Don't even know where to start. With Eight Ball, with Jess, with the road?

I think about how scared I was last night in the desert. The most frightened I've ever been. I figure I've got nothing to lose, and so I turn to a clean page and write:

> Darkist place I ever ben.
> Midel of the California Dessert.
> No lights for miles.

I know my words are an embarrassing jumble, but I feel better putting them on paper. Besides, what does it matter? No one will ever read them anyway.

12

By Friday morning I was wound up like a spring in
the backseat of a new car. Everybody at the garage was in a
crappy mood, or maybe it just seemed that way. After Jess
brought her Beemer in for that tune-up, I didn't expect to see
her again. No reason our paths should ever cross. Even so, every
time a car pulled up to the shop, I stopped what I was doing to
see if it might be her.

"Expecting somebody?" Kip said after I'd looked outside for
the fiftieth time that day.

"Your mama . . ." I started to say more, but then thought
better of it.

After lunch I finished replacing the muffler on a Hummer,
and Gomez asked Wade to move it out to the parking lot until
the owner came for it. Wade hopped inside the massive SUV
and proceeded to back over a Jag waiting for a brake job.

"You know what that's gonna cost me?" Gomez screamed as
Wade stared in horror at the mangled front end of the Jaguar.

"I'm sorry," he muttered.

"You're supposed to be making me money, not costing me a fortune in body work!"

"I'm sorry."

"Give me one good reason I don't fire you right now!"

"I'm real sorry." Wade's face turned bright red, and his entire body started to shake.

"What am I going to do with you?"

"I dunno."

"Jesus, Mary, and Joseph, just sit over there out of the way and try not to destroy anything else until I decide what to do."

I followed Gomez to his office behind the front lobby. "I'll fix the Jag on my own time," I offered.

"It needs a whole new front end. We don't do body work," Gomez said, sitting behind his desk and rubbing his hands through his thick peppered hair.

"You can take it out of my paycheck. Whatever it costs. Please, just give Wade another chance."

"Why are you doing this? You're not the one who ran over the car. Give me one good reason I shouldn't run him off."

"Wade got beat up real bad in juvie. He was in a coma for three days."

"Holy Mother."

"He's never been the same since. His coordination is messed up, and he gets double vision."

"Why didn't somebody tell me?"

"Wade doesn't like people to know. He doesn't remember how it happened, and it makes him nervous to talk about it."

I pictured the way Wade had looked when I'd run back to the shower room with the guard, sprawled out on the tile in a pool of his own blood, and I prayed Gomez didn't ask me more, because then I would have to explain how it was me they had been after and how I had run.

The old man picked up a photograph sitting on his desk, a picture of his youngest son, who had been killed in a drive-by.

"Maybe I could try Wade at the front desk."

"Thank you!" I said, jumping to my feet and pumping Gomez's hand in gratitude. "You won't regret this."

When I walked out of the office, I was surprised to see Wade standing outside at the corner in front of the shop, smoking a cigarette. The traffic light turned green, and he started walking. I ran outside after him and caught up with him on the other side of the street.

"Hey, where you goin'?"

"Nowhere." He kept walking without looking up.

"You can't just leave work."

"Why not? Gomez is gonna can me anyway."

"No, he's not. I just talked to him. He's gonna put you at the front desk."

Wade stopped suddenly, a cold and hard look in his eyes that I'd never seen there before. "What did you tell him?"

"Nothing," I lied, but Wade wasn't buying it.

"Stay out of my business," he screamed, and then he took off down the street.

I had to run to keep up with him. "Wade, don't do this. You need this job."

"No, *you* need this job," he said. "Now that you're trying to play Mr. Johnny-Be-Good." He spun around to face me. "Don't go out drinkin', Wade. You know it's a violation of our probation, Wade. Can't keep any weed around the house no more, Wade. What happens if we get caught? Can't be seen with the gang. Gotta keep our noses clean. Well, I'll tell you somethin', I'm sick and tired of tryin' to keep my nose clean. If you're what guys turn into when they go straight, I'd rather stay crooked."

His words hit me like a punch in the face. I knew I'd been holding my act together pretty tight, but I didn't think it showed. "Wade, come on, don't say shit like that."

A Honda Civic drifted around the corner and then skidded to a stop next to us. The window slid down to reveal Two Tone sitting in the passenger seat. The driver was an associate of the BSB.

"Got the stuff?" asked Wade.

Two Tone smiled and held up a baggie filled with pot.

"Wade, don't do this," I said, but even as the words were coming out of my mouth, I felt the desperate need for a joint. Felt the edge that had been growing sharper inside of me. Knew a toke would smooth down my jagged borders. Took a deep breath and imagined calmness filling my lungs.

"Eight Ball's got a party goin' on down at the Krazy Eights Klub. Want in?" Two Tone asked.

"Wade, don't be an idiot," I said, coming back to myself.

"But I am an idiot," he said, pointing to the scar on his forehead where the guys in juvie had bashed his head against the bathroom mirror and knocked him unconscious. "That's what you told Gomez, ain't it? Let Wade the idiot sit at the front desk and answer phones. Maybe he won't drop 'em." Wade turned to Two Tone. "I'm in," he said. As he got into the backseat of the Honda Civic, Two Tone flashed me a smile that said he had won this round.

Wade rolled down the back window, looked at me, and said, "I'm not like you."

Then he closed the window and the Civic sped away.

13

I WAKE UP COVERED IN SWEAT AND SHAKING FROM THE same old dream.

A room with blue curtains and a cuckoo clock that keeps ticking louder and louder like a bomb, until a screaming bird explodes through the door and I wake up.

Why is it that a stupid clock scares the shit out of me?

I look around and try to get my bearings.

It's dark. I'm in the passenger seat of the Mustang. Baby Face is asleep in the back. I remember we're on the run.

Look around for Wade, but he's nowhere to be seen.

Highway is nowhere in sight.

I wonder if Eight Ball has found us, killed Wade, and is somewhere outside, waiting for me.

My eyes adjust to the darkness of the place, and I see moonlight reflecting on water; a shadowy figure sits on the edge of a rock fence, reading a sign by the flame of a Bic lighter. I get out of the car and approach cautiously.

"Wade?"

"Pretty, ain't it?" he says, flicking off the flame.

"Where are we?" I try to hide the rage I feel bubbling up in my throat as I wonder where in the hell he has brought us.

"Santa Rosa. The Blue Hole. Sign says Billy the Kid used to stop here to clean up before goin' into town."

"I said not to take any detours."

"I needed a smoke," he says, pulling a pack of Kools out of his shirt pocket and lighting up. "Why are you in such a hellfire hurry to get to Texas, anyway?"

"I gotta see my father."

"He's locked up. Ain't goin' nowhere."

"Wade . . . ," I say with a sigh, but then I don't finish. How can I explain that after eleven years in prison my father finally *is* going somewhere, and that if I don't hurry it will be too late?

"Give me the keys," I demand. "I'll drive the rest of the way."

"Fine," says Wade, throwing them at me, crushing his cigarette on the stone fence and stomping off to the car.

"We'll go to the Grand Canyon on our way back home," I promise him when I get back into the car. "We'll stay all day."

"We ain't ever goin' back home," he tells me. "And you know it."

BOXES

We built walls of cardboard
thinking they would keep us safe.
And they did.
Until the flames
came.

14

IT WAS A HOT FRIDAY NIGHT IN SOUTHERN CALIFORNIA,
and everybody I knew was getting stoned or drunk. I got into
the Mustang with Baby Face, and we drove down Rosecrans
from Downey to Compton to Manhattan Beach and then went
south to Hermosa Avenue. As soon as I left one town, I was in
another, each one a totally different world, as if an invisible box
surrounded its edges, keeping everybody in their proper place.

Most of the time.

The rich stayed rich. The poor stayed poor. The troublemakers stayed in trouble.

I wondered what my father was doing. Pictured him sitting
in a cell. Wondered if he ever tried to turn his life around or if
he knew that once you start down the wrong path, there's no
going back.

I knew it was a stupid, crazy thing to do, but I started
cruising Hermosa Avenue looking for Jess, no plan of what
I'd say if I found her. No idea how I'd explain being in her
neighborhood.

I knew if I went home and spent the night sitting alone on my bed, staring at the walls, I'd get myself in trouble. I had some phone numbers. Girls I could have called. Knew any of them would come over and help ease the loneliness that was becoming a black hole inside of me. They'd bring weed, too. The good stuff. But then I'd wake up the next morning and I'd be more alone than ever, or else I'd find myself with a girl I didn't recognize, because daylight had turned her into something cold and hard.

I kept driving until I saw a sign near Pier Street that caught my eye—THE JAVA HUT. I noticed the picture of the hut before I noticed the words. I recognized it from the logo on Jess's friends' shirts, and I wondered if they worked there. I parked and went inside, knowing the chances were one in a million that Jess would actually be there, which of course she wasn't. I ordered an iced coffee and started walking Baby Face toward the Strand. There were people dancing around a bandstand just south of the pier, cops patrolling on bicycles, and vendors selling food out of booths. Some kind of Fourth of July Beach Bash. The Fourth wasn't till Wednesday, but they were getting an early start.

Farther down the beach, Baby Face and I passed couples dancing to music from stereos, kids playing volleyball in the sand, and couples holding hands and rollerblading. Here I was, out with my dog. A total loser. At least I'd showered.

I looked at all the faces, hoping to accidentally bump into Jess, but finally gave up and went back to my car when it started to get dark.

I put Baby Face in the back while I sat up front and rolled down the windows.

That's when I saw her coming out of the Java Hut with Jason.

They walked down the sidewalk arguing and stopped right beside my car. They didn't see me, but I scrunched down in the seat, anyway.

"Come on, baby," Jason said, stopping not eight feet in front of me. He pulled Jess close and rubbed up against her. I could tell he'd been drinking. "You don't need to take a stupid SAT prep course. My parents gave me the keys to the cabin. Don't you want to spend the week with me, alone?"

Jess pushed him away. "Have you heard anything I've been trying to tell you? If I don't get a decent score I'm gonna have to take the test again."

"I hear you all right. The stupid SATs are more important to you than I am."

"It's a little bit harder to get into Stanford than UCLA, especially since I don't have an uncle in the registrar's office."

"Yeah, well, this is supposed to be the time of our lives, and I'm not having much fun. I have needs, and you haven't been taking care of them." He grabbed her hand and guided it toward his crotch. I wanted to jump out of my car and belt him.

"Take care of yourself!" Jess told him, pulling away.

"That's what I been doing, and I'm getting damn tired of it."

"You're disgusting! Is that all you ever think about?" she said, and then she turned and ran in the opposite direction.

"You aren't the only girl out there," he yelled after her. He got inside a red Jeep parked beside my Mustang and drove right past her. I wanted to follow him and run the bastard down, force him off the road into a ditch where he belonged. But then I saw Jess running down Hermosa Avenue all alone, and I wondered what I should do. I could have offered her a ride, but I figured it would freak her out for me to suddenly show up out of nowhere, so I got out of the Mustang and followed her on foot, keeping my distance.

The avenue got more deserted the farther away she got from Pier Street. I wondered where she was going. Then I saw a black van cruising in her direction. The driver looked familiar, and I realized it was Spider at the wheel, with Ajax beside him. I ducked behind a car as he passed. With their tattoos covered up and their belts cinched tight, they almost looked like they belonged. It surprised me how smooth they could act when they tried.

Ajax got his nickname from his squeaky-clean record. His father is a judge up in Sacramento and pulled a lot of strings to keep his son from soiling his legal reputation.

I waited and watched in silent horror as they flipped a U-turn and started following Jess.

Jess saw the van and tried to dart down a side street, but Spider made a quick turn, sped up, and pulled in front of her. Ajax threw open the passenger door, jumping out of the van and blocking her path down the sidewalk. Spider walked around the back of the van and came up behind her.

Jess was trapped between them. "Get away from me," she yelled.

"Is that any way to act?" said Ajax. "We just want to invite you to a party."

I ran toward them with no idea what I'd do when I reached them. Jess saw me, and her look of confusion followed by betrayal almost froze me in my tracks.

She thought I was with them.

What else could she think? Why else would I show up there on that dark street at the same time?

"So, what's the hap, sweetheart?" Ajax asked, his voice echoing off the empty pavement as Spider threw open the van door.

"Leave me alone!" screamed Jess. Ajax took a step toward her and she raised her arm, bringing a set of keys across his face. Then she turned to run.

"Ouch! Shit! Bitch!" Ajax yelled, pressing his hand to his bleeding cheek. Spider stepped out to block Jess's path and started pushing her toward the open van. "You like it rough. We can play it rough," he told her. They weren't even trying to be smooth tonight.

I was still a good fifteen feet away and knew that by the time I reached them, they'd already have her inside.

"Spider!" I yelled, having no idea what I'd say next, but at least it was enough of a distraction to make Spider look up and stop trying to force Jess into the van.

I slowed down as I walked toward them, trying to give myself time to sort out what I was going to do. I couldn't just order them to let her go. They might hurt her to spite me.

I put on the biggest smile I could manage. "Spider, what up, homie?" I thrust my hand toward him, and he reflexively reached out to grab it before he thought about what he was doing, letting go of Jess, giving her just enough time to wiggle away from him and edge past me, hurrying back to the avenue, frantically punching the numbers on her cell phone. Ajax and Spider started after her, but I stepped in front of them. "Whatcha doin' down at the beach? I thought Eight Ball was havin' a thang down at the Krazy Eights."

"Lookin' for party favors," Ajax said.

My stomach tightened. "Man, you better watch your asses," I warned. "Five-oh is thick up in here."

"Dat a fact?" Spider asked, giving me the once-over.

"Guess the city put out extra security 'cause of that Fourth of July thang going down at the beach," I said, though what few cops there were all seemed to be at the party.

"We 'preciate your concern," Ajax said, eyeing me suspiciously. "Come on, Spider. Let's bounce."

They got back into the van, and only then did I allow myself to turn around and look in the direction Jess had gone. She was just rounding the corner. To my horror, Spider sped off in her direction.

I ran full-out to the corner and rounded it to see the black van heading down the street, Jess nowhere in sight. Where had she gone?

Then I saw her, sitting in the passenger seat of Jason's red Jeep as it drove past me. She turned toward me, hand pressed against the glass, eyes cold and unreadable.

15

WE PASS A TOWN IN TEXAS CALLED HEREFORD, AND THE
whole place smells like cow shit. I roll my window up to keep
out the stench, but it doesn't help.

We hit Amarillo around midnight, the first real city since
Albuquerque. Wade is asleep in the back with Baby Face, but I
don't have any problem finding Highway 27.

It ends up being a long stretch of darkened two-lane highway. The only light for miles is the reflection of my headlights
off the stripes in the road. My eyes burn, threaten to close. It
would be so easy to fall asleep and slide off onto the shoulder.

A semi truck honks and I realize I've drifted across the center stripe. The truck is all decked out with red and blue lights
for the fourth of July. It brings back a long-forgotten memory
of Christmas, the year I turned six. I was supposed to be in bed,
but I was up waiting and watching for my father or Santa Claus,
whoever came first.

Dad had been gone a lot, making extra runs to California for
his trucking company, working overtime for holiday money.

He had promised me a brand-new BMX bike, and I had no doubt he'd come through. He was always returning from the road with special presents for me and Mom—a cap gun for me, a new dress for her.

There was a boy up the hill I used to play with. Can't remember his name. T.K., J.T., something like that. He was older than I was by a few years, and I must have annoyed him, but when you're in the country, friends are few with lots of miles between. One day right after Thanksgiving we were making tunnels in the dirt out behind his house with our Hot Wheels, and I was bragging about how my mother was going to take me all the way to Austin to go see Saint Nick at the mall. He told me I was a baby for still believing in such things. "Don't you know your daddy is Santa Claus?" he said.

Christmas Eve Mom kept telling me to get into bed and stay there or else Santa would get mad and wouldn't come to visit our house, but I didn't care. My father never minded me waiting up for him, so I figured if my dad really was Santa, I was safe. If he was just some fat guy dressed in red, I'd take my chances.

Mom kept looking out the window, worried. It had started to snow, which it never did in Quincy, and the dirt road leading up to our house was getting icy.

Mom finally quit arguing with me and let me sit on the couch with her, watching out the window and holding my hand so tightly I thought she might crush the bones.

It was late, and I'd fallen into that place between waking and dreaming when I heard the cuckoo clock belch out twelve long, shrieking birdcalls. I looked out the window and saw the most amazing sight.

The huge outline of a sleigh all lit up in red and green and white, bigger than I ever imagined, rolled to a stop in front of our mobile home. There were no reindeer; it was powered by diesel and moved on wheels, eighteen of them. When I saw my father walking up the gravel driveway, pushing a new red bike, I turned to my mother and told her breathlessly, "It really is true. My daddy is Santa Claus."

I ran outside and jumped on the bike, without even stopping to say hello. Then I rode up and down the driveway, pumping my legs as fast as I could, catching snowflakes on my tongue, feeling the cold wind biting through my Spider-Man pajamas.

Up close you could tell it was a truck with lights arranged to look like a sleigh, so it was easy for me to understand how other kids got confused. I also understood why lately, my father had been so secretive about what he was keeping in the back of his truck.

It was about a month later that the police came and took my father to jail, and all my dreams went with him along with my belief in things like happiness and hope.

Christmas and Santa Claus.

16

WADE NEVER CAME HOME THAT NIGHT. SATURDAY MORNING
I told Gomez he was sick, hoping I could cover for him long
enough to talk some sense into him. I had just returned from
cashing my paycheck and was about to leave for the day when
Jess walked into the front lobby. She looked around and then
proceeded to the front desk, where Gomez was going through
the invoices.

"My car is making a funny noise," she told him. She didn't
even look in my direction, which was hard since I was standing less than three feet away. I wondered why on earth she'd
come back. I was pretty sure after what had happened the night
before she would never want to see me again.

"How long?" asked Gomez.

"It's been doing it for a while. I forgot to mention it when I
was here." Only then did she glance at me, but she looked away
just as quickly.

"What kind of funny noise?" Kip asked as he came to stand
beside me.

"Kind of a chirp, chirp, chirp, like a little bird."

"What kind of bird?" Kip asked, smiling playfully.

I mouthed the words *Leave her alone.* She looked like she'd been crying.

"Oh, and the steering wheel has started shaking, but only when I'm coming off the freeway," Jess added.

"Rotor could be going," I told her.

"Can you fix it?" she asked, finally looking me full in the face.

"Sure."

"I thought you were leaving," Gomez said, trying to hide a smile.

"Just pull her into the bay," I said to Jess, ignoring him.

She nodded and walked back out to her car.

"Third time's a charm," said Gomez. "If you don't ask her out, you're a fool."

"She has a boyfriend."

"Then why did she conveniently forget to mention her funny little noise? She wanted an excuse to come back and see you."

"She's not here for the reasons you think."

"Son, you got no idea why she's here."

I walked back into the garage and saw Jess standing next to her car, chewing on her thumbnail, and I realized Gomez was right. I had no idea why she was there.

I put her car up on the lift, took off the right front wheel and the caliper underneath, and then slid off the rotor.

"Were those guys last night friends of yours?" she asked.

"Nope." I walked past her to the brake lathe and started shaving off the warped edge of the rotor. When I walked back to her car, I was surprised to find her still standing there.

"But you knew them. Those guys from last night," she said as if there had been no pause in the conversation.

"Yep." I slid the rotor back in place.

"They were going to hurt me?"

"Yeah," I said without looking up at her.

"And you stopped them."

It wasn't really a question, so I didn't answer her.

"What were you doing there?"

"Heard there was a big party down at the beach. Thought I'd check it out," I lied, though it sounded like a good enough explanation.

"You were following me."

I took a deep breath. "Sort of." There was no use denying it.

"Why?"

"I saw you fighting with your boyfriend. I got worried. Wanted to make sure you were okay."

"You saw that." Her face turned three shades of red, and she started pacing back and forth in front of the car. I would have given anything to be able to read her mind, but she just stoped and stood there in silence.

It was almost impossible finishing my work with Jess watching me, but I managed somehow.

"Car's finished," I told her, after I checked the brake pads.

"That was quick." She almost seemed disappointed.

"I could take longer if you wanted."

Her cheeks turned red again. "No, that's great. I need to get home, anyway."

We walked up front and she bought a soda while Gomez filled out her invoice.

"Did you ask her out?" Gomez whispered.

"Nope, and I'm not going to."

Gomez totaled the bill, and Jess paid him with her father's credit card. "I think Dylan should follow you home," he said.

"Really?" She looked up at me.

"Make sure the brakes are working okay," Gomez told her. "We usually like to test-drive cars before we let 'em go, but we're about to close."

"I'll meet you out front," she said. I couldn't read her, and it was making me crazy.

"What are you trying to do?" I asked Gomez after she had gone outside.

"Give you a jump start. You need to get your act in gear, son."

"She's out of my league. We don't even play in the same ballpark."

"Have you seen the way she looks at you?"

"She looks at everybody that way."

"You're a good kid, Dylan." He patted me on the back. "Not very observant when it comes to girls, but you'll figure it out." Gomez walked back to his office, leaving me to wonder what the heck he was talking about.

I went to the bathroom. Peeled off my grease-stained work shirt and washed my armpits in the sink. Combed my hair. Studied my reflection in the mirror.

Girls always told me they went crazy over my eyes. The rest of me may have been dark and hard but at least I had nice eyes.

I went back into the garage to get Baby Face. I worried that I looked like I was trying to show off my arms by wearing the white tank top. Figured my filthy blue work pants and black boots would counter the effect. Thought about putting my dirty work shirt back on. Sniffed it and decided against it.

I found Jess outside, sitting in the Beemer, top on, air-conditioning running. I realized that by the time we reached Hermosa Beach I'd be sweating like a pig again, since the air conditioner in the Mustang was busted. I was saving money to put in a new system, but by the time I got what I needed it would probably be winter.

Jess rolled down the window.

"My car's out back." I said. "I'll pull it around front and follow you." Jeez, what was I getting myself into?

I expected her to tell me she'd changed her mind or to forget about it or to take a hike. Instead she looked up at me with her green eyes and said, "Thank you." It made me feel proud, and I figured, what the heck. I'll follow her home. Who knew what might happen.

17

"**Can you explain to me where in the livin' hell we** are?"

I look up to see the morning sun shining on Wade, who is standing outside the Mustang. Baby Face is next to him, on her leash, growling at a cow on the other side of a barbed-wire fence. I get out of the car and look around. Realize that I've driven right off the road onto the shoulder. I must have fallen asleep and taken my foot off the gas.

We're out in the middle of nowhere. The landscape is so flat that I look in all directions and see nothing but brown grass and sky.

It's creepy, like one of those movies where you're the only person left on Earth or where the mutated locals hack you to pieces and then barbecue your body parts.

"Ten miles to Plainview," I say, squinting to make out the name on the road sign.

"And you complained about me takin' detours," he says. "Why don't you let me drive?"

"Maybe I should," I say, getting back inside the car on the passenger side.

"Looks like we've landed on another planet," he tells me as he puts Baby Face back inside the car and sits behind the wheel.

"We have," I reply. "This is Texas."

18

I PARKED ON HERMOSA AVENUE AND MET JESS AT THE PIER.
I'm not exactly sure how it happened, but we started walking
and talking and pretty soon I was buying her and me and Baby
Face chili dogs from a beachside vendor.

"My dad used to be a beach vendor," she said as we walked
along the Strand eating our hot dogs. "He had a T-shirt truck,
and he'd park it by the pier down in Newport Beach."

"Is that how he made his millions?"

"Yes, as a matter of fact."

"You pulling my leg?"

"Think about how many people buy T-shirts," she said,
giving me a sideways smile. She had a spot of mustard on her
chin. I wanted to reach over and wipe it off, just for the excuse
to touch her face, but I didn't. "I mean, he had to move up,"
she explained. "But it all started out of the back end of a truck.
His dream was to get us out of our little apartment and buy
my mother a beach house. Before long he was renting a booth
in a mall in L.A. and we were moving to north Downey. Then

my mom started selling real estate. Dad finally saved enough
money to get a storefront on Hollywood Boulevard."

She was talking a mile a minute and I was glad, because I
couldn't think very clearly. Didn't want to say something stupid. She was walking a little ways ahead of me, backward, like
she was leading me somewhere. Her skirt was blowing in the
wind coming off the water, so she looked like she was floating.
Watching her move was hypnotizing. "But you ended up here,
so it was worth it," I said.

"Yeah, sure," she said, like she wasn't sure at all. Then she
got real quiet and looked out at the water.

We kept walking until the sun started to set. I figured I
should be heading back to my car before I wore out my welcome, but all of a sudden Jess stopped and said, "This is my
place."

"This?" I looked up at a house not eight feet from the short
fence separating it from the beach. I couldn't believe it. She
had a place right on the Strand. It didn't have much of a yard,
but then she didn't really need one. It was narrow and tall. All
the houses there were. But I knew it had to cost a fortune for its
location alone. I had a sudden feeling of panic like I used to get
when the cops came around checking IDs at the bar, like I was
pretending to be somebody I wasn't. "Don't you gotta meet your
boyfriend or something?"

"He's gone to Big Bear for the holiday."

"What about your folks?"

"My parents are out of town until after the Fourth."

My parents are out of town. Those words coming from a girl
would usually sound like music to my ears, but something
about the way Jess said it made me feel nervous.

"Jess, there you are," a voice said, and Jess's smile faded as Katie and Alice walked up to us. "Alice and I have been texting you for half an hour. Did you forget about the sale down at Chico's?"

"I think I'll pass," Jess replied.

"Come on, Jess. Don't be like that. You know we're fundage impaired."

"Hey, aren't you that guy who fixes cars?" Katie asked, looking at my grease-covered work pants as if she couldn't believe I ever left the garage.

"Yeah, they let me out every now and then," I said.

"Where's Jason?" Alice asked.

"Gone for the weekend," Jess said, lifting her chin in defiance.

"I see," Katie said, looking me up and down. "Guess you've got a thing for bad boys."

"We're friends," said Jess. "Not that you would understand what that means." Jess turned to me, and the look in her eyes was so deep and warm it seemed to melt away all the years between Long Beach and Hermosa. I was twelve years old again, wanting nothing more than to find a way to make her laugh.

"With a boy who looks like that, there's no such thing as *just friends*," said Katie. "But we can take a hint. Come on, Alice. Four's a crowd."

When they had left, Jess turned to me. "Do you ever look at the people around you and wonder how you ended up with them?"

I thought of Wade and how I'd met him during in-school suspension at Downey High School. "All the time."

"Come on," she said, hopping over the brick fence and leading me into her backyard. She sat on a porch swing and I sat down next to her, facing the beach.

This was a place I could get used to.

"I love to watch the sun set over the water," Jess said, looking out at the flame red horizon.

"Yeah. It's different every day."

She looked surprised.

"I like to unwind on the weekend by driving up the coast," I told her.

She nodded, then reached out and touched my right hand, tracing the crude tattoo of the cross with her fingertips. The sensation of her skin against mine was like an electric shock.

"Ellee. Is that your girlfriend?" she asked, reading the letters beneath the cross.

"No."

"But it is a girl."

"A woman."

"Really?"

"No. It's not the way it sounds."

"You have her name tattooed on your hand. She must be important."

I wondered how much I should tell Jess about Ellen Carter. I knew if I hung around her much longer I was going to fall hopelessly in love, and that would be terrible because we would never end up together, not in a million years. Maybe if I told her the grisly details of my past, I could scare her away and avoid the heartache.

"When I quit school my uncle Mitch got me a job with a friend of his, a guy named Jake Farmer, who owns a used car lot in East L.A. Last summer he got me and Wade to start chopping cars for him."

"Chopping cars?"

"Stripping down stolen cars for parts. Taking out the CD players, radios, anything of value."

"Oh." Jess raised an eyebrow. "Did your uncle know?"

"No," I said, though I'd never been sure exactly how much Mitch knew about Jake's side business. He and I never talked about it, even after I got busted.

"Jake said me and Wade would never get caught 'cause he had us working out of an abandoned warehouse. He said even if we got arrested, we'd never do time because we were juveniles."

"What does this have to do with Ellee?"

"Ellen."

"Your tattoo says Ellee."

"Wade was afraid we'd get caught, and he got a little sloppy with the nail."

"The nail?"

"That's how you do 'em in jail. Either that or a piece of wire. You gotta poke the skin and dab in the ink that you make with lead shavings and toothpaste."

"I see," she said, taking a deep breath. Good! It was working. I was obviously scaring her. Any minute she was bound to tell me to get lost.

"Ellen was an innocent old lady who got in the way of the gangbangers who stole her car. So they ran her down. She'd left her cell phone in the glove box, so it was easy for the cops to track the GPS to the warehouse with me and Wade the next morning. That's how I know Ajax and Spider. They're in the gang." I didn't mention that Ajax was the one who'd killed

Ellen. I realized that if I'd ratted him out he'd be behind bars, and the streets would be safer for Jess.

Of course, I'd also be dead.

"I made a bargain with God. If he let Ellen Carter live, I'd clean up my act and go straight."

"What happened?"

"God didn't keep his end of the bargain."

"Wow." Jess was quiet for a long time. Plotting her escape, I assumed. She pretended to watch the sun sinking into the sea, leaving streaks of red and gold. It was almost dark, and here she was sitting in front of her beach house with an ex-convict.

I watched the people going by, laughing and talking. Not sad, desperate people, but folks with hope and a future. I wondered what it would feel like to be a person with a future. All I'd been thinking about for the past few months was surviving. Keeping my nose clean. Holding down a job. I wished I could erase the tattoo. Wished I could erase myself and start over. But even if I did, what would I do differently? Why couldn't I have found Gomez *before* I found Jake Farmer?

"What about you?" Jess finally spoke. "Did you keep your end of the bargain?"

"I'm trying."

Jess looked up at me. "That's so . . . unbelievable."

"It's all true. Believe me."

"I believe it happened, I just can't believe you would tell me. I mean, my friends would never confess anything like that. They can't even admit they buy Prada knockoffs. It's like we're always in this huge competition for who has the perfect life. I'm so sick of it. Sometimes I feel like we're all in a big popularity parade, all dressed up, marching behind the horses."

"You want me to leave?" I braced myself for rejection.

She looked surprised. "Why?"

"Aren't you afraid of me?" I'd seen people cross the street to avoid me and my type.

"Should I be?" She didn't seem afraid at all. She didn't even seem disappointed.

"No."

"Then I guess I'm not."

"So you don't want me to leave?"

"No. I don't want you to leave. In fact, what I really want . . ." She looked down at her sandals.

"What?"

She still wouldn't look at me. "Dylan, would you stay the night with me?"

I felt my mouth fall open as I suffered a mild heart attack. That was *not* the reaction I was expecting from her.

"No. It's not like that. I'm not coming on to you. That's not what I mean. I'm sorry. I shouldn't have asked you that." She was trembling like a kitten left out in the rain, and I suddenly realized what she wanted. What she needed.

She was afraid of being alone. If two mongrels like Ajax and Spider had tried to force me into a van, I'd be scared too.

"Sure. I'll spend the night with you. I'll spend the whole week if you want."

"Are you sure?" she asked. It was weird, the idea of a girl wanting to be with me because she thought I was safe. I remembered the way her boyfriend had treated her, and I made a promise to myself that I would never be like that.

"I don't expect anything," I said. "You're safe with me."

"I know. I don't know how I know, but I do." She smiled,

took my hand, and led me into her house.

Jess input a code on the security pad so we wouldn't set off the house alarm. Then she locked the back door. She proceeded to walk through the entire first floor, turning on every light, looking in every corner, which is exactly what I would do if I'd been accosted by gangbangers the night before. "My room is upstairs," she told me. "It used to be a separate flat, but my parents connected them."

When we reached the staircase, Jess picked up a black trash bag filled with clothes. "Oh, maybe you could use these. I was supposed to take them to Goodwill for my father."

"Thanks," I said, looking down at my dirty work clothes, realizing I wouldn't be going home to change.

When we reached the second floor, Jess said, "Home sweet home." She pointed to a large room with a small kitchenette in the corner, set off by a bar and four stools. There was a small bathroom next to the kitchen, but everything else seemed to be in the one room, a futon facing a wide-screen television, a beanbag chair next to the futon, and a shelf filled with books and movies. There were piles of books and clothes everywhere.

A huge full moon was glowing through a plate-glass window in the wall behind the television. "I bet that's one awesome view during the day," I said, trying to make conversation. Not really sure what I was supposed to do next.

"You must think I'm a total wimp to ask you to babysit me."

"Nope," I said, turning back to her. "I think you're alone . . . and scared."

Jess wrapped her arms around herself and sat on the edge of the futon. Baby Face curled up on the carpet and laid her head on Jess's feet, looking up at her as if to make sure she was okay.

I left the window and went to sit beside her. There was an afghan folded on the table next to a pair of pajamas. I unfolded it and wrapped it around her shoulders. It was cold on the beach after the sun went down. Farther inland the concrete soaked up the sun and never let it go, but here you could feel the temperature drop after the sun set.

"My parents are never here."

"What do you mean?"

"After a month of haze and gloom my mother decided she didn't like the beach—or my father. They both have separate apartments in the city now, close to their jobs. They're always taking separate vacations. As soon as I graduate they're going to sell this place and probably get a divorce."

"Wow. Is that how the rich abandon their kids?"

"Yeah, with a credit card. I don't mind. It's better than having them here fighting all the time. But last night I thought every sound was an intruder."

"So I'm filling in till Jason gets back."

"It's not like that. He doesn't know about my parents. God, if he did he'd be trying to move in with me."

I tried to wrap my mind around what she was saying. I wanted to ask her why she confided in me when she couldn't talk to her boyfriend, but I didn't.

"No wonder you look so tired," I said, touching the dark circles under her eyes. "Don't worry. I know just what to do." I got up to leave.

"Where are you going?" she asked.

"To my car. I'll be right back."

I walked down to Hermosa Avenue, got the Mustang, and parked it behind Jess's house. Then I found my copy of *Poetry*

Through the Ages in the trunk. By the time I returned, Jess was
already in her pajamas—a pair of shorts and a tank top. She
didn't seem to have any idea how sexy she looked.

"I'll read you to sleep," I told her, looking hard at the book,
trying to avoid looking at her body. "I do it for my mother all the
time. She says my voice is a natural sedative."

"It may not be that easy. I'm an incurable insomniac."

"That's okay. I know a lot of Yeats."

"You like Yeats?"

"My mom used to read me a lot of poetry when I was little.
What, I don't strike you as the sensitive poetic type?"

"Not really."

"I try to hide it."

"You do a good job." She was smiling again. God, I loved the
way her mouth twisted up at the corner, like we were sharing a
secret joke.

I had left my reading glasses at home, so I couldn't keep up
my old ruse, but I opened the book to page fourteen—to "The
Mermaid"—another Yeats poem—and pretended to read anyway.

> "A mermaid found a swimming lad,
> Picked him for her own,
> Pressed her body to his body,
> Laughed; and plunging down,
> Forgot in cruel happiness,
> That even lovers drown."

"I thought mermaids were supposed to *save* men."

"They are," I told her. "But sometimes a guy doesn't mind
drowning."

19

"What do you mean we're lost?" I ask Wade.

"Lost. L-O-S-T, lost. It's what happens when you take the wrong damn road and end up in the middle of some godforsaken place called *Rankin*." He points out the window to the vast fields of dead grass and oil pumps.

"You said to get on 87 headin' out of Lubbock."

"I said to take 84, but it don't matter, 'cause we ain't on either one."

We had wound through an endless maze of country back roads, passing through nowhere towns with nowhere names like Needmore, Welch, and Punkin Center before Wade finally admitted he didn't have any idea where we were.

We've been driving around like that for two hours, and both of our tempers are flaring.

"Can't you find *Rankin* on the map and then figure out what road we're on?" I ask.

"There's hundreds of little piss-ass towns on this map. Why don't *you* try to find it?" he says, tossing the map on the dashboard. "I wanted to head for Colorado. Find some mountains where it was cool, but no, you insisted we had to go to Texas. Couldn't even stop to see the damn Grand Canyon. I gotta be turnin' yellow before you even stop to let me piss."

"I told you, I need to find my father."

"Why do you gotta find him now, after all these years, now that we're on the run?"

"I got my reasons."

"What reasons?"

My patience has reached its end. I am tired, angry, hungry, and shaking inside. I am dangling at the end of a frayed, worn rope, and I know I wouldn't be running at all if it wasn't for Wade, so who is he to question me?

"What reasons?" he says, as if I didn't hear him the first time.

"Ask him stuff."

"Like what?"

"Like how I ended up on this friggin' road out in the middle of bumfuck nowhere with you, Wade. How I ended up lost in some Texas hellhole. How I ended up with you, goin' nowhere, just when I thought I was goin' somewhere. Just when I was getting my life together. Just when all the pieces were starting to fit."

Wade stares at me for the longest time. He looks like he's trying to hide the fact that I've hurt his feelings, but then I realize he's suppressing a smile. "Well, shit, Dylan. If that's all you wanted to know, you didn't have to drive all the way to Texas. You could have just asked me. I can tell you the answer to that."

"Really?" I say, white-knuckling the steering wheel so I don't clock Wade. "Then please tell me. What's the answer, Wade?"

"You can't read."

A slow panic starts settling over me. "What are you talking about?"

"It was sittin' there, plain as day, when you were in the middle of blamin' me for how sorry your life turned out."

"What was sitting there?"

"The sign for San Angelo, you dumb shit. It's comin' up in about ninety miles." He grabs the map from the dash and traces the highway with his finger. "From there we get back on 87. Take 87 to Fredericksburg, then 290 all the way through Austin until we hit Quincy, just north of Brenham." He tosses the map back onto the dash. "You see, Dylan, that's your problem. You're so busy starin' at the problem, you don't see the solution. Look for trouble and you find trouble. Look for a solution and you find San Angelo."

The irony is that signs are one of the few things I *can* read. I try to keep my hand from balling into a fist, afraid that if Wade tries to spout any more of his wisdom, I will kill him. I turn on the radio, hoping to drown him out, but all I get is static. I check my CD case, but all I have with me is Aerosmith and *West Side Story*, which I'm sick of.

"Want me to drive?" Wade asks. "I won't take any detours."

I slam on the brakes and come to a dead stop right in the middle of the road. "Sure. Why not? My life is one big fucking detour," I yell. Then I bang my head on the steering wheel and I can't help it. I start to cry.

"Dylan?"

I think of last Sunday, not even a week ago. I had woken up on the beanbag chair at Jess's house. Found her and Baby Face curled up asleep on the futon. Put on her father's clothes. I'll never forget the look in her eyes, when she saw me cleaned up

and respectable . . . like I was somebody. I made her breakfast
and thought about how easy it would be to pretend I fit into her
life. Then I told her I had to go home to get some things.

Saw a car parked out in front of my house with Texas dealer
plates.

Went inside to find my uncle Mitch sitting with my mother,
holding her hand as she stared blankly at the wall, all the life
gone from her eyes. I asked what was wrong, and he told me
he'd brought her some bad news.

About my father.

"Dylan, you okay?" asks Wade as a gas truck passes us, blaring its horn.

"They're gonna kill my father."

"Who?"

"The State of Texas."

"What are you talkin' about?"

"They're gonna kill my father by lethal injection in less than
two weeks."

"How can they do that?"

"He's on death row somewhere in Texas. I don't even know
where."

Wade gets real quiet. Doesn't even comment when two
pickups pass us.

"Why didn't you tell me?"

"I didn't know how."

Wade nods as if this makes perfect sense. "Want me to
drive?"

"Yeah, maybe you should."

THE ROAD TO HUNTSVILLE
By D.J. Dawson

I injured my back during the UT homecoming
game my sophomore year and lost my football
scholarship, along with my dream of going pro.
Then I found out my girlfriend Mollie was pregnant, and we both quit school to get married. I
needed to support my new family, so I took a job
driving an eighteen-wheeler, delivering cattle
feed from Texas to California.

I became addicted to painkillers. Then I
began self-medicating with illegal drugs.

Soon after I agreed to start transporting
cocaine for a Colombian drug cartel. I was convinced I could do five or six runs, get the money
I needed to buy my own rig, and be done with the
whole business. I thought I could quit anytime I
wanted, but I was wrong.

I asked an old friend to help me get out. One
thing led to another, and before I knew what
was happening, I found myself in the middle of a
drug raid with a dead cop. I did not pull the trigger, though that's what I'm here for, but I wasn't
innocent, either. I was running drugs and as a
result, a good man is dead. A woman was left
without a husband. Children were left without a
father, including my own son.

One day they will come for me, bind me in
iron shackles, lock me in a white prison van,

and set me on the road to Huntsville. It is a
journey of forty miles down a country highway
that weaves through the Sam Houston National
Forest. A road lined with pine trees and wild-
flowers. A road paved with desperation, hopelessness, and fear.

I know what's at the end. It's a redbrick fortress called the Walls. And one day soon that is
where the prison van will take me to die.

I won't offer you a tired admonition to avoid
my path. I won't advise you to stay on the
straight and narrow. I won't suggest that you
make good choices. I won't even tell you to do the
right thing. You can get that kind of advice from
teachers and parents and TV evangelists, and if
you are like me, you wouldn't listen anyway. I
just make one suggestion.

Know what path you're on.

20

MY UNCLE MITCH TOOK ME OUT TO A LOW-RENT BAR THAT
didn't check for IDs.

"Tuesday, July seventeenth. That's the date set for the execution," he told me, downing a tall glass of Budweiser. He was already on his third and didn't even notice I hadn't touched mine. If there was ever a good time to start drinking again, I was pretty sure this was it, but I'd promised Jess I'd come back that night, and I wasn't about to show up at her house drunk.

"I want to see my father," I told him.

"Bartender, get me a double," my uncle yelled to the man behind the counter.

"I *need* to see my father."

"I've always respected your mother's wishes on that matter," Mitch said, tapping the table, the diamond ring on his middle finger flashing. Mitch is a man who likes finery. Tailored suits and expensive shoes. Lots of gold.

"Where is he?"

"Like I said, I've always respected—"

"I got a right to know some things!" I yelled, pounding my fist on the table.

Mitch looked at me coolly, his eyes narrowing. "You're on probation. You can't just pick up and go to Texas."

"Work it out so I can." I knew my uncle was used to pulling strings when it came to getting what *he* wanted. He could at least try to help me. "You owe me."

"Excuse me?"

"Your friend Jake Farmer, he's the one who had me and Wade choppin' cars. I served eight months in juvie because of him."

"You tell anybody?" he asked me.

"No."

"That's good," he said, and that's when I realized Mitch had known all along what Jake Farmer was up to.

"I gotta get out of here," I said, and I ran out of the darkened bar into the glaring daylight. It was so bright it took a full minute for my eyes to adjust before I could make out where I'd left my car. Light is funny that way. Too much of it can blind you.

TIME

Time
goes round and round
the spinning clock,
until the fateful day
time
folds its tired hands
and
stops.

21

IT'S ALREADY SEVEN O'CLOCK WHEN WADE AND I PASS A sign that says QUINCY: POPULATION 700.

"Damn," Wade says. "There was more people than that in our freshman class."

The heat of this place is ten times worse than California, because it's wet and sticks to every pore in your body. There's a sound outside like a pulsing electric hum, and I remember the insects that used to come out on summer nights. My grandmother called them Sick Katies.

"Main Street," Wade says, reading the sign. "Want me to turn here?"

"Yeah," I say, thinking there should be more to the town but realizing this is it. I thought after eleven years they might have put in a Dairy Queen or a Super Wal-Mart, but the place looks just like it did when I left. It's like a time warp.

Wade turns, and the Mustang hobbles down a brick paved street. There's the Baptist church and the post office, the Ford dealership, the drugstore, and the grocery store no bigger than Gomez's garage.

"Pull over here," I tell him, pointing to the drugstore.

"Why?"

"I need to ask for directions." All of a sudden the idea of visiting my grandmother is making my stomach do flip-flops. The familiarity of this place is unsettling. Memories tug at me, and I can almost see my mother walking out of the grocer's with bread and eggs.

"Why do you need directions? I thought you used to live with the old lady," Wade says as he parks in front of the drugstore.

"It was a long time ago." I get out of the car. "We'll be right back," I inform Baby Face.

Bells hanging off the door handle jingle as we walk in. The entire right side of the store is filled with over-the-counter drugs. On the left is an old-fashioned soda fountain with red vinyl bar stools permanently attached to the ground. A group of old men, farmers by the look of them, sit at a table playing cards.

Three teenage boys wearing coveralls, with sunburns from the eyebrows down and hair flattened from grimy baseball hats sitting on the counter, share a basket of tortilla chips and drink out of huge red plastic cups. They are covered in dirt and sweat and look like they've just finished a long day's work. A red-haired boy puts about fourteen packets of sugar into his drink and stirs.

Wade and I sit next to them on a couple of stools as a plump girl with blond curls and a red apron hands us menus. She smiles at Wade. "You boys from out of town?"

"Downey, Cal—"

"Arizona," I say.

The timer on a toaster oven dings, and the girl goes to retrieve a boxed pizza, which she slices and puts in front of the boys sitting next to us. "Thanks, Dorie," says the redhead.

"Don't tell people where we're from," I whisper to Wade. "What if someone comes lookin' for us?"

"Ain't nobody comin' lookin' for us in this town. I guaran-damn-tee you that."

"What can I get you fellas?" Dorie asks us.

"A couple of Cokes," I reply. "And can you tell me how to get to Levida Dawson's place?"

"Levida. Don't think I know anybody named Levida."

I can't believe it. With only seven hundred people in the town, she's got to know my grandmother, unless . . . is it possible she's moved away? Maybe she wasn't the woman on the phone.

"Oh, sure you know her, Dorie," says one of the boys. "A. Devil Dawson."

"Oh, you mean the Devil Woman," says Dorie. "Sure, I know her. Everybody knows the Devil Woman. Lives out on Farm Road 67. Crazy as all get-out. Plays the organ at my daddy's church, even though we've all warned him she's possessed." She turns to Wade again. "My daddy's the preacher at First Baptist, if you're ever in need of a church home."

Wade smiles at the word *home*, as if he's just been invited to move in.

"Why you lookin' fer the Devil Woman?" the redhead asks, swiveling on his stool to face us.

"We're traveling Bible salesmen," I answer.

He laughs. "Well, y'all be sure you hold them Bibles up nice and high to protect yer heads. The Devil owns a twelve gauge and she ain't afraid to use it. She don't cater much to visitors, either."

"She don't cater to nobody but that damn pig of hers," says the black-haired boy sitting next to him. He turns to me. "She took her son on a five-state shootin' spree when he was barely ten years old. That's what turned him into a cold-blooded killer."

"No, it ain't. It's 'cause she kept him locked up in that barn, feedin' him pig slop."

Wade's eyes grow as big as two silver dollars.

"Don't listen to them," Dorie tells him, sliding to-go cups filled with soda in front of us. "Red and Dakota just like to spin tales." Wade pulls out his wallet to pay her, but she touches his hand, smiles, and says, "It's on the house."

"I ain't spinnin' no tale," says Dakota. "They're gonna fry D.J. Dawson's ass over in Huntsville in ten days, at six o'clock in the p.m."

"They don't fry nobody's ass no more," Red corrects him. "Not since they retired Old Sparky to the Texas Prison Museum. They're gonna give him a lethal injection. Put him to sleep. He deserves a helluva lot worse for what he done."

I'm suddenly dripping in sweat. Someone opens the door, and the buzzing sound from outside fills the room. I drink the soda in one long gulp to keep from catching on fire, and then I stand to leave. "Come on, Wade."

"What did he do?" Wade asks Red, making no move to get up from the bar stool.

"Killed a cop. Tornado T.'s daddy. Tornado, you okay?"

Only then do I notice that the third boy, a husky flax-haired kid, has taken all the tortilla chips from the basket and mangled them into dust while we've been talking. He stares straight ahead, breathing hard, like he wants to hurt somebody. He turns to look at me, and his eyes are cold and dark.

"You idiots," Dorie tells Red and Dakota. "Ain't you got no feelin's a'tall?"

"We gotta go," I say, grabbing Wade by the collar and pulling him out of the drugstore. By the time we get into the Mustang I am shaking so badly I can barely drive.

"That was your father they were talkin' about," says Wade.

"Yeah."

"Is he really a cold-blooded killer?"

I take a long, slow breath, trying to steady my nerves. "I don't know. Do you wanna go home?"

"Home?"

"Back to California. You don't have to stay here. California's a big place. You could hide from Eight Ball somewhere up north. It might get dangerous here."

"It's dangerous everywhere."

"Colorado, then. Start over."

He looks out the window as if he's thinking it over. Remembering California, maybe. He finally says, "I can't do that, Dylan."

"Why not?"

"'Cause you're the only family I got." He smiles at me, and I know we are in this together until the bitter end. Even if it would be better for us both if things were otherwise.

I find Farm Road 67, a dirt trail heading off into nowhere. The Mustang bumps along, leaving a cloud of dust behind us.

We pass a brick house with a white picket fence, a shack

that leans to one side, and a double-wide mobile home. Then I spot a mailbox up ahead with the name DAWSON on the side. I come to a stop and see that the mailbox is full of bullet holes. The name LEVIDA has been crossed out and replaced with A. DEVIL scrawled in red paint.

"Do you think she really has a shotgun?" asks Wade.

"Everybody out here has a shotgun," I tell him as I pull onto the gravel drive leading to a farmhouse, about fifty yards off the road. We see a series of signs painted on planks of old barn wood. Wade reads them out loud as we pass. "'Keep out,' 'No trespassing,' 'Reporters go home,' 'Enter at your own risk and suffer the consequences.'"

We're about twenty feet from the house when I hear the blast of a shotgun and feel something hit the front of the Mustang. "Shit!" I yell, spinning the car around as fast as I can, no easy task on the narrow dirt road. Another round of shot hits the back end. I try to race back to the farm road.

I hear an engine and look back to see a tractor roaring toward us.

"Look out!" Wade yells, as the tractor rams us from behind, scoops up the rear end of the Mustang, and starts shoving us toward a ditch. "Damn! She really is crazy!"

"Why can't you people leave me in peace!" yells the woman behind the wheel of the John Deere.

My car goes nose first into a ditch. Wade and Baby Face and I scramble to get out, crawling back up the ditch to find ourselves facing the barrel of the shotgun. The woman from the tractor is standing in the dirt with her finger on the trigger. She's wearing men's overalls and has wiry gray hair going in twenty directions. There's a big fat pig beside her.

"I don't give no interviews."

The pig raises its snout and snorts as if to emphasize her point.

"Please!" I say, raising my hands in the air. "We're not reporters."

"Oh, yeah? If you ain't reporters, then who are ya?"

"I'm Dylan Dawson."

"What did you say?" She closes one eye and aims straight for my head.

"I'm Dylan Dawson," I repeat, shaking so badly I fear I'll piss on myself.

"Horseshit. Dylan Dawson is in a maximum security prison."

"I'm his son. I'm Dylan Junior."

The old woman's body goes slack. She drops her shoulders, puts the shotgun at her side, and turns pale, as if she's just seen a ghost. I'm not sure if she's going to cry, faint, or have a stroke.

"Well, boy, you got timin'. That's all I can say." And with that statement, Levida turns around and starts walking back toward the farmhouse. The pig grunts at us, then turns to follow her.

Wade and I look at the tractor the old woman has left in the middle of the road. Look at the Mustang sitting in the ditch. Stare at each other, wondering what to do. It's clear we aren't going anywhere anytime soon.

"You might as well come on up to the house," Levida yells, never breaking stride or looking back. "Guess you'll be expectin' me to feed you and give you a place to stay."

"Is that an invitation?" whispers Wade.

"As close as we're gonna get."

22

I WOKE UP AND LOOKED AROUND, TRYING TO GET MY BEAR-
ings. Heard the sound of the ocean, a dog whine. Realized
I was sleeping on the front porch of Jess's beach house with
Baby Face next to me. Looked up and saw Jess standing
over me.

"What are you doing out here?" Jess asked. She had the
afghan wrapped around her shoulders.

I tried to piece together how I'd ended up there after my
talk with Mitch. Had I gotten drunk and blacked out? I could
tell from the soft blue light of morning that dawn was just
breaking.

"Why didn't you come back? You said you were going to
come back. I've been waiting all night for you."

"I did come back. I'm right here," I said, sitting up. It suddenly started coming together in my mind. How I'd driven up
and down the Pacific Coast Highway till well after midnight,
nearly talking myself into buying a case of beer, but getting more and more worried about leaving Jess alone. Finally

deciding to spend the night on her front porch so I could keep an eye on her place without the embarrassment of her seeing me cry, which I'd done most of the night.

"Come inside," she told me.

"I can't."

"Why not?"

"I'm not somebody you should be hangin' around with."

"Why?"

I told her about my father being on death row in Texas; my mother, who wouldn't talk about it; and my uncle, who had set me up with a job he knew was illegal. Words came gushing out of me. I finally got through to the end of it. "Trouble just seems to follow me. You'd be better off not getting too close."

"Oh, Dylan," she said, kneeling down beside me and touching the crude blue cross on my right hand. "I know you've been in trouble. I know your family situation is bad." She took my hand in hers and squeezed it. "But I also know that you are the most decent person I've ever met. You're the only real and genuine person that I know."

There was a light in her eyes that reached all the way to the corners of my soul, telling me that I could start over. That I could leave my past behind and be worthy of a girl like Jess. It was like a small explosion shaking me all the way down to my roots.

She pulled me to my feet. Tilted her head up toward mine. For a moment I thought she was going to kiss me, but she didn't. Instead she smiled and said, "Now come inside, silly."

"I can't," I said, looking at my watch. "I gotta go to work."

"Tonight, then? Promise me you'll be back tonight."

"I promise."

When I got to work, I was surprised to see Wade sitting up front, answering the phones. It made me wonder about his weekend with the BSB. Whatever had happened, it was bad enough to make him come back to the garage.

"You didn't come home last night," he said.

I punched my time card. "Won't be coming home for a while."

"Your mom left."

I spun around to face him. "What are you talking about?"

"Your uncle Mitch took her to Texas."

"What?" I couldn't believe she would leave the state without even saying good-bye.

"He told me he was bringin' her to his place so he could take care of her. She didn't look right. Is somethin' goin' on?"

"No," I hurried back to the garage before he could ask me any more questions.

The day was a roller coaster of emotions. When I thought about my mother, I felt guilt and anger. When I thought about my father, I felt anger and dread. When I thought about Jess, all I wanted was to forget about everybody else.

By the time three o'clock rolled around and I was clocking out, I felt exhausted.

I ended up at the probation office, pacing back and forth in front of Mr. Grey's desk. "I appreciate the gravity of your circumstances," he told me. "I can't promise you anything, but if you'll get these forms filled out and return them to me as soon as possible, I'll try to push it through juvenile court so you can get permission to visit your father."

I picked up the pages and looked them over. I knew I'd never fill them out. He wasn't going to be able to help me. "Thank you for your time," I said.

I threw the pages in the trash on the way out.

On the drive from Mr. Grey's office to Hermosa Beach, I had to admit to myself that the only way I would be able to see my father was if I violated my probation and drove to Texas without permission.

I was not inclined to put myself in jeopardy for a man who had never done anything for me. I had too much to lose. By the time I arrived at Jess's house, I had convinced myself that seeing my father didn't matter. What would be the point anyway? He would be dead and gone in a few days. So much the better for me. Maybe then I could finally let go of my past and start over.

I showered at Jess's house. It was weird, being naked in her bathroom, knowing she was on the other side of the door. When I was done, I put on a pair of khaki shorts and a short-sleeved polo shirt from the sack Jess had given me. "Who are you pretending to be?" I asked the respectable-looking guy in the mirror. I didn't recognize him, but I sort of liked him.

Half an hour later I was walking down the street with Jess, enjoying how every guy who passed us looked at her in admiration and then me in envy. *I could learn to get used to this,* I told myself, and stood a little taller.

"Karaoke!" I pointed to a storefront across the street. "Come on." I was so excited that I started trying to cross in the middle of traffic.

"No," she said, pulling me back onto the sidewalk and heading off in the opposite direction.

"Jess, what's wrong?"

"Nothing. I just don't sing much anymore."

"Aren't you still in chorus?"

"I gave it up my junior year."

"You're kidding me, right?"

She gave me a sideways glance and picked up her pace. "To get into a decent university you have to have four years of math, four years of science, four years of language arts, a foreign language, history, government, econ. I don't have time for singing anymore."

"Don't you need extracurriculars?

"I'm in the debate club, and I do DECA."

"What about your voice?"

"Who cares about my voice? There are more important things going on in the world. I want to make a difference. I'm going to law school. I want to become a public defender."

I couldn't believe she'd give up singing to work with scumbags like me. "By the time a guy ends up in front of the judge, it's too late to make a difference."

"It's never too late to make a difference," she said.

We had arrived back at the beach and we stood there, staring out at the vastness of the ocean. I don't know why, but it made me think of possibility. Maybe she was right. Maybe it wasn't too late.

"All I'm saying is that with your music you could have an influence on people before they end up in trouble."

"Yeah, right," Jess said, laughing.

"What's so funny?"

"After *West Side Story*, my mother thought maybe I should work with a talent agent. I signed with a guy in Beverly Hills, and within two weeks he had gotten me my first job singing on television."

"Wow."

"In a chicken suit." Jess started to sing, "Come on down to Yummy Buckets. . . . Try our tasty chicken nuggets."

"That was you? You were the dancing chicken that came on after the late-night news?"

"I confess."

"I loved that song."

"Yeah, very funny. I had to wear that stupid chicken suit for hours. That's what show business is really like. I used to think that words and music could change the world, but look at the people who have made it. You see their faces all over the tabloids talking about their latest stint in rehab. I'm not like that."

I brushed a strand of hair from her face. "No, you're not like that. You really could change the world."

Something shifted then. I wasn't sure what, but Jess stared up into my eyes long and hard, like she was looking for something she hadn't even realized she'd lost. Then she cupped my face in her hands. "It's amazing."

"What?"

"Your eyes are so clear. I think I can actually see my reflection."

"Look closer," I told her.

She edged toward me. I leaned toward her.

"Closer."

She stepped up on her tiptoes, her lips so close to mine I could feel her breathe.

"Closer . . ."

She covered my lips with hers, pulled me close, and kissed

me like I'd never been kissed before. It was warm and wet and wonderful.

It was better than sex. It was like sinking into a crystal clear sea and coming out new. She opened her mouth to let me in and in that moment, my heart imploded and nothing else mattered.

23

"RISE AND SHINE," A VOICE BELLOWS, AND I OPEN MY eyes to come face-to-face with Levida's pig, Charlotte. Levida is standing behind the pig, holding a basket and a pitchfork.

I look around. Realize I'm in Levida's barn. Know I've been dreaming again of the room with the cuckoo clock and the blue curtains.

"If you're gonna stay with me, you boys will have to earn your keep," Levida says, prodding Wade with a pitchfork and dropping the basket on the ground. I sit up and rub my aching ribs.

My grandmother lets Charlotte sleep in the house. That stupid pig has her own bedroom, while Wade and I are relegated to the barn. Levida gave us sleeping bags to spread across the hay, but it was too hot to sleep inside them.

I look at my watch. Only six o'clock and already so humid I can feel the sweat beading on my forehead.

Levida stands with her hands on her hips, surveying the barn. "We'll start with those stalls," she says, pointing to what I can only imagine used to be pigsties. From what she told us last night, the only pig she has left is Charlotte. Levida started selling off the land when my grandfather died. From the looks of the barn, she's been taking it apart piece by piece as well. Several of the outer boards are missing, and all the doors are gone.

Levida grabs a sledgehammer and starts hammering away at the old pigsties. "Been wantin' to tear down this old barn for a long time. Now I got the manpower to do it."

"Lev—Gram . . ." I'm not sure what to call her. "Ma'am, with all due respect, I didn't come all this way to tear down your barn. I came to see my father." I tense reflexively as I prepare to dodge the sledgehammer, but Levida sets it down and stares at me as cool as a cucumber.

"Well, seein' as how your car is sittin' in my ditch with two flat tires, you might be needin' to borrow my pickup truck."

"I hadn't thought of that."

"So you might try to be a little more amenable to helpin' out around here. Besides, it's Sunday. You ain't goin' nowhere until after church."

"Church?" Wade says, perking up, though I know he doesn't have a religious bone in his body.

"I figure you boys can get in a good two to three hours of demolition before you have to get cleaned up for Sunday services. Oh, and let me know if you find anythin' interestin'."

"Like what?" I ask. I can't imagine finding anything of interest if I searched the entire county.

"There's biscuits in the basket for your breakfast and some old clothes that belonged to your father in the box," she says as she kicks a box left beside my sleeping bag. "Come on, Charlotte."

Charlotte grunts at Baby Face, who cowers in fear of the massive pork chop and tries to hide under my legs.

Wade and I spend the morning tearing apart the stalls in the barn and stacking the old boards outside. Then we get ready for church.

I sort through the box of clothes my father left behind. Old jeans, some dress pants, T-shirts, dress shirts, and even a pair of brown cowboy boots at the bottom. I try on some pants and a shirt and realize my father is much larger than I am. The shoulders hit me halfway down the arm and all the pants sag around my waist, the way I used to wear them when I was a wannabe gangbanger. I have to cinch them up with a belt to look anywhere near respectable. Wade tries on a pair of dress pants and leaves them to sag around his scrawny waist. I toss him a belt. "Better cinch those up if you want to make a good impression on the preacher's daughter."

It's weird, wearing my father's stuff. Even weirder than wearing the clothes Jess gave me. It's like D.J. Dawson is suddenly standing somewhere behind me, but every time I try to get a good look at him, he slips away.

It's while we're having punch and cookies in the church foyer and waiting for the eleven o'clock service to begin that I realize where all the pieces of Levida's barn have gone. They're hanging for sale in the church thrift shop with Bible verses painted on them.

Dorie intercepts Wade at the coffee urn, and before the morning is over he has fallen in love and gotten saved, in that order.

Levida plays the church organ like a bat out of hell. She looks like one too, in her flowing black dress, swaying violently to the music and working the pedals with both legs. Her hands are so gnarled and arthritic, I don't know how she does it, but she manages to play all morning without missing a beat.

I have never been a religious person, but as I sit there in the sweltering heat of the Texas Hill Country, watching Wade get dunked in a baptistery below a crude wooden cross that looks suspiciously similar to an old barn door, and listening to Pastor Bob talk about mercy and redemption, I am filled with hope. Not the kind of expectation that comes from knowing you can pull yourself up by your own bootstraps, but the trust that comes from utter failure, from knowing you are pathetic and small and you've got no place to look but up.

"Jesus died in your place," the preacher says, after Wade comes up out of the water. "He was put to death like a common criminal to save your eternal soul." I look at my cross tattoo and a disturbing thought comes to me—I have permanently inscribed my hand with a symbol of execution.

I make another bargain with God. If you will get me out of the trouble I'm in, I'll never get off track again.

There is a potluck after church, fifty different varieties of food spread out on tables in the church basement, the only semi-cool place in the building.

"You're D.J. Dawson's kid, aren't you?" I hear, just as I finish my fried chicken and zucchini bread. I look up to see Red, the boy from the drugstore, standing in front of me with a paper plate full of roast beef and potato salad, his fists clenched so tightly around the rim he's bending the thing in half. "Aren't you?" he says again, making no attempt to hide the hostility in his voice.

I don't know if he's figured this out on his own or if the church gossip mill has provided him with the information, but there is no use denying it. "Yeah. I'm D.J. Dawson's kid."

He starts to shake, and I see he's fighting hard to contain his rage. "Then you better watch your ass." He turns and walks away.

I don't head out for Huntsville until nearly two. My clothes are in the wash, so I've sorted through all my father's old stuff, wondering what a guy should wear when he's visiting somebody on death row. I keep on the pants I wore to church but exchange the plaid shirt for a short-sleeved white dress shirt and tie. I eventually give up on the tie because I can't figure out how it works.

I ask Wade to go with me, to help me find the prison, but he won't because he's afraid he won't make it back in time for evening church at six o'clock.

"Plus, Dorie's dad holds a class for new converts at five," he tells me.

I can't imagine there are a lot of new converts in a town this size, but I let it pass.

It's surprisingly easy for me to find Huntsville, even though the road I'm traveling changes numbers three times before I get there. It's almost easier *not* having Wade navigate. The gears on Levida's old pickup truck grind every time I shift, and the suspension needs to be tightened. I'll give the truck a tune-up when I get back to Levida's place.

The town of Huntsville surprises me. I don't know what I was expecting. Some big industrialized city with factories and lots of barbed wire, maybe. What I find instead is a sleepy college town with green hills and pine trees, on the edge of a national forest. There's a town square surrounded by brick buildings. There's even an old opera house. It feels homey in a strange way.

I stop a kid on a bicycle and ask him where to find the prison.

"Which one?" he replies.

"What do you mean, which one?"

"There's nine prisons in and around Huntsville," he tells me, as if this is something I should already know.

"Nine prisons." I let what he's saying settle over me.

"That's the Walls right there," he says, pointing to a towering redbrick building down the street. Something about the brick fortress sends a chill down my back in spite of the heat.

"Thanks."

"That's where they kill 'em," says the boy.

"Kill who?"

"The guys on death row. Every couple o' weeks or so they send one up. Streets fill with reporters and TV cameras. My dad says the lights around town used to flash when they used Old Sparky. Now they just put 'em to sleep quiet-like with an injection."

"Thanks," I say, rolling up my window, eager to end the conversation and be on my way.

I drive right up to the front of the building. Redbrick walls flanking it on either side tower thirty feet or more above me.

I remember juvie and how when the door slid shut and locked behind me, I knew I was a prisoner. I wonder if the law is looking for me now. Consider that once I walk into that building, they might not let me back out.

I get out of the truck reluctantly. See a huge old-fashioned clock right above the front door, as if to remind all who enter here of the importance of time, or maybe that they are about to lose it.

I walk up the porch steps with their shiny brass rails to a double glass door bearing the state seal of Texas. Take a deep breath and go inside. Find myself in a small foyer. There is a wood-paneled wall on the right and a counter on the left about chest high, with a sliding window opening into a room filled with weapons and restraints. I hear voices talking over a police radio inside the room and see a woman, dressed in a gray uniform.

Straight ahead from the entrance, through a window separating the two rooms, is an amazing sight—a huge cage surrounded in shining brass bars. A man dressed in white pants and a white shirt, who I assume is a janitor, looks up at me briefly, then goes back to shining the brass with a cotton rag. The whole interior of the place gleams.

I walk over to the counter on the left and find two logbooks with the word VISITORS written on them. Wonder if I should give them my real name or an alias.

"Can I help you?" the guard asks me.

"I'm here to visit Dylan Dawson," I say. "Senior," I add, wondering if there is any possibility the two of us will get confused and I'll end up trapped in this place. "He's on death row."

"Death row is over in Livingston, forty miles east, but you can't visit on Sundays on any account. That's reserved for folks visiting members of the general prison population."

"Livingston. I thought he was here in Huntsville."

"Nope, they just bring 'em here for execution." The casualness of the way she says it makes the perspiration beading on my skin run like a river. I feel the white shirt sticking to my body like flypaper.

"So I came all this way for nothing?"

She shrugs. "They wouldn't have let you into the prison dressed like that anyway."

"Like what?"

"Can't wear anything white inside," she tells me, pointing to my shirt. "That's what the inmates wear. In fact, most people around these parts avoid that color altogether. You don't want someone to think you're an escaped convict."

"No, ma'am," I say, glancing over at the man in white polishing the brass bars, realizing he must be an inmate. "Anything else I should avoid?"

"No open-toed shoes. No cell phones. No paper money. I assume your name is on his visitation list."

"I don't know," I say.

"They won't let you in if you're not on his list."

"How do I get on the list?"

"You can write a letter to the prisoner. He tells the warden to put you on his list. Then the prisoner has to write you back to let you know it's okay to visit."

"But he's my father. I haven't seen him in eleven years, and they're gonna kill him in nine days."

Only then does the woman's expression soften. "Dawson," she says as if the name is suddenly ringing a bell. "Is your daddy D.J. Dawson?"

"Yeah, do you know him?"

"Everybody knows him. He's been all over the papers since they announced his execution date. That's a tough break, kid."

"Can't I just call him?"

"It doesn't work that way, but if you've got somebody else who's going in to see him, they could ask him to put your name on his list."

"I could ask my grandmother," I say, but even as the words come out of my mouth, I have my doubts. After all, Levida didn't bother to tell me there was no visitation on Sundays. The only thing I know for sure is that I won't be writing any letters.

"You gotta help me see my dad," I tell Levida as she ladles black-eyed peas into soup bowls and butters up slices of cornbread to go on the side.

Levida takes a seat at the kitchen table next to Charlotte, who gets her own pan of cornbread in a huge metal bowl on the floor. "It's the Lord's day, so before we eat, we read from the Good Book," she says to me and Wade and Dorie, who has joined us for dinner and sits so close to Wade she is nearly on top of him.

"Did you hear me?" I ask her. "I said—"

She silences me with a look and hands me a black leather Bible.

"I can't," I tell her. "I don't have my reading glasses."

She narrows her eyes but doesn't say anything, just hands the book to Wade, who happily complies. "'He was led as a sheep to slaughter; And as a Lamb before its shearer is silent, So He does not open His mouth. In humiliation His judgment was taken away; Who will relate His generation? For His life is removed from the earth.'"

"Amen," says Dorie.

Levida gives me a sideways glance, and I can tell she's chosen this particular selection for my benefit, though I have no earthly idea why. I get up from the table, shove in my chair, and head for the door. Levida jumps up from her chair and beats me to it, blocking my way out. "You will not disrespect the Word of the Lord in this house!" she says, shaking a finger in my face.

"Why didn't you tell me my father is in Livingston? Why didn't you tell me he couldn't have visitors on Sundays? Why didn't you say my name has to be on some stupid list before they'll even let me in?"

"Why didn't your mama tell you?" Levida spits back at me, venom in her eyes.

I don't know, but there is no way I am going to try to explain my mother to Levida. "I want to talk to my father, and I need you to help me get in to see him."

"Why should I?"

"I'm his son. Your grandson."

"Oh, yeah." She puts her hands on her hips as if she couldn't care less.

I lower my voice so Wade and Dorie can't hear me, though they are so engrossed in each other they don't even seem to notice our conversation. "Don't you think he might want to see me before he dies?"

"I wouldn't know."

"What do you mean?"

"I haven't talked to him in eleven years."

"Are you telling me you've never been to visit him?"

"Went once. Haven't been back since." There is a hardness in her eyes that I don't know how to read. I can't tell if it's a reflection of her frosty, bitter heart or if it's covering some pain too deep for words. The only thing I can see clearly is that she will be no help to me at all.

"I just want to know what kind of man he is," I say. "Before it's too late."

She studies me with her stone eyes and rubs her chin. The icy crust around her heart seems to thaw just a little. "Come with me." She grabs my arm and leads me to a room at the back of the house, takes a ring of keys out of her pocket, and unlocks a door. Turns on the light. We step into a room filled with trophies and pennants. I blink. It's like some kind of shrine to my father. There's a football jersey pinned up on the far wall, and to my right, a huge photograph of my father in his football uniform. His high school graduation. Some college photos.

I walk toward it. This is the face I have not been able to remember, but how could I have ever forgotten? It is the same face as mine. The same square jaw and dark hair. The same thin lips and pale blue eyes. I realize in amazement that I don't have my mother's eyes at all. My eyes are my father's.

That night in the barn I stay up until four o'clock in the morning, till the batteries in the flashlight burn out, looking at the scrapbook of clippings Levida has given me.

Pictures and articles of my father's football team winning the state championship. Stories about his college glory days. Newspaper accounts of the murder trial and conviction. Letters to the editor. Even a piece from *Newsweek*.

Not one of which I can decipher beyond the title and first three sentences.

I pull the paper filled with Jess's handwriting out of my back pocket. I try to read it, but the flashlight is dead, so I just slip it under my pillow in the darkness, wondering if I'll ever see her again.

When I finally go to sleep, I dream of clocks.

But this time it isn't the bird that bursts through the door, it is my father.

He has come to tell me that time is running out.

WORDS

I carry a message
        that I cannot read.
        The words may be haunting
or tender or sweet.
Though what it says
I do not know,
I still carry it with me,

        wherever I go.

24

I WOKE UP IN THE BEANBAG CHAIR AGAIN. JESS AND BABY
Face were snuggled up next to each other on the futon, still set
up like a couch. I imagined what it would feel like, lying next to
Jess like that.

Dogs can get away with anything!

Couldn't believe I'd spent another night in the home of a
gorgeous girl without sleeping with her. But it was okay. I'd
decided to do things right for once, no matter what that took.
I was following her lead. Since that first kiss on the beach, she
hadn't touched me. If she was waiting for me to make a move,
it wasn't going to happen. I was too afraid of messing things up,
breaking the spell, waking up from the dream.

Jess opened her eyes. Yawned. Look up at me. Smiled her
crooked grin. God, she was beautiful. "I can't believe how easy
it is to sleep with you here."

"It's not me. It's Yeats," I said, pointing to the book lying on
the floor, trying not to watch how the T-shirt clung to her body.

"The two of you make a good team," she said.

* * *

I had to work, and Jess had another day of SAT cramming, so I didn't see her again until that night. She wanted to drive down to the Redondo Pier, but she wanted to take my car. I warned her that my air conditioner was busted and the radiator was on the way out, but she insisted.

"My first car was a Mustang," she told me, rubbing her hand against the dashboard like it was made of gold.

"Mine too." First and only.

I remembered the day my uncle Mitch took me to the auto auction in Santa Barbara and told me to pick any car I wanted—under $4,000. The old Mustang was a classic, but nobody was bidding on it because it was a putrid shade of piss yellow. Mitch got the thing at a steal for $3,800, and I used my first paycheck to paint it midnight blue.

"What's this?" she said, thumbing through my journal just as we pulled into a filling station for gas.

"Nothing." I grabbed it out of her hands and tossed it onto the backseat, next to Baby Face. "Just some poems."

"Yours?"

"Yeah, but they're pretty lame, so don't read 'em. Want a Coke?" I asked, trying to change the subject.

"Sure, okay," she said.

I went into the mini-mart, and when I returned I noticed that my journal was lying on the floor of the back. I wondered if Baby Face had knocked it off the seat or if Jess had read it. I'd die of embarrassment if she saw her name above that last poem. I studied her face for signs, but she just smiled at me and thanked me for the Coke.

Later, when we got back to her house, I went into the bathroom to change for bed. At home I slept in my underwear, but I was wearing shorts and a T-shirt for her benefit.

When I came out I was surprised to see she'd already slipped into her pajamas—the tight-fitting T-shirt and cotton shorts. She was sitting on the futon, which she'd made out into a queen-size bed. My legs went weak as I sat down beside her, thinking of all the things that could happen on a bed that size. She was looking through my copy of *Poetry Through the Ages*, which I guessed she'd taken from my car, though I hadn't seen her do it. "Why are some of these page numbers circled?" she asked.

"Fourteen, thirty-eight, twenty-two. They're my mom's favorites. She gave me the book for my birthday." I suddenly wondered if I'd looked too eager in sitting down beside her, and I started to stand. She grabbed my arm and pulled me back down next to her. "Read me this one," she said, handing me the book.

My instant reaction was panic. I hadn't pretended to need glasses the previous night, so I couldn't very well rely on that trick now. But then I looked at the page number and realized it was one of the Yeats poems my mother had circled in blue ink, thirty-eight. A poem I knew at least. "Okay," I said.

> "I saw a staring virgin stand
> Where holy Dionysus died,
> And tear the heart out of his side,
> And lay the heart upon her hand . . ."

I never understood who "Dyin' Isis" was. Mom had mentioned the god of wine, but she was drunk at the time, so I might have misunderstood. I did understand what a virgin was, though I'd never been with one. When I finished the poem, Jess looked up at me expectantly, like she had something on her mind and I was supposed to figure it out. Like she was trying to tell me something.

Then it hit me. "Are you a virgin?" I asked, but then I realized how rude that sounded and tried to cover my tracks. "A virgin who's gonna tear out my heart?"

"Yes . . . no . . . wait." She looked at me. "I'm not going to rip out your heart."

"Thanks for clearing that up," I said stupidly, my heart beating erratically.

"Is that okay with you?" she asked softly.

"Okay with me?" I didn't know how to answer, but I could see by the look on her face that it was very important to say the right thing. Monumental. Life-changing. "No, it's not okay at all," I replied.

"Why not?" She looked down at her toes.

"I *want* you to rip out my heart."

She smiled, pressed her hand to my chest, and said, "I could never do that."

You already have, I thought as I took her hand in mine. "Jess, I already told you. I don't expect anything."

"That's good to know."

"All I really want is to be here with you, just like this."

"You mean it?"

"Yes." It was a lie, but I knew it sounded good.

She kissed me then—long and deep and hard, and I knew I'd answered her well. "Will you stay close to me tonight?" she asked.

"Of course," I said, feeling so light and dizzy I feared I would float right off the bed.

"Thank you." She lay down with her back to me, which wasn't quite what I'd been hoping for. I lay down next to her, not knowing where to put my hands. She pulled my arm around her body and held it close to her heart. I had to keep it in a fist to prevent my fingers from wandering into dangerous territory. I wanted desperately to be a gentleman. It took me a while, a long while, but I finally started to breathe normally, after I realized nothing more was going to happen. Especially after I heard her snoring.

I have a very sedating effect on women.

The only problem left was what to do with my boner. Keep it at a safe distance, was all I could think to do. Difficult with her so close. I lay awake well into the night, unable to believe I was holding this incredible, beautiful girl in my arms. I wanted to stay there forever. Avoided the temptation to run my hands across her sleeping body. Maybe it was enough just to be close to her. I pressed my face into her hair and breathed her into me. "I love you," I whispered. "Stay with me forever. Please."

We lay there in the silence, but it didn't feel like silence, because words were starting to invade my brain again. Let me love you, girl who came from the sea. Let us swim to the bottom of the ocean where we can be anything and where no one can find us. We will grow gills and breathe salt water. We will sprout fins and scales and make our home in underground caves. Or else we will drown there. But either way, I will be happy.

25

I SLEPT LATE BECAUSE IT WAS THE FOURTH AND I DIDN'T
have to go to work. I reached out for Jess and found myself
hugging Baby Face, who responded by licking my face.

Not exactly the greeting I was hoping for.

At least not from my dog.

I sat up, looked around. Saw Jess sitting at the bar, writing
something.

"You're awake," she said, bouncing off the bar stool and
walking toward me, paper in hand. She was fully caffeinated
and already dressed, wearing a pair of cotton shorts over a
one-piece bathing suit that fit her like a glove. I wondered if
she had any idea the effect she had on guys like me.

"I have something I want you to read," she said, holding
out the paper.

I made no move to take it from her hand. "I don't have my
glasses."

"Don't be silly. Since when do you wear glasses?"

I wanted to crawl under the futon and die, or at least

make a quick escape out the window.

"I know what you need," she said, smiling. "I'll get you some coffee." She left the paper on the table and returned a few minutes later with a steaming mug.

I drank it very slowly, with Jess looking up at me the whole time. When I finally set down my mug, she put the paper in my hand.

The words she'd written immediately began dancing. "What is it?" I asked. It could have been a grocery list or a suicide note for all I knew.

"A poem. Maybe the beginning of a song. I'm not sure. I used to write a lot of songs."

"You did?" I said, stalling for time as my stomach did flip-flops.

"Go on, read it."

I tried to read it. I really did. I made out the first few words, but I was so shaken with her sitting there that I forgot what I was reading the minute I came to the end of the line. Something about people and what they say about you. After that I was completely lost. I didn't know what else to do so I just kept staring at the paper.

"You hate it," she said, looking suddenly like she might cry.

"No. Not at all. It's . . . it's beautiful."

"You really think so?" She scooted closer.

"Absolutely."

"Do you feel the same way?" she asked, and it felt like her future happiness rested on my answer.

"Most definitely," I told her, praying that was the right reply.

"I'm *sooo* glad," she said, taking my palm and pressing it against her lips. I stroked her cheek with my thumb. Felt her breath between my fingers. Moved my hand down her neck. Traced her collarbone with my fingertips.

I was wearing running shorts and had nowhere to hide my reaction. "Excuse me," I said, jumping off the futon before she saw and hurrying to the bathroom. Not coming out for a good long while.

A change had come over Jess. I wasn't sure exactly how or why, but I wasn't complaining.

She couldn't get close enough to me. Couldn't help touching me. Every now and then she would even stop in the middle of the sidewalk to pull me close and kiss me.

All day long I kept touching my back pocket, where I'd carefully tucked the poem she wrote. I felt like I held a treasure map I couldn't decipher, but it didn't really matter because I already had the treasure. Nothing mattered anymore except being with Jess.

That night as we slow danced on the beach with the band playing love songs and the fireworks exploding over the ocean, she pressed her body into mine and kissed me as if we were the only two souls in the world, even though the beach was crowded with people. Every time the sky lit up, a little explosion went off inside of me. She had to feel the reaction she was having on my body. No hiding it now.

When the band stopped playing to take a break, Jess grabbed my hand and led me out past where people were sitting on blankets, watching the light show. She led me up under the pier and found an empty place on the sand. Then she lay down, right in the middle of God and Southern California, and pulled me down on top of her.

I was trying to prop myself up on my elbows, afraid I might

crush her, but Jess wasn't afraid. She pulled me closer, took the full weight of me on her.

We were both fully dressed. Nothing was going to happen out here on the beach. Then again, her futon was just a few blocks away. I was losing myself in her, completely and absolutely, and I kept thinking that if I stayed here long, I might not be able to leave.

Later, as she was tugging me along the boardwalk back to her house, we stopped to kiss every few feet.

I'd had girls come on to me before, but I'd always known that if I wasn't around they would have found someone else. This was different. Jess was hungry for me and only me.

Those girls had also been stoned or drunk, which I figured made me look a lot hotter to them than I really was. Thinking back, I realized I'd always been stoned too. All of a sudden I wondered if I would know what to do straight.

My head was spinning. I felt like I'd been drifting, lost at sea all my life, and now that I'd found dry land, I couldn't quite get my bearings.

Why hadn't I brought any condoms?

Would she have any?

I doubted it.

What if I got her pregnant and ruined her life?

What if I gave her some disease?

What would she look like naked?

Would she regret this tomorrow?

What had she written on the paper in my pocket?

A million statistics from health class rushed through my head. Then she kissed me and I forgot them all.

She tasted like an ocean breeze.

What if I was misreading her?

Wasn't it just last night she had me reciting a poem about a virgin?

What did that look in her eyes really mean?

What if her father came home, found us together, and killed me?

Why hadn't I brought any condoms?

Was it possible I was dreaming?

What had she written on the paper in my pocket?

When we got inside Jess's house, she quickly locked the door behind us and then pulled me straight up the steps to the second floor, where Baby Face ran out of her hiding place in the kitchen to greet us, probably frightened by the fireworks. She jumped up on the futon, wagging her tail.

Jess pulled me onto the floor so that we were both kneeling on the carpet, unbuttoned my shirt, and started kissing my chest. Her lips were like fire. "Oh God!" I groaned.

And then the phone rang.

"The machine will get it," she said, as she untied the bathing suit strap around her neck. I reached up to help her.

"Jess, are you there?" came a voice over the answering machine. "Jess, pick up. I've got to see you. Baby, I've been such an idiot. I'm on my way over."

"No!" Jess jumped up and ran to the phone, leaving me on the floor.

"Jason, what are you doing? . . . At this hour? . . . No . . . no. This really isn't a good time. . . . No, I don't want you to come over right now. . . . I don't have to give you a reason. . . . Have you been drinking? You haven't? You sound funny. . . . What's wrong? Jason, are you . . . crying?"

Jess looked down at me and her face filled with remorse, as if she'd suddenly realized she'd woken up under a cardboard box with some bum. She turned her back to me and lowered her voice, and I knew what was happening.

I was waking up from the dream.

"I know you didn't mean what you said," she murmured. "I know you're sorry. . . ."

I buttoned my shirt and started throwing my belongings into my bag.

"What are you talking about?" she asked him. "A ring?"

I zipped up my bag and sat on the futon, waiting, breathing, just trying to keep breathing.

"Why did you do that?" she asked him. "I know that we *talked* about it but . . . Yes . . . I know you do. . . . Yes, I know. . . . I know. . . ."

My heart stopped beating as I listened.

"I love you, too," she whispered.

I love you, too. The words burned themselves onto my brain. Maybe she didn't mean it, but she'd still said it.

"Okay," she told him. "I'll see you in a few minutes."

She hung up the phone and turned back toward me, but didn't look me in the eye as she retied her bathing suit straps.

I put the leash on Baby Face. "I should be going," I said. "Will you be okay?" I could hardly speak, so strong was the desire to crawl in a deep hole and die.

"He's not as bad as he seems."

I wanted to tell her exactly what I thought of Jason. I'd seen his type a hundred times. He'd probably spent the entire weekend with some other girl before he woke up and came to his senses about Jess. But I knew from experience that when you told somebody they shouldn't want something, they wanted it all the more. "I'm sure he's a great guy."

"Really? What makes you think so?"

"You wouldn't love him otherwise."

She started to cry. "I don't want you to go," she said, but I left anyway, and she didn't try to stop me.

I drove down to Huntington Beach. Crying. Cursing. Screaming out the window at the night.

Jason had cried on the phone with her, hadn't he? Why hadn't I cried in front of her? Why did I always have to play the tough guy?

When I got to Huntington Beach, I parked at the pier. Got out of the car. Took the piece of paper out of my back pocket. Knew that whatever was written there was lies. Like the lie she told me when she said she wouldn't rip out my heart. Her claw marks were all over it. I tried to tear up the note. Tried to hate her.

Couldn't seem to do either one.

Got back in the car. Realized what I really needed was to get very, very drunk. Unfortunately, my fake ID was back at home in Downey.

Put the car in gear and drove, playing "Dream On." It all came flooding back to me. My uncle had set me up. My father was about to die. My mother, who had never bothered to tell me he was on death row, was having some kind of mental breakdown. My best friend was on the verge of handing his life over to a gang, and the only girl I'd ever really loved was with somebody else at that very minute. I'd gotten her all warmed up for Jason.

All I had wanted was to escape from my pathetic life, and for a few days I had, with Jess.

When I got home, it was two a.m. and no one was there. At first I was worried about my mother, but then I remembered she'd gone to Texas with Uncle Mitch. I went into the garage bedroom I shared with Wade and looked through the boxes where I kept my clothes. I'd thought the fake ID was in the bottom of a box of jeans, but it wasn't. I turned over both of the mattresses, ripped through Wade's girly magazines, tore the pockets off of clothing. Completely trashed our room before I realized it was three a.m. and the bars were closed.

Went looking through the kitchen for the bottle of Crown Royal I knew Mom kept hidden. Remembered I'd poured the last one out. Started throwing dishes and cursing her. Cursing me. I asked myself what kind of mother puts their kid out in the garage. Then I felt guilty because I knew I wasn't exactly the ideal son, and I wondered if she was okay. She had looked so hopeless the last time I saw her. Was it possible she still loved my father, maybe a little bit?

Jess was better off without me. I should be happy for her, right?

I felt all the old rage bubbling up inside of me. I had changed my clothes, but I was still the same inside. No good. If she stuck with me, Jess might end up like my mother one day. That would be worse than this, I tried to tell myself.

I went to the box room. I don't know why. Maybe I was pissed because the boxes were filling my old room. Maybe because it was my mother's way of keeping things in order, and I was sick of pretending the world could be arranged.

I dumped the contents of all of the boxes into the middle

of the floor; the old tax returns, birth certificates, never-been-opened kitchen appliances. The fancy clothes Uncle Mitch bought her but she never wore. Then I tore all the boxes apart and tossed the pieces on top of the pile, sat down in the middle of it, and started to cry so hard my whole body was shaking.

"Bad day?"

I looked up to see Wade standing in the doorway, and I never felt so relieved. Good old faithful, predictable Wade. From the look in his eyes, I could tell he was trashed.

"You got any weed?" I asked him.

"Nah, smoked it all. Think I got a few Kools left." He reached into his back pocket and pulled out a pack of cigarettes. Walked over. Offered me a smoke and a light.

I inhaled deeply, imagining it was something stronger. Felt my whole body relax. An overwhelming tiredness came over me. I thought about dropping the burning cigarette into the middle of the room and watching everything go up in smoke as I sat in the middle of the bonfire. Knew I wasn't quite that crazy.

Wade sat beside me on the floor and lit a cigarette for himself. "What happened?"

"I tried to be somebody different from who I am and it didn't work out."

"The world ain't set up that way. Folks say we oughta be better than we are, but deep down they just want us to stay in our places. With our own kind. Messes up the natural order, otherwise."

"Guess I figured that out the hard way."

"Did you love her?"

I wasn't sure how Wade knew there was a *her*. He surprised me like that sometimes.

"Yeah."

Wade nodded his head. Looked at his watch. "We're supposed to be at work in five hours."

"Don't remind me," I said as I grabbed one of Mom's fake fur coats and made a pillow out of it.

"We could call in sick."

"Nah. That wouldn't be right. Gomez is the only person who ever tried to do right by us."

"Whatever you say, but after work we're gonna find ourselves a party. Pick up some girls. Get blown in every way possible."

"Whatever," I said, my eyelids heavy with sleep.

"It'll be just like old times," he told me. There was a hint of something desperate in his voice, but I wasn't really listening, because by that time I was too far gone to hear any hint of danger.

26

I WAS SO DISTRACTED AT WORK THAT I FORGOT TO REPLACE
the drain plug in a Volkswagen van. I must have looked pretty
bad too, because nobody bothered me or accused me of pulling
a Wade.

"I scored us some weed," Wade told me after taking a
lengthy lunch break and spending most of it at the pay phone
out front. "Found us a party over in Compton. All we gotta do is
bring a couple of bottles."

"Sounds great," I said, trying to smile. Truth was, I already
felt like I had a hangover and wasn't looking forward to tomorrow morning, but I'd promised Wade I would party with him,
and it seemed to mean a lot to him. He walked around all day
smiling and saying things like, "Good to have you back" and
"Just like old times."

"You okay, son?" Gomez asked me when I nearly poured a
quart of oil into the radiator of a Jimmy.

"Don't call me son. I'm not your son. I'm not anybody's
son," I said. Then I grabbed an old oil barrel we used as a trash

can and went out back to empty it so I wouldn't have to look at the hurt in his eyes.

I had just dumped a bunch of boxes and old rags into the dumpster when I turned around to see a fist coming straight for my jaw. It knocked me backward and I fell to the ground. No sooner had I landed on the asphalt than I felt arms lifting me, holding me while the first guy used my stomach for a punching bag.

I lifted both my knees and drop-kicked my attacker, who flew back about four feet, hit a wall, and came back swinging.

Meanwhile, I threw the two guys who were holding me off balance by forcing them to support my full weight. Then I shoved them in my attacker's path.

He stumbled to the ground, and I finally got a good look at his face. It was Jess's boyfriend, Jason.

Great! I could only imagine what Jess had told him about me—that I'd tried to force myself on her? That my gangbanger friends had tried to kidnap her?

Jason came at me swinging, along with his two cronies who were big guys like him and just as full of rage. "Somebody needs to teach you a lesson. Girls like Jessica don't end up with trash like you," Jason yelled.

I grabbed a piece of pipe out of the dumpster and swung it in front of me to keep the three of them back. "You don't deserve her any more than I do," I told him.

"What did you do to her?" he screamed at me.

"None of your damn business," I shouted, but I panicked as I wondered again what she had told him. The events of the last few days raced through my mind. Had I moved too fast? Misread her? No, she had definitely been the one to come on to

me, but maybe she didn't remember it that way. Maybe the guilt
of seeing her boyfriend put the whole weekend in a different
perspective.

"Oh yes, it is my business," he said, picking up a piece of two-
by-four lying by the wall. "I bought her a damn ring, and when
I get to her house she tells me she wants to break up with me."

"She broke up with you?" I said in disbelief, dropping my
guard.

Jason's two friends took the opportunity to grab the pipe
and force my hands behind my back. Jason started whaling on
me with the board, but I was too dazed to feel anything for the
first couple of blows.

"I had to find out from her friends she'd left me for a lousy
grease monkey," he said as the board came down hard across
my ribs. The whole scene seemed so unreal that I couldn't help
it. I started to laugh. Which just made Jason angrier. He sliced
the board across my mouth, and I wasn't laughing anymore.

"Stop it!" someone screamed, and I looked up to see Jess
running out of the back of the shop, followed by Kip and
Gomez, who was carrying a tire iron. Gomez knocked Jason off
his feet, while Jess started beating the guys holding me with her
handbag. "Let him go," she screamed at them.

"You heard the lady," said Kip, picking up the piece of pipe
I had dropped.

The two thugs released me, and I fell to the ground. Only
then did the pain set in, but the sight of Jess kneeling down in
front of me made it worthwhile.

"I'm so sorry," she said. "I didn't tell him anything. I swear."

"I suggest you pick up your friend and get him out of here,"
Gomez warned Jason's cronies. "Before I call the police."

They helped Jason off the ground and started moving him to his car. "Jess, you can't leave me for *him*," he pleaded.

"I already have," Jess told him.

She had left her fancy rich boyfriend for me? Had I heard her right, or had the blow to my head left me loony?

Jess turned back to me. "Are you okay? Oh my God. You're bleeding." She took a tissue out of her purse and dabbed the side of my face. Then she kissed me on the lips so tenderly I was instantly lost. Little voices were saying things to me like, *You're not good enough, you'll drag her down, you don't belong with her*. But I ignored them all. I wrapped my arms around her and pulled her close, even though my entire body was aching. Because in that moment I believed something different from what the voices in my head had been telling me all my life. I believed I could be a better person than who I'd always been.

By that time every guy in the shop was standing outside watching us, and they all began to cheer, except for Wade, who stood at the back of the crowd with his hands in his pockets, looking like he'd just lost his best friend.

"I couldn't stand watching you walk away last night," Jess told me. "But I was so afraid something bad would happen if you stayed. And now look at you." She started to cry and wiped my face again. "This is all my fault."

"I'm okay," I said, trying to get up and grabbing my side in pain.

"All right, Romeo," Gomez said as he and Kip helped me to my feet. "I'm taking you to my doctor to have a look at those ribs."

Jess looked around and seemed to notice for the first time

that we had an audience. She quickly stood up, then leaned toward me and whispered, "Tonight. My place."

"Tonight," I said, and then I watched her walk away.

The doctor x-rayed me and said my ribs were bruised, but not fractured. Mr. Gomez paid him out of his own pocket and then drove me back to the shop. "Thank you," I told him, feeling bad for what I had said to him earlier. He was the only person who had ever acted like anything even close to a father.

"Is she worth all that pain?" he asked me, smiling.

"Definitely," I said, still reeling from the events of the day. "But I don't deserve her."

"Then be somebody who does."

"That's what I intend to do."

By the time we got back to the shop it was closing time. "What about the party?" Wade asked me, looking like a wounded puppy.

"I don't think that's gonna work out," I told him. It would have been easier if he'd gotten angry. Then I could have stood my ground, told him to leave me alone, but it was the sad, lost look in his eyes I couldn't stand.

"But we had plans," he said.

"Plans change."

His lower lip started to quiver as if he was going to start crying right there in front of me. It took so little to make him happy and so little to crush him. It was exhausting, being so responsible for his happiness.

"Come on, Wade. Can't you see I got a good thing going?"

"You can't be somethin' you ain't," he reminded me.

"I gotta try."

"But I'm the one who set up the party. I'm supposed to bring the booze, and now I don't even got a ride. Can you at least give me a ride?" He was so pathetic. What could I say?

"Sure, Wade. I can give you a ride." And with those eight words, my fate was sealed.

Wade showered. Combed his hair. Got dressed. Checked his watch. Decided he didn't like his hair. Spent a half hour trying to get it right. Then, just as I thought we were finally going to leave, he checked his watch again. Decided he didn't like what he was wearing.

"I've got a couple of things to take care of," I explained to Jess on the telephone, after Wade started changing his clothes yet again. "Then I'll be right over, I promise."

"I'll be waiting, as long as it takes," she told me. "I'll stay up all night, just come to me as soon as you can."

I looked around at the dismal room, the dirty throw rug we'd tossed over the grease stain in the middle of the garage, the one window with the threadbare curtain, the cinder-block wall we'd built where the garage door used to be, the lone bulb that served as our main light source. It was so pathetic compared to Jess's house I almost felt guilty for leaving Wade behind.

Almost.

"Okay, it's time to go," Wade said at 8:35 on the dot.

Finally.

I thought about taking a change of clothes to Jess's house, but then remembered the bag filled with her father's rejects. Didn't want to look like I was moving in. I put Baby Face in the backseat and we were on our way.

"You can wait out here," Wade said as I pulled up in front of a liquor store on Rosecrans Avenue. "I'll just be a minute. And keep the engine runnin'. I don't wanna be late to the party."

Then why did you change your clothes four times? I wanted to ask him, but I kept my mouth shut.

Wade went into the store and didn't even walk over to the liquor aisle. He just stood in front of the candy, next to the register.

"Wade, what the hell are you doing?" I said, even though I knew he couldn't hear me.

That's when I saw him draw a gun and point it at the guy behind the counter.

"Shit!" I yelled. "Wade, are you crazy?" I screamed.

Before I had time to think what to do, Wade had handed the man a pillowcase, which the clerk filled with money and handed back. Wade ran outside, jumped in the car, and screamed, "Drive. Drive! DRIVE!"

I peeled out of the parking lot as fast as I could, nearly hitting a Volkswagen. I could hear sirens in the distance. Wondered if they were already coming after us. Wondered if the guy in the store had pressed a silent alarm, gotten my license plate number, had Wade's picture on the surveillance camera. Realized I'd just become an accessory to armed robbery.

"Wade, what the hell were you thinking?"

"Get on the 710," he said.

I didn't really have much choice if I wanted to put some distance between us and the crime scene, so I did it.

He was clutching the pillowcase full of money to his chest, and the hand holding the gun was shaking so badly I was afraid he was going to accidentally shoot me. "Would you please put that thing down?" I said.

He looked at his hand. Didn't even seem to realize he was still holding the gun. Tossed it on the floor.

"Wade, what is going on?"

"Take this exit," he said.

"Wade!"

"Do it!" he yelled.

I took the exit. Didn't know what else to do. When I was sure we'd lost the cops, I pulled to a stop in front of a park. Got out of the car, went over to the passenger side, and yanked Wade out by the collar. Threw him up on the hood of the Mustang with him still clutching the bag full of money.

"Is this some sort of fucking game to you, Wade? You turn eighteen in two months, and my birthday is next week. We're not going to juvie this time. They're gonna lock us in with the big boys."

"Ajax got a hookup. We ain't gonna do no time. He promised."

"What are you talking about?" I looked around the park, saw the graffiti covering the trash cans, and realized we were smack dab in the middle of Compton.

About that time the black van pulled up alongside us and parked on the curb. Ajax, Spider, Eight Ball, and Two Tone all got out, along with some other guys from the BSB carrying twelve-packs of beer like they'd just arrived at a party.

That's when I realized. This was the party.

"What up, cuz? You got the goods?" Eight Ball asked Wade.

"Right here." Wade handed him the pillowcase, his hands still shaking.

Eight Ball looked inside, smiled, and slapped Wade on the shoulder. "You done good."

"Dat's my man," Two Tone said, knocking fists with Wade.

Ajax pulled out something that looked like an electric toothbrush, with a needle coming out the top where the bristles should have been. "Okay. You boys proved yourselves. Time to tat up."

The full impact of what was happening hit me. Ajax wasn't holding a toothbrush. It was a homemade tattoo gun. And this was an initiation. So Wade had robbed the liquor store to get into the gang. But why did he have to drag me along?

Ajax grabbed my right arm and held the needle against it. I jerked away from him. "No!"

Eight Ball's smile disappeared. "Whatchoo mean, no? You done the crime. Now you in. We had an agreement." He looked at Wade. "Both of you or no deal."

Wade turned to me. "Come on, Dylan. You know this is where we belong. This is where guys like us always end up. Here or in the gutter, and I don't wanna end up dead in no gutter."

"You decided this all on your own. You didn't even hit me up on it!" I screamed at him. "You had no business!"

"You told me he was down," Eight Ball said to Wade, his eyes cold and dangerous.

"Fo' sho he is," said Wade, posing like a tough guy. "He's just a little sideways right now. Some rich bitch got him twisted. He'll come around."

I grabbed Wade by the face, wanting to crush his jaw in my fist. "Don't you ever call her that. I'm not coming around, Wade. I don't want any part of this." I turned to Eight Ball. "What I told you in the garage is solid. I'm going legit."

The BSB looked from one to another as if they were having a silent conference among themselves. "We cool wit' dat," said Eight Ball. "'Course, we can't offer you no protection from the po-po if you ain't in." He glanced at Ajax, who nodded. "If you in, this never happened. You ain't in, you on your own."

He was blackmailing me. If I joined the gang, my life would belong to them forever. But if I didn't, I would go to prison.

"I'm not tatting up," I said.

Eight Ball looked at me long and hard, but I wasn't backing down. "Okay," he finally said, his voice full of resignation. "You can roll."

"That's it? You just gonna let him fly?" said Two Tone.

Eight Ball raised a hand to silence his younger brother. "Go on," he told me.

I walked to my car in relief. "C'mon, Wade."

"Wade ain't goin' with you," Ajax said.

"You still letting me tatt up?" Wade asked.

Ajax set the tattoo gun on a bench and pinned Wade's arms behind his back. "Not a punk-ass lying piece of shit like you."

Spider reared back and gave Wade such a punch to the gut that he doubled over and couldn't breathe. Then he grabbed Wade by the hair and forced him to look at Eight Ball. "We had an agreement, and you didn't follow through," said Eight Ball. "Now we gotta teach you a lesson. Two Tone, take care of him."

Spider helped Ajax hold Wade while Two Tone took a switchblade out of his pocket, beaming at the opportunity.

"No, please," said Wade, starting to cry as Two Tone tossed the blade from hand to hand, smiling.

My mind went back to juvie. To one night when I was in the shower and all of a sudden I looked around and no one else was there except three guys with swastika tattoos. They grabbed me and threw me on the floor, and the next thing I knew, Wade came into the bathroom carrying a shank he'd made from a tin can lid stolen from his job in the commissary. He was like a crazy man, cutting and slashing at them. Screaming at them to leave me alone. Then one of them pulled a pipe off the sink and started swinging.

I had run, thinking Wade was right behind me, and didn't slow down until a guard stopped me and asked me what had happened to my clothes. I looked back and realized Wade wasn't there.

"Leave him alone," I yelled at Eight Ball.

"I told *you* to go," Eight Ball said. "Don't push me."

Two Tone lunged playfully at Wade, laughing when he winced. Then his eyes turned ice-cold as he held the blade against Wade's throat.

"Stop!" I grabbed Two Tone from behind, spun him around to face me, and gave him an uppercut to the jaw.

One blow. It wasn't even that hard, because I was still aching from the bruised ribs. It was the way Two Tone fell. Slow motion. His head hitting the park bench. Neck twisting awkwardly. A look of realization in his eyes just before they closed.

Eight Ball fell to his knees beside his brother, followed by Ajax and Spider. I grabbed Wade and pulled him toward the Mustang. Eight Ball felt for a pulse. Began weeping. Cradling his brother in his arms. "No!" he screamed. "No, no, no." Then Eight Ball looked at me, eyes smoldering in hate. "You killed him."

He grabbed the blade from Two Tone's limp hand and came after us, but I was already slamming on the gas.

I got on the 710 and headed north. Got off in South Gate. Took side streets till I found the 5. Got on and off of highways going north and south, east and west. Every time I had the chance to merge onto another highway, I did. No rhyme or reason. No plan. Just trying to make sure we weren't followed.

I knew I couldn't go back home. Couldn't go to the garage. Couldn't go to Jess, even though she was still waiting for me. It wasn't until we were just north of San Bernardino and Wade asked, "Where are we going?" that I knew.

"We're going to Texas."

THE HEART OF TEXAS

In the heart of Texas, there's a town,
a sleepy town nine prisons strong.
Commit a crime and you'll go down
to Huntsville, where the days are longer,
steel bars strong there, hope all gone
there. Huntsville, where they right the wrongs
done in the heart of Texas.

27

FIRST THING MONDAY MORNING I HEAD OUT FOR
Livingston. I don't know if they will let me in to see my father,
but I have to try. After I get to Huntsville, I stop to ask for directions. Then I take highway 190 through Dodge and Point Blank.
Can't believe the names of these Texas towns.

The Polunsky Unit sits outside Livingston in a big clearing surrounded by chain link and barbed wire. I approach the
parking lot and am stopped by a guard in a polo shirt, who gets
out of a pickup when he sees me coming. Not very official-
looking. There isn't even a guard hut at the entrance. Just a
picnic table. I'm guessing the guy stays in his truck because it
has air-conditioning.

He asks for my ID, and I hold my breath as I imagine an
all-points bulletin with my name in flashing red letters, and
hope the legal system doesn't work that efficiently. I don't really
know if the law is after me or not. Maybe the liquor store clerk
didn't get my license plate number, and maybe Eight Ball won't
tell the cops how his brother died.

As I sit in Levida's pickup, waiting, I watch the guards standing in their towers with their rifles and imagine how hot they are going to be in a few hours. I'm already sweating, and it's only ten o'clock in the morning.

The man in the polo shirt gives me back my license, asks me to sign a visitor's log, and lets me into the lot. I drive up to a concrete building and park. Then I go inside, passing through a metal detector before I reach the guard behind the window at the counter.

"Hello, my name is Dylan Dawson Junior. I'm here to visit my father, Dylan Dawson Senior."

"I'll need to see some ID," she tells me.

I give her my license, which she looks at briefly and returns to me before thumbing through a notebook. "Dylan Dawson Junior. Yep, there you are," she says.

"I'm on the list?"

"Yes. Is the prisoner expecting you?" she asks.

"No," I say, but then I wonder, how long ago did my father put my name on that list? How many years has he been waiting for me to show up?

Another guard arrives to escort me to the visitation area. We walk outside through an automatic door to another, larger concrete building. The main part of the prison, which we are now entering, is surrounded by rolls of razor wire, and I wonder if I'll end up in a place like this for killing Two Tone. I wasn't trying to kill him, just trying to protect my friend, but the law doesn't always see things the way I do. My whole body is trembling uncontrollably, and I pray it doesn't show. This place is three times the size of juvie, and I know the men inside have had a lot more years of hard time.

We enter the unit and walk down a long hallway until we arrive at the visitation area. "Enjoy your visit," the man says, like he's some kind of Disney tour guide. Then he returns to the front of the prison. I enter the room, tell my name to the gray-haired guard inside. "I'll have them bring the prisoner," he says, and then he picks up a phone and says my father's name.

There is a row of brown plastic chairs facing a wall of glass, divided into little cubicles. Visitors sit in the chairs talking over telephones to prisoners perched on metal stools on the other side.

One of the visitors is a tall man in a polyester suit and alligator boots, who reminds me of my uncle Mitch. I look through the glass to the man across from him and instantly recognize the pale blue eyes from the photographs at Levida's house. His hair is different, a crew cut, and the face has been worn by the years, but I know instantly who he is.

"He's already up here," the guard tells me, but I'm already walking toward the man in the boots, who looks up at me as I approach. "Can I help you, young man?"

"I'm here to see Dylan Dawson."

The man on the other side watches me through the glass.

"I'm his lawyer, Buster Cartwright. Who are you?" the man asks me.

I hear my father's voice faintly, over the telephone, answering for me in a soft drawl. "He's my son." He reaches out his hand, pressing it against the glass, as if trying to touch me. He smiles, and I see a tear making its way down his cheek.

"Well, I'll be," says the lawyer, sizing me up. "You're the spittin' image."

I press my hand up against my father's, and I'm suddenly

close enough to the glass to see my reflection, blurred by the tears now filling my eyes. I wipe them away with my fist and take a good look at my father. He's bigger than I thought he'd be, even larger than in his football pictures. His chest is huge, and his biceps strain against the white cotton prison shirt. A massive presence of a man. Even so, there is nothing hard or cold about him; in fact, he radiates a warmth that I can feel through the glass.

"I been waitin' a long time to talk to you." I hear his voice coming over the phone in the lawyer's hand.

I pick up the second of the two phones on my side of the glass, hanging on the partition separating the cubicles. "I'm sorry it took me so long to get here," I say.

"It's okay. You're here now. That's all that matters." He gives me a smile as deep and wide as the Pacific Ocean.

I sit down, and before long we're talking to each other as if I've just stopped by to visit any old divorced parent and not a man awaiting execution. He asks me about school.

"Not much to say," I tell him over the red telephone. I still can't believe I'm sitting here across from him, after all this time. It's like we've never been apart.

"Do ya get good grades?" he asks. His Texas drawl isn't harsh and crude like Levida's, but smooth as apple butter.

"I quit school a while back," I confess. He nods in understanding, but the lawyer, who has made no move to leave, raises a disapproving eyebrow.

"Do ya have a girl?" my father asks me.

"Yeah," I say, thinking about Jess, picturing her sitting by the plate-glass window, looking out at the ocean, waiting for me. I know I should call her, but what would I say? She's got to be steaming mad by now. Maybe that's for the best, for her to hate me, and then forget me.

"Tell me about her," my father says.

I tell him how I first met Jess in the church choir and how we were in school together at Downey High until I dropped out.

"Go on," my father encourages.

Before long I'm telling him all about Jessica Jameson, describing her eyes, her smile, her incredible voice. I thought it would hurt, talking about her, but it actually helps ease the pain, as if, somehow, she's not so far away anymore.

When I get to the part about Jess kissing me on the Fourth of July and taking me to her beach house, I look at my father and wonder what it is like, seeing people only through a wall of glass. Never touching them. I wonder if anyone besides his lawyer comes to see him, and I can't even imagine how lonely he has been all these years.

"Well, don't stop in the middle of the story, boy," says the lawyer, who I've forgotten is still there. "Tell us what happened next."

I look at my father. "Her boyfriend called to tell her he was coming over, and I left."

"Damn!" says the lawyer.

"That's too bad." My father shakes his head.

"Tough break, kid," says a third voice softly, over a microphone, and I turn to see the gray-haired guard, who has obviously listened to the entire conversation.

"Not much privacy in here," my father says.

After that intrusion I stick to neutral topics that I don't mind everyone overhearing. I talk about my friendship with Wade, my job at Gomez & Sons, my car—carefully avoiding subjects like the time I served in juvie, the fact I'm violating my probation, how I've become an accessory to armed robbery and accidentally killed someone.

"Mechanicking is a good trade and a respectable occupation," my father tells me. "But what about the girl? That can't be the end of the story."

"She came by the shop last Thursday."

"Yeah."

"To tell me she broke up with her boyfriend."

"Then what?" says the lawyer, who is really starting to annoy me. He's wearing some kind of sweet cologne that smells like cheap wine, and as it mixes with his body sweat, the odor becomes nearly unbearable, like the rotting fruit from a distillery.

"She said she wants to be with me."

"Attaboy," the lawyer says, slapping me on the back.

"Good goin'," the guard chimes in.

Only my father seems to notice I'm not smiling. He lowers his voice to almost a whisper. "Are you okay, son?"

Son. That single word turns me inside out. *Why did you have to be here, Dad,* I want to ask him, *when I needed you so badly at home?*

I bite my lip, hoping the tears I feel gathering behind my eyes will stay there and not spill all over my face. I want to tell my father everything. Know he's the one person in all the world who would understand, but I can't say anything with the guard listening to our every word. All I can do is shake my head ever so slightly and hope the gesture doesn't reveal too much.

"Mr. Cartwright," my father says to the lawyer, "why don't you give my boy your number, in case he needs to contact you for *any* reason?"

"Contact me?" the lawyer replies, looking from me to my father. "Oh," he says. "Yes, let me give you my card." Mr. Cartwright opens his briefcase, pulls out a card, and hands it to me.

"I think I'll make a couple of phone calls while the two of you catch up," Mr. Cartwright tells us, closing his briefcase, and then he leaves. Finally.

"You've got ten more minutes," the guard informs me over the microphone.

"Ten more minutes," I say. "It's hard to believe two hours have passed."

"Where are you stayin'?" my father asks.

"Levida's place."

"With your grandmother?"

"Is that okay?"

"Sure. Why wouldn't it be?" He rubs his chin, avoiding my eyes.

"Why doesn't she ever come to visit you?" I ask.

My father glances at the guard. "She has her reasons."

I nod, knowing he can't say any more, but wondering what reasons she could possibly have.

"She put you to work yet?"

"She has me and Wade tearing down the barn."

"Tearin' down the barn! Why?" he asks.

"She uses the wood to make signs she sells at the church."

"Is that the reason?" His voice is tighter than a hangman's knot.

"I think she might be looking for something," I say.

My father takes a long, slow breath. "She won't like it if she finds it."

"In that case, if I find anything, I'll just keep it to myself."

"Good."

"Time's up," says the guard.

"Promise me you'll come back tomorrow," says my father.

A tornado couldn't stop me from being at the prison first thing in the morning, but all I can manage to say is, "I'll try." I've learned how easy it is for plans to turn out different from what you expect.

I walk outside to where the pickup is parked, leaving the artificial light of the prison. It hits me instantly, how hot and wet the air is as it hangs heavy in my lungs.

I'm anxious to put some distance between myself and the rolls of razor wire. I pull the keys out of my pocket, and the lawyer's card falls to the ground. I pick it up.

I feel someone hit me hard across the back and spin around to see Buster Cartwright smiling. "C'mon, I'll buy you lunch. Let's get outta here. This place gives me the jitters."

He heads for a Cadillac the color of a banana, parked nearby, but I make no move to get into the pickup or follow him. He turns to me and says, "You do want to know about your daddy, don't you?"

I am ripped down the middle. On the one hand, I want nothing to do with this clown of a lawyer. But more than that, I want to know what he is trying to do to save my father.

"C'mon, I'll take you to Bubba's Smokehaus."

"What's that?" I ask.

"Best barbecue in three counties."

At the mention of barbecue I realize how hungry I am, having left Levida's place before breakfast. I figure it won't hurt anything to talk to the man, so I get into the pickup and follow the Cadillac to a place on the outskirts of town that I think at first is a dilapidated old barn, until I see the rusted sign for BUBBA'S.

Bubba's isn't much better on the inside. The tables look like something my grandmother might have made, and peanut shells cover the wooden floor, which creaks and crunches as we walk across it.

A waitress in jeans and a Bubba's tank top leads us to a table with a bucket of peanuts sitting in the middle of it. Mr. Cartwright grabs a handful and tells the waitress, "Bring us a platter of beef ribs, Texas toast, slaw, and some calf fries as an appa-teaser."

"What are calf fries?" I ask him, when the waitress leaves to give our order to a man in a greasy white T-shirt who is covered in tattoos.

"Texas oysters."

"What's that?"

"Bull nuts."

I look at the pail of peanuts.

"You really are a city boy, aren't you?" He laughs. "When they castrate a bull calf, they cut off its balls," he explains. "Tenderest meat on the beast."

The waitress returns with a platter of small round fried things.

"Try some," Cartwright says, pushing the platter toward me.

"No thanks." I'm starving, but there is no way I'm going to eat some animal's private parts. "What are you doing to help my father?" I ask him. "Are you filing an appeal?"

"Filed eight of 'em. They all ran out," he says, wiping his chin. "But don't you worry. No way they can kill Dozer Dawson."

"Dozer?"

"The Bulldozer. That's what the governor calls your daddy. Old football nickname."

"The governor of Texas knows my father?"

"Your daddy is a politician's wet dream."

"Excuse me?"

"Literacy, border control, drug trafficking; your daddy's book covers the governor's entire political campaign. Heck, he could be his speechwriter."

"My father wrote a book?"

Cartwright puts down his napkin and stares at me like I just arrived from another planet. "You didn't know your father wrote a book? Where you been all these years, boy?"

"California."

The lawyer shakes his head as if I've confirmed his suspicions, opens his briefcase, and hands me a hardcover book. "*The Road to Huntsville* by D.J. Dawson. That there is an autographed copy."

I look at the back of the book and see a mug shot of my father. "When did he write this?"

"In prison. Became a self-educated man. Just like Malcolm X."

"Self-educated?"

"Couldn't read beyond a third-grade level before he got locked up."

My surprise must be obvious, because Cartwright says, "You don't know anything about your daddy a'tall, do you?"

"No," I admit. "Not much."

"Your daddy's book is read in every government class in Texas. Ten thousand high school students have already signed a petition asking Governor Banks and the prison review board to grant him clemency, and the list is growing every day. It's an election year. Billy Banks can't let your father die. It would be political suicide."

"You really think so?" I ask, as a great weight lifts from my chest.

"Your daddy is one of the state's leading spokesmen on the war against drugs," Cartwright explains as a huge platter of ribs arrives. "He was an illiterate drug addict when they sent him up."

That's not how I remember my father. I remember a man I thought was Santa Claus.

"Now look what he's accomplished. You can't kill a role model like that." Mr. Cartwright tucks a napkin into his shirt collar and grabs a rib off the platter. I do the same.

I wonder if the poems and phrases floating around in my head could become a book someday. So what if I can't read a textbook or a job application? If my father learned to write, I could do it.

"Do you believe my father is innocent?" I ask.

Cartwright shrugs. "I don't work with many *innocent* folks, but all the evidence in the case against him was circumstantial," he tells me between bites. "The cops never even found the murder weapon. If it wasn't for the fact that your daddy's friend, Travis Seagraves, copped a plea and took the stand against him, the DA would have had a hard time making a case. Seagraves's testimony made your father sound like a hardened criminal. The guy had some kind of ax to grind."

The ribs are huge and slathered in sauce so spicy I have to ask for my Pepsi to be refilled three times. These are the best ribs I've ever eaten. I decide that this is the first place I will bring my father when he gets out of prison.

When we're done eating, Cartwright sits back in his chair and lets out a huge belch. I have to wonder where my father found this backwoods lawyer. The waitress takes away our empty plates and returns with steaming hot towels we use to clean our faces and hands. They are soon covered in grease and sauce, and I try to imagine how the restaurant will ever get them white again. I know they will, though, just as I know the slate will be wiped clean for my father . . . and for me. What did the preacher say? "'Though your sins be as scarlet, they shall be as white as snow.'"

"Of course the governor may take it to the last possible minute," Mr. Cartwright says. "Milk the case for all the free publicity he can get. And there is a growing contingency of people on the side of the dead cop's family. But don't you worry. I got the whole thing under control."

By the time I get back to Quincy, it's nearly four o'clock in the afternoon and I'm drenched in sweat. As I make my way down Main Street, I see a sign on a storefront I didn't notice before. It says SEAGRAVES FEED STORE. I park out front, go inside, and walk up to the man at the counter.

"I'm looking for Travis Seagraves," I say.

"He's out back taking inventory," the man tells me.

I walk out back and find a man about my father's age, writing on a clipboard while two other men unload sacks of feed from a semi truck.

"Excuse me, are you Mr. Seagraves?" I say.

"Who's askin'?" he says, without looking up from his work.

"Dylan Dawson."

His head snaps up in my direction.

"Junior," I add. I've never been Junior before, and it's a little hard getting used to, but I'm realizing how important it is to make that distinction.

The two men unloading the truck share a look.

"T.J.!" Seagraves calls to a guy on the other side of the yard, who stops what he is doing to walk over to us. The resemblance between the two is unmistakable. This must be his son. Seagraves hands him the board and the pen. "Take over for me for a couple of minutes."

T.J. looks at me like he recognizes me, and then nods at his father.

"Follow me," Seagraves says. Then he leads me back through the store and up a flight of stairs to an air-conditioned office. He plops himself down in a chair behind a desk, opens a small refrigerator, and pulls out a bottle of Budweiser. "Want one?" he asks.

"I don't drink."

He takes half of the bottle in one swallow and then eyes me suspiciously, as if he doesn't trust any man who doesn't consume alcohol. "You sure you're the Dozer's kid? He never turned away from a beer."

"I'm sure."

"I hear they're fixin' to put him out of his misery."

I tense up like I've been hit and instinctively ball my hand into a fist, but then I let it go, remembering what happened the last time I hit someone. I don't like Travis Seagraves one bit. The man is hard and crude, which I can tell from his walls, covered in pictures of naked women. But I could forget all that if he didn't talk about my father dying as casually as Cartwright talks about castrated bulls.

As Seagraves finishes his beer, an old newspaper clipping, hanging among the centerfolds, catches my eye. It's the same photo I saw at Levida's house, with the three boys holding the state cup, but two of the boys have been cut out of this photo. The one who remains looks an awful lot like T.J. "You played football with my father."

"I did a lot of things with your father, most of which landed me in a world of shit."

"You testified against him," I remind him.

"Didn't have much choice, once your father led them out to the landing strip on my family's ranch, but I didn't tell the cops anything new. Just confirmed what they had already figured out."

"Which was what?"

He tosses the bottle in the trash can and gets a fresh one out of the fridge, narrowing his eyes.

"It's old history. Read the police report, or better yet, ask your daddy. Ask him what he and Jack Golden did with the money."

"Jack Golden. You mean the policeman who got killed?"

"Jack Golden the dirty cop who was in knee-deep with your daddy."

"Knee deep into what?" I say, wishing I'd asked more questions of Buster Cartwright.

"You seen Janie Golden's big fancy house out on Farm Road 66? I think it just about says it all. You don't buy a house like that on a widow's pension."

"What does that have to do with my father?"

"Jack was your daddy's connection to the Colombians."

And now I understand.

"After the shooting, I figured it out. Jack was on the border patrol. I think he found out Dozer was gonna double-cross him the way he was planning on double-crossin' me. Your daddy controlled all the money. Wouldn't tell me where he kept it. He liked keepin' everything secret. His border connection set up the deal with the Colombians. We used an old landin' strip on my family's farm and hid the drugs in the sacks from the feed store. Dozer made the drug runs in his truck and collected our share of the money. Said he was keepin' it safe until we were finished and then the three of us would square up. Said we'd do a few runs and then we'd all be rich, but that ain't quite the way it worked out. I never saw a dime. Did you?"

"Me?"

He stands up so quickly his chair crashes to the floor. Then he walks around the desk toward me, fists clenched like he's ready for a fight. I stand, ready to run, my own chair toppling backward.

"Jack Golden's widow got her hands on that money some-how. What about your mama? She got her a big fancy house somewhere?"

"I don't know anything about any money," I say, backing toward the door.

"I was the smart one." He spits out words like venom, taking one step toward me each time I take a step closer to the door. "I was the one who helped Dozer make it through high school. He may have been a good athlete, but he was as dumb as a doornail. 'Do it for the team,' the coach told me. 'If we make it to state, the college scouts will see all of y'all, but it was only your stupid daddy who got the scholarship. And what did he do with it? He pissed it away, while I got stuck here in Quincy shoveling horse feed." The vein pulsing in his neck is a fire hose about to burst. I consider that this would be a good time to run, but I'm afraid to turn my back on him, so I just keep backing up, reaching my hand behind me, praying I find a doorknob.

"That money was supposed to be my ticket out of here. So the next time you're over in Livingston, you can just tell Dozer Dawson he got what he deserved for double-crossin' Travis Seagraves."

I find the doorknob and I'm out the door, running out of that place as fast as I can. I get into the pickup and gun it down the brick-covered street, passing Red and Dakota, who are out in front of the Chevy dealership, painting big white letters on the windows of the cars. Big white letters that say DIE DAWSON.

It is hard to believe that a place this small can hold so much hate, and I have the terrible feeling I've only just seen the surface. *Oh Jess, why couldn't I have stayed with you?* I'm in too deep now to ever go back.

When I turn off onto the dirt road to Levida's farmhouse, two things catch my eye, or rather the absence of two things.

First off, my blue Mustang is no longer in the ditch; in fact, it's nowhere in sight. Second, the entire roof of the barn is gone, along with most of the south wall. I pull up beside the barn, where boards and rusted nails lay in piles like bones waiting for the vultures. Wade greets me as he swings a sledgehammer against the wood. "What do ya think?" he asks, sunburned, covered in sweat, and beaming with pride as he points to the barn.

This is his one talent, tearing things apart. He is quick, efficient, and total when it comes to destruction. "Beautiful," I tell him. "You might have a future in demolition. By the way, where's my car?"

"Me and your grandma towed it up to the shop," he says, nodding to a metal building behind the house. Wade takes a long drink from a thermos filled with water and then pours the remainder of the contents over his head, shaking his wet hair.

"Did you find anything interesting?" I ask.

"Yeah, sure. Lots of stuff."

"Really?"

"C'mon. I'll show you."

I follow Wade to an old pigsty filled with rusted farm tools, old Sears catalogs, and a sheet of plastic that catches my eye because of its bright colors. I pick up the plastic and discover a bull's-eye filled with bullet holes.

I am instantly six years old again, bumping down the dirt road in the white pickup with my father. In the back is the bull's-eye, covering a bale of hay. We stop out in the middle of the field, and my father drops the bale. Then we get back in the truck and drive about fifty yards away. Share a piece of chocolate cake and sandwiches, in that order, that my mother packed us for a picnic lunch.

Then we get out of the truck, and my father puts a gun in my hand.

"What's this for?" I ask him.

"Birthday present for your mother, little man, but she didn't like it much. Says she won't have it in the house, but you gotta know how to handle firearms when you live in the country, so me and you are gonna have a little tutorial."

He takes another, larger gun out of the truck and uses it to show me how to clean mine, load it, and lock and unlock the safety. Then we shoot up the bull's-eye. Or rather, he shoots up the bull's-eye. I mostly scare a lot of rabbits. The gun is heavy, but it's small and fits my hand, making me feel big and important and powerful.

"You okay?" Wade asks, bringing me out of my daydream.

"Yeah. You find anything else?" I say, looking around the dilapidated barn.

"Nope."

"If you do, let me see it first, before you show my grandmother. Okay?"

"Sure, but what am I looking for?"

"I don't know, but it's important."

While we eat a dinner of chicken-fried steak, potatoes, gravy, green beans, and peach cobbler, Levida insists on reading to us from the Bible. "'In the beginning was the Word, and the Word was with God, and the Word was God.'"

Her Bible reading seems a strange substitute for conversation, but then I figure, she probably doesn't talk to people much and maybe has forgotten how. She reminds me of the bag ladies in downtown L.A., and I wonder what would happen to her if she didn't have this old farm.

Wade and I clean the kitchen from top to bottom while Levida gives Charlotte a shower. It's nearly ten o'clock when we settle down in front of the television. Baby Face curls up at my feet, seeking protection from the pig, who plops down in the middle of a braided rug, arching her pink neck in delight as Levida squirts her with a water bottle she keeps next to her recliner. "Thatta girl," she says, scratching Charlotte's ears, and the pig lets out a squeal of pleasure that nearly bursts my ear drums. "Pigs don't got no sweat glands," Levida explains to me and Wade. "Most people think they're dirty animals, but they ain't. They prefer to be clean, don't you baby." She kisses the pig's nose. Charlotte grunts in reply. "But they gotta find a way to cool themselves down. They don't like to wallow in the mud. They only do it when they have to."

I can't believe she's telling us all about this pig's glandular problems when she doesn't ask once about my father. Doesn't even inquire whether or not I was able to get in to see him.

"Pigs are much smarter animals than dogs," she says, giving Baby Face a look of scorn as my dog peeks out from between my legs. "Pigs are anatomically closer to humans too. Insulin comes from pigs. Why, the valves from a pig's heart can even be transplanted into humans."

I'm sure my grandmother could have her entire heart cut out and replaced with a pig's and no one would know the difference.

On the television, the news comes on, and protesters holding up signs saying SAVE THE DOZER fill the screen. Levida's eyes go wide, and she turns up the volume.

A reporter, a brunette in a skirt and high heels, approaches a tall blond man walking out the doors of the state capital. He starts shaking hands with the media gathered on the steps, but stops as the pretty brunette reaches him.

"Governor Banks," she says to him, "a lot of your constituents are pushing for you and the prison board to grant clemency to Dozer Dawson. He's become a hero to a lot of young people for what he's been able to accomplish in prison. Not to mention the fact that his upcoming execution is fueling the already heated death penalty debate. Can you tell us what direction you're leaning on this issue?"

The governor steps in front of the camera, like some kind of TV celebrity; he almost smiles, but not quite. Looks straight at the reporter, who seems to blush, though she tries to hide it. "So what is your position, Governor?" She thrusts her microphone toward him.

"As you know, Marianne, there are a lot of things to consider in this case. I'm giving it a lot of deliberation. I will say that mercy is a cornerstone of all civilized societies. That and man's ability to redeem himself."

The other reporters press in, pushing microphones in his direction, trying to get his attention. I would think he'd be running for his car, but he keeps his eyes focused on Marianne. They look good together on the television, and I figure that the governor knows this, that he's a smart man, that he will do just what Cartwright said and milk my father's case for all the publicity he can get.

Marianne says, "What about the fact that America is one of the only industrialized countries in the world that hasn't abolished capital punishment? What about the fact that Texas leads our country in executions? Twenty-four people were killed by lethal injection in Huntsville last year alone. That's an average of one every other week." Marianne is on a roll now, unaffected by the piercing green eyes of the governor. "How do you feel about people accusing you of sanctioning government-endorsed murder?"

If her words fluster the governor, he doesn't show it. He steps right up to the camera and fills the TV screen, blocking out Marianne and the other reporters. "I am a humble servant of the citizens of Texas, and I'm called upon every day to make difficult decisions," he says, as if he's been waiting all day for the opportunity to give this speech. "I don't make the laws, but I did take an oath and give my promise to the people of this fine state that I would enforce them. It wasn't me who sentenced D.J. Dawson to death. It was you . . . a jury of his peers." He says this last line looking straight at the camera, as if placing the blame squarely on anyone who might be watching. And then he is gone, with a crowd of reporters clamoring after him.

The screen goes black, and Levida sets the remote down with a shaking hand, stands, and says, "It's bedtime. Y'all better get on out to the barn." Then she makes a clicking sound to the pig, and they both wander off down the hall.

I thought she might invite us to stay in the house, what with an entire roof and most of one wall of the barn gone, but I was wrong. Wade and I go outside, and as soon as he lies on top of his sleeping bag, he's asleep. The night is hot and thick and the sounds of crickets, hoot owls, and vermin in the nearby bushes keep me awake. I know there are wolves that occasionally make it down from the hills into Los Angeles. I don't want to even think about what kind of creatures could be lurking out here in the dark in the middle of the sticks. Probably the same ones lurking around during the day, but I've learned that dangerous things like to wait till night to surface, when you can't see them coming.

I turn on the flashlight, filled with new batteries, and look through the pages of *The Road to Huntsville*, trying to make out the story of my father's life by the photographs, but all they show is his small prison cell, the narrow place in the prison yard surrounded by chain-link fence where he is allowed to stretch his legs, and the visitation room I've already seen.

I look back through the newspaper articles in the scrapbook, find the picture of my dad with Travis Seagraves and the third kid holding the championship trophy. Back when he was my age and had no idea where he was going to end up. I finally put all the pages away, open my leather binder, and start to write—slowly, haltingly—hoping maybe my own words will help me find the answers to the ones I cannot understand.

> I met a stranjer just this morning.
> He wuz not who I xpected.
> Thay sed he wuz a murderer,
> But thay wer misdirected.
> He had a smial a mile wide.
> In prizen wite wuz clad.
> The momint that he lukked at me,
> I new he wuz my dad.

28

I SPEND THE NIGHT DREAMING OF WHEELS THAT TURN INTO clocks that turn into screams. By the time I wake up, I'm covered in sweat and feeling like I haven't slept at all. I check my watch. It's early, only six o'clock. Wade is curled up asleep next to Baby Face. I pull on a pair of pants from the box of clothes my grandmother gave me, rummage around, find a Grateful Dead T-shirt, decide it might not be appropriate, given the circumstances, and then choose a plain blue cotton shirt.

I figure I might as well be on my way to Livingston, since I have nearly two hours of drive time ahead of me. I fire up the farm truck Levida has let me borrow and am heading toward the highway when I spot a sign for Farm Road 66. I remember what Travis Seagraves told me about Jack Golden's widow and the missing money, and I make a quick turn. I drive about a mile before I see a huge three-story rock house. The sort of place you might find in Beverly Hills or Malibu, not out in the middle of the Texas Hill Country. I think about my father rotting away in prison because of a cop who double-crossed him for drug money, and it makes me want to blow out all the windows in that big fancy house and set the whole stupid thing on fire.

I turn the truck around, hitting the gas as hard as I can. The truck is an eight cylinder and can really move when you push it. I pass the drugstore on Main Street, and through the plate-glass window I see the same old men drinking coffee. Men who have been around. Men who would know the history of the town.

I stop, back up, and park out front, not sure what will happen, not sure what I will say or do, knowing only that my father might be dead soon.

I walk inside. In addition to the old men at the table, there are a host of younger men, farmhands by the looks of them, buying sodas and doughnuts for breakfast.

I order a Pepsi from Dorie. "How's Wade?" she asks, but I ignore the question. I have more important things on my mind than Wade's love life.

"I just drove past a mansion out on Farm Road 66," I say to her, but loud enough so everyone in the place can hear. "I didn't know you had rich people living here in Quincy."

"That place belongs to the Golden widow," Dorie whispers, looking around at the faces of the men, who have all stopped to stare at us.

"The Golden widow!" I say. "She must be made of gold to afford that place."

"Jack Golden's widow," Dorie corrects me. "The dead cop."

"Now where on earth would a dead cop's widow get all that money?"

"An anonymous donation," a man says, stepping out of the crowd. He puts his hands on his waist like he's trying to intimidate me, but it has no effect.

"Who are you?" I ask him.

"Arnie Golden. Jack was my brother. Who the hell are you?"

"I'm Dylan Dawson," I say with pride. "Dozer Dawson is my father."

Arnie's face turns bright red, and everyone in the drugstore moves back against the walls like they're getting ready to watch a shoot-out. Arnie looks around at the people lining the store, and I get the feeling he wouldn't hesitate to kill me if there weren't so many witnesses. "Then I offer you my condolences," he tells me. "Seein' as how he'll be dead in a few days." He turns and starts walking out the front door, like I'm not even there, like I'm nothing, and this action enrages me more than his bitter words.

"Your brother was a dirty cop. You know it. I know it. This whole town knows it."

Arnie Golden stops. I can see the muscles of his back flinching through his white cotton shirt. "Boy!" he says without turning around. "If you value your life, you might consider another occupation besides slander." Then he is out the door.

"Are you crazy?" Dorie whispers. "Do you have any idea who Arnie Golden is?"

"The brother of a dirty cop."

"He's a Texas Ranger."

Out the window I see him walk across the street and get into a patrol car. He puts on a pair of sunglasses and looks back at me through the window of the drugstore. I can't see his eyes, but I can tell he's glaring at me. So is everyone in the room.

"What possessed you to say a thing like that?" my father yells, after I tell him about my encounter with Arnie Golden. I thought he'd appreciate me standing up for him, but I was dead wrong. He looks like he wishes I wasn't here. "Are you out of your mind?" His anger cuts straight through the glass between us.

"The prisoner will please keep his voice down," the guard says over the intercom.

"Everybody knows Jack Golden was dirty," I say.

"Jack Golden was a decorated hero of the Gulf War. He was a respected police officer and a loving husband and father. He didn't deserve to die, and he sure as hell doesn't deserve to have his name dragged through the mud. Who put such nonsense into your head?"

"Travis Seagraves." I feel like I'm five years old, ratting out the class bully to save my own skin.

"I should have known." He curses under his breath.

"I just wanted to help."

"Do you really think it will *help* to drag a murdered cop's reputation through the gutter?"

"The prisoner will either lower his voice or return to his cell," warns the guard.

"But you didn't do it," I say. "Did you?"

"Mr. Cartwright is trying to focus public attention on all the good I've accomplished since I've been in prison. We're not going to dredge up an old murder, do you understand me?" There is a look of warning in his eyes. "Tell me that you understand!"

"I understand," I say, well aware that he hasn't answered my question. Afraid to ask it again.

"Good. Now you go home and think about that. Think real hard, and then you decide whether or not you can come back here on those conditions, because if you can't, I got nothin' more to say to you." He stands to leave, and I feel a thud in my chest as my heart drops into my gut. "I'm ready to go back," he tells the guard with a coldness that chills me to my very core.

"Wait!" I plead. "Our time isn't up."

"You think about what I told you," my father says, and then he disappears through a metal door, leaving me staring at an empty chair.

When I was eight years old, my mother enrolled me in a summer school program for underprivileged kids called Youth Solutions, and every Friday we went on a field trip, no place exciting or that cost any money, always places that were cheap or free and "educational." One day they took us to a meat-packing plant, and we toured the freezers where the sides of beef were hanging. The girls were freaked out by the headless cows hanging on meat hooks, but I soaked up all that cold air. When the rest of the class left, I stayed behind, and being the troublemaker I was, I shut the door so they wouldn't find me. Only then did I remember my mother's warnings never to crawl into refrigerators left behind in the town dump, because once you got in, you couldn't get out and would suffocate to death. I started yelling and screaming, "Don't leave me, don't leave me!" I was pounding on the door, too scared to realize there was a round lever I could have pushed to get out. They couldn't hear me, but they found me when the teacher was doing the head count for the trip back to school and realized I was missing. I was only in the freezer about ten minutes, but I would have sworn it was ten hours.

As I watch the metal door close behind my father, I find myself standing up and pounding on the glass. "Don't leave me!" I yell, even though I know he can't hear me.

"Young man, step away from the glass," says the guard. I stop banging, pressing my hand against the place where just yesterday my father's hand had been. I close my eyes and try to imagine that my father is still there across from me, and to my horror, I cannot picture his face at all, even though I was just looking at him.

"Please move away from the glass," the voice says again, more insistent this time.

I hurry outside to the pickup truck, open the door, and grab my father's book, turning it over to look at his photo on the dust jacket, and I see his face, but it's not him. I cannot see the man who is my father. He is a phantom. A vapor. And all of a sudden I cannot feel my legs, as if I'm a vapor too. As if I don't exist.

I put the truck in gear and drive to the nearest pay phone, desperate to hear a voice that makes me feel solid and real.

"Hello."

"Jess!"

"Dylan? My God, Dylan. Where are you?"

"Texas," I say, so relieved to hear her voice that I don't think of the danger of confessing where I've gone.

"What happened to you? It's been five days! I waited for you all night. Then I went to the garage looking for you, and while I was there the police came around asking questions."

"The police?" So much for wishful thinking.

"They've started showing your picture on the news, along with Wade's. Mr. Gomez says that if you're in some kind of trouble he can help you, but you have to turn yourself in."

"I can't do that," I say. "I'll be turning eighteen in less than a week. When they send me away next time, it won't be to juvie."

"Dylan, whatever happened, we'll get through it. You are one of the best people I know."

"You should get out more." The bitterness rolls off my tongue before I can stop it.

"Don't be like that. I want to be with you. I *need* to be with you. You look at me and I feel like for the first time in my life, somebody sees me. Please come back. We can find a way through this. We have to find a way through this."

"I love you, Jess," I tell her, the words fighting their way up through the tears choking me. "But sometimes that's not enough. You have to forget me."

"No!" she yells, but I'm already hanging up the phone.

About ten miles before I reach the town limits of Quincy, I look in my rearview mirror and notice a blue Escalade coming up fast behind me. It signals like it's going to pass, so I edge the old Ford over to the shoulder. The Escalade pulls up alongside me, into the oncoming lane, and just hangs there. I can't figure out why, but then I look up to see Red at the wheel. Dakota, who is in the passenger seat, smiles at me, and at the same moment, the Escalade pulls into my lane, edging against the Ford, trying to push me off the road.

I fight to keep the tires on the pavement. Try accelerating to get past the SUV. It pulls back behind me and I breathe a sigh of relief as I approach a hairpin curve, but then Red guns the engine and the Escalade rams me from behind, and the Ford goes flying into the grass on the shoulder of the highway.

My head hits the steering wheel, and I guess I pass out for a minute because the next time I open my eyes, I'm outside of the truck being held by Red and Dakota while Tornado Tim pummels me with his fists.

"You are nuthin' but trash," Tornado says, punctuating each comment with a blow from his fists. "Your pig grandma is trash." WHAM! "Your slut mother is trash." WHAM! "Your drug addict daddy is trash." WHAM! WHAM! WHAM! "He shot down my father like a dog, with a damn pussy gun." WHAM! WHAM! WHAM! WHAM!

My knees give way and I start to collapse to the ground, but Red and Dakota lift me back up.

"You about done, Tornado?" Red asks, looking up at the highway. I look up too, wondering why there doesn't seem to be any traffic, wondering why someone doesn't stop to help me. Maybe no one sees me. Maybe I really am nothing.

"You don't want to kill him or nothin'. Not out here in broad daylight," says Dakota.

"What if I do?" Tornado says, reaching into his pocket, pulling out a snub-nose .22 and holding it against my forehead.

It's all over now.

"Where did you get that?" Red looks nervous.

"From my mama's purse," Tornado replies. Then he moves the gun down my face until it is in my mouth. *God no! Please don't let me go like this.*

"You want to know what it feels like to be shot in the face with a pussy gun, feelin' your brains scramblin' around in your head while you try to call for help, only you can't scream, 'cause your tongue is gone? That's how my father died. That's what your father did to him."

A mixture of tears and sweat pours over my face, stinging my eyes, mixing in my mouth with the taste of metal.

I struggle against the two boys holding my arms. Why won't they let me go? Tornado is going to pull the trigger, and my brains will be gone before I even hear the crack of the pistol.

Through my tears I see something shiny approaching, and at first I think it's another gun, but then I realize it's the noonday sun glinting off a Texas Ranger badge pinned to a white cotton shirt.

"What in tarnation do you think you're doin'?" Arnie Golden screams at his nephew, grabbing the gun out of his hand.

Tornado Tim seems to crumble and dissolve right there in front of me. Arnie Golden puts his arms around him, and Tornado weeps like I've never seen anyone weep before. "His father killed my daddy," he cries.

"I know he did," Arnie says, holding Tornado tight in his arms, glaring at me as if my presence has not only reopened old wounds, but rubbed gallons of salt in them as well.

"I just want somebody to pay," says Tornado.

"They will," says Arnie. "But right now you need to head on home."

"Yes, sir," Tornado says, wiping his eyes.

"And the two of you." Arnie looks at Red and Dakota, who let go of me to stare at their shoes. "Make sure he stays there. You want Tornado to end up in jail over the likes of him?" He points at me like I'm not even human, and his words hit me harder than any of Tornado's blows. I am worse than nothing. I am a black stain.

"No, sir," they reply.

"Then get out of here."

They nod, and the three boys walk up the hill to the Escalade and drive away.

"Thank you," I say weakly.

Arnie turns on me, grabs my throat, and pushes me up against the Ford. "I have done you one favor, boy. Don't expect another. Now our families are square."

"Yes, sir," I say, as if I understand, though I have no idea what he is talking about.

"Do you think my friends at the justice department would ask any questions if you ended up with one of my bullets in your head?"

"No, sir."

"You're damn right they wouldn't." His hand is shaking against my throat, and I half expect him to kill me right there on the highway, but he doesn't. He lets me go and steps back. "My brother was a damn fine man. Those people at the state house in Austin act like they've forgotten how he died, but I haven't forgotten and that boy sure hasn't forgotten. Blood never forgets. Do you hear me? Blood . . . never . . . forgets!"

He turns and walks away, gets to his patrol car, turns back to me, and says, "If you want to know where that money came from, ask your grandma. She's the one who left it on my brother's doorstep. I saw her do it, sneaking up to the house in the dark, thinkin' she could use drug money to pay for her son killing Jack. My sister-in-law would have never taken it if she knew where it came from, and if you breathe a word of this to anyone, I will kill you with my bare hands. Do you understand? Does that answer your questions?"

"Yes, sir," I tell him.

"Good," he says. "So don't be asking any more of them." He gets in his patrol car and drives away, leaving me with even more questions that I'm not supposed to ask.

I get into the truck and just sit there. I'm shaking so badly, I can't even get the key in the ignition. I think of that .22 in my mouth and remember a gun just like it.

My father and I had just gotten home from shooting at hay bales in the field, and my mother was outside working in the garden. We were standing in the kitchen, next to the pantry. My father opened the door and pulled out a burlap sack filled with peanuts. He was the only one who ate them, because my mom couldn't stand them. He took the gun out of my hand and nestled it into the bag among the hulls and shells. Looked out the window at my mother, still digging in the dirt. "Your mama doesn't like the idea of having a gun in the house, so this is gonna be our secret, okay, little man?"

I smiled and nodded, proud to be called a "little man." Proud to share a secret.

"She's a city girl," he explained. "She doesn't understand. But me and you understand, don't we? The country can be dangerous. Things can happen. You gotta be prepared."

THE ROAD TO HUNTSVILLE
By D.J. Dawson

I spent three months sitting in an Austin court-room, studying the faces of the twelve men and women chosen to determine my destiny. I didn't know their names or occupations or histories, but as I sat there day after day, I tried to figure out who they were, just as they were sitting there trying to figure out who I was. I thought if I could see them as real people and not just numbers on a chair, maybe they could do the same for me.

There was Bill the insurance salesman, Tony the potter, and Jimmy the tattooed guitar player, who all nodded their heads in agreement when the court-appointed psychiatrist quoted studies showing that drug rehabilitation programs are a greater deterrent to crime than capital punishment.

Laura the librarian and Randall the construction worker smiled wistfully as Coach Rogers described how proud the whole town was when we won the state cup.

Julie the housewife, Jojo the hairdresser, Cotton the dairy farmer, Daniel the soccer coach, Bryan the nurse addicted to painkillers, Janie the realtor who dreamed of owning a house in the country, Michael the unemployed janitor.

I made up entire histories for these people.

Imagined I'd see them on the street one day after I got out and we'd strike up a conversation. Until the day the DA showed the pictures of the homicide scene, and Laura the librarian wept as she looked across the room at Jack Golden's widow.

That was the day I knew I was never getting out.

29

I PULL MYSELF TOGETHER AND DRIVE TO THE FARM, PARKING down by the barn so I can wash the blood off my face before my grandmother asks me what happened.

I can't really call the place a barn anymore, because Wade has demolished another wall. With only two opposing walls left standing, the structure looks like some kind of oversize goalpost.

"What happened to you?" Wade asks as I turn on the water hose.

"Ran into a rough patch of bad road."

"Looks like the road ran into you."

"Dylan Junior!" Levida yells, and I look up to see her standing by the shop, holding a wrench and wearing coveralls soiled with grease.

"Coming!" I yell back, quickly finishing my cleanup. "What in the world is she up to?" I ask Wade.

"Fixin' your car."

"What?"

"Guess she felt bad for shootin' it up."

"I doubt it." It's hard to imagine Levida feeling bad about anything.

I hurry up to the shop and find Levida inside, looking under the hood of the Mustang. "I need you to tighten down the wheels," she says, handing me a lug wrench.

I take the lug wrench, not noticing it's covered in grease until my hands are stained. Levida has exchanged my two rear tires with replacements that look like they came off one of her farm vehicles. They are huge, in contrast to the tires in front, and make my car look like a giant blue beetle with its butt in the air. "What have you done to my car?"

"I'm fixin' it," she tells me, tinkering with something under the hood. "Your radiator's busted."

"I know, but I can't afford a new one." I tighten down the lug nuts. Arnie Golden's parting words still echo in my ears, and I wonder how I can casually bring up the subject of her delivering drug money to Jack Golden's widow without getting hit upside the head.

"Young people today," she says, shaking her head. "Want to just throw everything away as soon as it isn't new and shiny anymore. Lucky for you I have a solder gun."

"Don't tell me you tried to patch a busted radiator with a solder gun."

"Oh, you think it's better to have to fill it up with water every time the thing goes dry? You're lucky you didn't burn up the engine."

I'm in no mood to argue with her, so I finish the wheels in silence. When I'm done, I walk over to where my grandmother is hunched under the hood. "Hand me a seven-sixteenths socket," she demands.

I look through the toolbox sitting out on a wooden work table, examining the numbers on all the handles, and hand her what she asked for. "Thanks," she says. "My tired old eyes ain't what they used to be. Can't hardly read those tiny numbers no more." She looks at me long and hard. I know she knows I lied about needing glasses, but I'm not about to admit it. What business is it of hers? Besides, after the day I've had, I don't care what she thinks of me.

She finally returns to her work and starts tightening the valve cover gasket. "I heard about you causin' trouble in town," she says.

"I was just asking questions."

"Humph!"

I wonder how a person who seems to be almost completely ostracized gets the town gossip so fast. I take a deep breath and say, "Arnie Golden told me you were the one who gave Jack Golden's widow all that money."

Levida throws the socket against the shop wall, and it echoes off the metal siding. Then she wipes her hands on a rag and puts them on her hips, puffing out her angry chest. "What are you doin' here, boy?"

"Helpin' you fix my car."

"Not here in the workshop, here in Quincy. Why did you come back after all these years?"

"It was drug money, wasn't it? Did he give it to you? Did you take it from him?" Maybe that's why my father couldn't split it with Travis and his "border connection." Maybe there's more money hidden in the barn, and that's why Levida has us tearing it apart.

She studies me. Wrinkles her nose in thought. Seems to

thaw ever so slightly, like an iceberg when the temperature rises to thirty-five. Rubs her forehead with her fist and leaves a trail of grease. "Jack Golden was your daddy's best friend. His mama and me went to school together," she finally says. "Jack and D.J. played football together at Quincy High School, but then you would have known that if you had read the newspaper articles I gave you."

I think of the third boy in the photo with my father and Travis Seagraves, and I realize it's Jack.

"Why was Jack Golden with my father that night?"

"I don't know. I wasn't there," she says, slamming down the hood of my car.

"But you do know *something*," I say, wondering why she has to evade every single question I ask.

"Oh, I know a lot of things," she says, pointing a black-stained finger in my face. "I know that your daddy couldn't do enough to make your highfalutin mama happy. Her always talkin' about goin' to New York City. Always wantin' fancy clothes. Never liftin' a finger to help around this place. He worked like a dog to afford all the fine things she thought she needed, but it was never enough. Then her brother started comin' round in his fancy blue Cadillac with all his talk of get-rich-quick schemes."

"You mean my uncle Mitch?"

"You got any idea what it's been like for me livin' in this town after your grandpa died and your daddy went to prison? Havin' to sell my land off piece by piece 'cause I didn't have any help workin' it? Havin' to live with the cold stares of the towns-people who used to be my friends?"

She grabs the edge of the work table to steady herself as she tries to catch her breath. "This town used to be a decent place to live, but it's been losin' itself, piece by piece, just like me and this farm."

"Why didn't you just leave?" I ask, thinking about how often my mother picked up and moved us. Wondering what it would be like to live in a place where everybody hated you because of something your kid had done.

She points out the window. "My daddy, my mama, and your granddaddy are all buried out on that hill. I ain't goin' nowhere till they put me in the dirt with 'em, so I don't need you stirrin' up trouble. Understand?"

"Yeah, I understand," I say, thinking how old she looks in the light coming through the shop window, with her greasy coveralls and her frizzled gray hair going in a million directions.

Levida grabs a rag from the workbench and tries to wipe the dried grease from her hands, but it doesn't help. They stay black and stained like mine.

I spend the rest of the afternoon helping Wade tear down a third wall in the barn, working like a crazy man. Sweat pours down my body like a river, and the glass cover on my watch actually steams in the heat, dragging on the hands until they finally stop.

That night Levida fixes us another huge meal. Pork chops, green beans, red potatoes, and something called red-eye gravy that she makes out of coffee and pork fat. I wonder if she puts on a spread like this when it's just her and Charlotte. From the way she treats the pig, giving her extra gravy on her potatoes, I wouldn't doubt it. Surely she's not just cooking like this for our benefit.

Dorie, who came by to visit Wade after her shift at the drug-store, stays to eat with us.

"There are only three animals more intelligent than the pig," Levida informs us. "The chimpanzee, the dolphin, and the elephant, none of which are worth a darn on a farm."

All through dinner Levida continues to barrage us with pig facts. Dorie keeps one hand under the table, and Wade keeps a smile on his face so big he can hardly chew his food. I've never seen him this happy, and I'm glad he's finally found love or lust or whatever this is.

"Pigs can run seven miles an hour. They can live up to twenty-seven years. Some of them can weigh as much as twenty-five hundred pounds, though Charlotte is a slim four-eighty-five."

Wade giggles, and even Levida isn't stupid enough to think it's because of her recitation of pig trivia. "What have you got to be so cheerful about?" she asks him, as a piece of cherry pie falls out of his mouth.

"I got religion now."

Levida glares at Dorie, who quickly loses her smile and puts both hands on the table.

"Be careful about gettin' too much religion," Levida warns him, looking from Wade to Dorie. "You don't want folks to call you zealous."

"Oh, don't worry, ma'am. I ain't the jealous type."

Dorie and Wade watch old Looney Tunes reruns, giggling and holding hands while Levida and I wash the dishes. At ten o'clock Levida turns on the news and sits on the couch next to Dorie, bringing an end to the girl's fun. She finally goes outside to the front porch with Wade for a very long good-night kiss.

I am surprised to see Arnie Golden on the TV screen in front of the Walls Unit in Huntsville. Tornado Tim stands beside him, along with a pretty black-haired woman I can only assume is Tornado's mother.

"When a good man like my brother is shot down and slaughtered, the scales of justice are tipped, set off balance, made unstable—and that's a dangerous situation for all of us. There is only one thing that will right those scales, and that's what we've been waiting for these last eleven years." Tornado and Mrs. Golden nod their sad heads in agreement. "The governor needs to understand that any lesser punishment for D.J. Dawson would minimize the value of the lives of the law enforcement officers who risk their necks each and every day for the people of this state."

"Damn!"

"Watch your mouth," Levida says. Then she turns off the TV and studies me. "Well, I don't guess you boys can sleep in the barn no more. You better go fetch your gear."

I can't believe my luck. I walk outside to find Wade with his tongue halfway down Dorie's throat. "C'mon," I say. "We're moving uptown."

Dorie says good-bye reluctantly. Wade and I go out to the barn with flashlights to gather our few belongings, along with the sleeping bags Levida has loaned us. It would have been nice if she could have decided to be hospitable while it was still light out.

When we walk back to the house, I am surprised to find my grandmother standing on the porch, holding a lantern. "Follow me," she says, and takes off down the dirt road that leads up a hill toward the family graveyard and into the darkness.

"Where we goin'?" Wade whispers to me as we approach the white picket fence that surrounds the row of wooden crosses.

For all I know my grandmother could be planning to shoot us and bury us with the rest of the family, but I don't think it would help to share this notion with Wade.

"There it is," Levida says as a single-wide mobile home appears in the glow of her lantern, over the hill, just beyond the graves. "Home sweet home." She strides toward it, finds a pile of empty beer bottles in her path, and kicks them out of the way. "Darn kids," she says, and then walks up the metal steps and opens up the door, which isn't locked, because the handle has been jimmied. I imagine late-night beer parties at an abandoned trailer, wonder if any liquor has been left behind, and try to push away the thought as Wade and I follow her inside to a darkened living room. "I'll fire up the generator tomorrow so you can have electricity. You can keep the lantern until then." She sets it down on a table next to an old coffee can filled with ashes and cigarette butts. Picks up the can. Shakes her head. "I shot the back window out of one of their trucks last month, but they don't ever learn."

By the dim light of the lantern I can see a couch and a table with names carved into the wood.

I remember it. This is the place where I lived with my parents. This was our home. It hasn't changed one bit, except for the vandalism.

The memories come washing over me in waves.

The couch, still covered in a hideous brown plaid fabric, is where I used to watch *Seinfeld* with my mother. Next to the couch are the pencil marks on the wall where my father used to chart my growth. The living room opens up across a bar into a kitchen. There is the pantry door next to the refrigerator. I think about the bag of peanuts my father used to keep on a shelf in the back, remember what was hidden there, and shudder.

"Sweet dreams," Levida tells us, but there is nothing sweet in the way she says it.

That night I dream of blood. Rivers of it flowing across the floor of the trailer. Blood dripping down the metal steps, finding its way into the dirt, where it cuts a trail all the way from the Hill Country of Texas to the sandy beaches of California and the Pacific Ocean, where it stains the whole sea red.

It's just like Arnie Golden told me. Blood never forgets. It has a memory of an ancient path toward home.

THE RIVER

Blood is a river.
    One drop follows another
        until they all reach the bottom
                of
                      the
                            deep
                        blue
                            sea.

30

IT IS THE EARLY MORNING HOURS, JUST AFTER DAYBREAK, when I hear a gunshot. I scramble to my feet from the couch, still half asleep. Look around the living room. Wade and Baby Face are curled up on the floor.

I look out the window, half expecting to see Tornado T. and his friends or maybe even Eight Ball, but no one seems to be out there.

Take a closer look at the window itself. See blood splattered across the blue curtains.

I kneel down next to Wade and shake him awake. "Are you okay?" I ask him.

"Let me sleep," he mumbles, rolling away from me.

I check Baby Face, thinking maybe she's been hit by a stray bullet, but she's perfectly fine.

I check myself, thinking maybe I'm in shock and dying and don't even know it, but I'm completely intact, except for my imagination, running wild.

I glance toward the door, wondering if someone is going to burst through at any moment, and notice the clock.

It's an old windup clock shaped like a house.

A cuckoo clock.

I stagger backward a step. See the graffiti above the clock.

THE DEATH HOUSE

This is the room of my nightmares.

This is the room where Jack Golden died.

I walk slowly back over to the window.

Inspect the curtain.

The blood is dried. Old. Black.

I slip on my shoes, don't even bother with a shirt, and run as fast as I can down the dirt road back to Levida's house.

She is outside hanging laundry on the clothesline and does not seem at all surprised to see me.

"What kind of game are you playing with me?" I say.

"I don't know what you're talking about," she says curtly, applying a row of clothespins to a flowered sheet. Levida picks up her basket and moves down to an empty place on the line.

I take the basket away from her. "What happened in that trailer?"

"I wasn't there!" she yells, grabbing the basket back, and then she throws it on the ground between us, sending socks and underwear flying. Her voice grows as quiet as a whisper but keeps its razor edge. "But you were."

With that she hurries back to the farmhouse, leaving the clothes behind.

I can see the clock. I can hear the gunshot. I can even see the blood on the curtains, but I can't see anything else.

I take a deep breath, try to steady my shaking limbs, and go inside the house to find my grandmother chopping potatoes, hacking at them with a butcher knife. "I was six years old," I manage to say, though my throat is as dry as a bone.

"That's old enough to remember," she says, without looking up.

"But I don't."

"Or maybe you just don't want to." She scoops the potatoes up in her hands and throws them into a pot filled with water, then finally looks me in the eyes. "Maybe all this runnin' around and askin' questions, nosin' into other people's business is to keep yourself so busy that you don't have to look at the truth."

I open my mouth to reply, but I cannot speak—because I have no answers.

"So quit asking everybody else questions, unless you're ready to answer some questions yourself."

I walk back up to the trailer, go inside, try very hard not to look at the curtains or the clock as I grab a shirt from the cardboard box. I look for Jess's note, but it has fallen out of yesterday's pants. Searching frantically, I find it under the couch. Open it. Look at the words to make sure they are still there; half-afraid they might have erased themselves. Jess is the only thing in my life that seems real, but she is a thousand miles away.

I carefully refold the paper. I hold it to my lips, then slip it into my pocket, and I am gone.

When I get to the prison I'm not even sure my father will want to talk to me, but his eyes fill with relief when he sees me through the glass.

"I was afraid you wouldn't come back," he says.

"I was afraid you wouldn't see me if I did."

"What I told you still stands. You can't go stirrin' up trouble with Jack Golden's family."

"I know. I won't."

"If they have any money, they came by it honestly."

"I know."

"Good. Now, on that subject..." A long, slow breath escapes him like the air from a leaking tire. "How have you and your mama been makin' out for money all these years?"

"Okay, I guess. Mom has a job singing at a nightclub in California. I've got a job too. Plus, Uncle Mitch sends us a thousand dollars a month and lets us live in one of his rent houses for six hundred. I never understood why he doesn't just send four hundred, but that's Mitch."

"Is that all he's doin' for you?"

"Yeah," I say, thinking it's a lot, but then maybe my father doesn't know what rents are in Southern California.

"Damn him," my father mutters under his breath.

It makes me wonder, was there money for my mother and me, like there was money for Tornado Tim and his mother? I can't ask with the guard listening.

"Was he your border connection?"

My father looks at the guard, and if I could read minds I'd guess he's wondering whether or not he wants to rat out my uncle. He finally looks back at me and says, "There are a lot of things I can't talk about."

I nod, afraid to push him too far, but at the same time hungry for answers and revenge. My life could have turned out totally different if we'd just had a little bit of money. I might have settled in a different neighborhood, done better in school, gone to college, ended up with Jess.

"Cartwright told me he gave you my book," my father says, intruding into my thoughts.

"Yes, sir."

"I think you'll find some of the answers you're lookin' for in chapter five."

"Chapter five." I groan. There is no way I'll make it through an entire chapter.

We sit in silence, all the unanswered and unasked questions thicker than the wall of glass between us.

"How's your mama?" he finally says. Today is the first he's mentioned her, and the look on his face surprises me, as if everything hangs on my response.

I think about how lost and desperate my mother looked the last time I saw her and wonder how she's doing at Uncle Mitch's house in La Puerta. I've hardly thought of her since I left California, and I'm suddenly filled with guilt. "She's okay," I lie.

"You said she was singin' at a nightclub in California. Is it a nice place?"

It's a cocktail lounge inside a bowling alley, but I'm not about to tell my father that. "Yeah. Pretty nice."

"Did she ever find someone?"

I'm not sure what he means, but then he adds, "Did she remarry?"

"No," I tell him, realizing that she never really looked. Wondering why, becoming conscious of the fact that I've been so wrapped up in my own grief and misery that I've never questioned hers.

He nods, as if this makes him sad for some reason. "Does she ever talk about me?" he asks, and then he seems to hold his breath while he waits for the answer.

"No."

He nods again, but this time there is the faintest hint of a smile on his face, even though he looks as if he could cry. "Good," he tells me. "Maybe when this is all over she can forget."

When I leave the prison I notice a large black vehicle coming up behind me, gaining speed. I've been so worried about my father I haven't planned what to do if Eight Ball catches up with me.

I killed his brother, and he will come after me. Then he will kill me. There are few things in life as certain as this. I wonder if Two Tone's dead, empty eyes haunt Eight Ball the way they haunt me.

The black SUV gets closer and I see that it is not a van, but a Jeep. I inhale a small breath of relief, but it is still clear that someone is following me. I wonder if Tornado Tim and his friends have decided to kill me in Livingston, away from the watchful eye of Uncle Arnie.

I pull off the main road and wind through the town, make quick turns onto various side streets. All the while the Jeep stays on my tail. Whoever is driving isn't even trying to hide the fact that they're after me. I take two more quick right turns and pull into a car wash before I lose the guy.

I drive to Huntsville, checking my rearview mirror all the way. I cannot stop shaking and realize that part of the reason is that I haven't eaten all day. As much as this place gives me the creeps with its nine prisons and its death house sitting in the middle of town, I decide to stop at a sandwich shop on the town square for lunch.

Maybe a small part of it is morbid curiosity. Leaning into

the thing you fear, like Uncle Mitch used to advise me. Out the window of the café I can see protesters lining the street on both sides leading up to the Walls Unit.

The waitress, an old woman with too much makeup and flaming red hair not even close to a natural color, delivers the roast beef sandwich I ordered.

"Can you tell me how to get to La Puerta?" I ask her.

"La Puerta!" says the waitress. "That's all the way down on the Mexican border. Two hundred and fifty miles. It'll take you at least four hours to get there. Why would you want to go all the way down there?"

"Family."

It's a slow afternoon. She shrugs, sits down in the chair across from me, and draws me a map on a paper napkin. "Take Interstate 45 to Houston. Then catch 59 to Victoria. Then you'll merge with 77. Stay on 77. If you find yourself in Mexico, you've gone too far."

"Thank you," I say, tucking the napkin into my back pocket.

"Looks like it's gonna be a big one," she says, looking at the protesters gathered down the street.

"A big one?"

"You can rate 'em by how early the protesters start lining up, how many TV cameras show up, how big the crowd gets—that sort of thing. Sometimes hardly nobody shows up at all. Like in the case of that child molester they killed last week. No sympathy for him. Raped two little girls, sisters, and left their bodies in shallow graves next to Ray Roberts Lake up by Gainesville. Washed up after the first heavy rain. After what he did to 'em, they had to use their dental records to identify the bodies."

I was starving half an hour ago, but now I look at my half-eaten roast beef sandwich and can't find the stomach to finish it. The waitress continues, "Used to always be a crowd, back in eighty-two after the state first started doin' executions again. Now they're so common nobody pays 'em much notice."

"Oh." I say. I wonder what it has been like for this woman, working in this diner all these years, with a front row seat to a constant parade of executions every other week. But then maybe it's not that much different from Southern California, where you learn to tune out the sirens and police helicopters and the murder statistics on the late-night news.

"Could I have my check, please?"

"Sure thang, darlin'," the waitress says, easing herself out of her seat and ambling toward the register like she has all the time in the world.

As I walk to the old Ford, the only thing on my mind is putting as much distance between myself and that redbrick fortress as possible.

31

WHEN I GET TO LA PUERTA, I ASK FOR DIRECTIONS TO Mitch's Motors and find a gigantic lot filled with used cars out in the middle of nowhere. There are so many Cadillacs of so many strange and varied colors, it looks like somebody burst open a huge sack of M&M's.

Behind the cars is a warehouse where I imagine barrels of flashy paint are stored. It looks a lot like the warehouse in East L.A. where Wade and I used to chop cars, only this one is three times as large. The entire property is surrounded by an electric fence.

"Señor Mitch is at home today," a man in a blue dress shirt informs me, pointing to a compound about a hundred yards farther down the road, surrounded by a brown stucco fence twelve feet high. He's wearing a semiautomatic secured in a shoulder holster. Pretty tight security for a car lot.

I get into the pickup and drive to the compound, where a man wearing another semiautomatic greets me in front of an electric gate. Behind him looms a sprawling adobe house covered in a Spanish tile roof. I think about Tornado Tim's big house in Quincy, remember the tiny rent house Mitch lets me and Mom live in, and wonder again about how different my life might have turned out if we'd had a little money in our pockets.

"I'm Dylan Dawson. I'm here to see Mitch Osterhaus. He's my uncle," I tell the guard.

The man eyes me skeptically, talks in Spanish over a two-way radio, then switches open the gate. "He says is okay," he tells me, flashing me a nearly toothless grin.

I park in front of the house and have to peel myself off of the vinyl seat before I get out. My body is covered in sweat, and it's all I can do to keep myself from sticking my head in the fountain covered in blue tile as I make my way to the front door.

I'm so thirsty I could drink the thing dry.

"Dylan, is that you?"

I turn and see my mother, standing by a row of rosebushes, holding a pair of pruning shears. "Mom?" I nearly don't recognize her in the big floppy hat. There is no sign of the distraught, catatonic woman I last saw in Downey. In fact, she looks completely recovered, but then gardening tends to do that for her.

"Dylan," she says, dropping her shears and running to wrap her arms around me. I hold her in my arms, wondering when she got so small. I want to hold her like that forever and make sure nothing ever hurts her. "I was so worried about you when I heard what happened," she says.

"What did you hear?" I ask, taking a step back.

She lowers her voice, even though there is no one around to overhear us. "Your uncle Mitch has a friend in California who said you robbed a liquor store. Is it true? Tell me it isn't true, baby," she says, pushing my bangs out of my eyes like I'm five years old.

"It isn't true," I say as I imagine Eight Ball using Jake to get to Mitch so he can find me. Maybe it was Eight Ball in the black Jeep after all.

"If you didn't do it, then why did you run?" she asks.

"I came to see Dad."

She lets go of me and looks away. "Did you . . . see him?"

"Yeah."

"How is he?"

"He asked about you."

She fidgets with her hair. "What did he say?"

"He asked me if you ever talked about him. I told him no." She looks away again, and I take her hand in mine. "Come with me to visit him?"

"I can't."

"He's a decent guy."

"Don't you think I know that?" she says, and starts throwing her gardening tools into a box.

"Well, well, well, the prodigal son from California." Uncle Mitch comes out the front door of the house wearing cowboy boots and a big Stetson hat. He's carrying a glass of wine and a white pill. He gives both of them to my mother, and I suddenly understand why her mood has improved so much. "I hope you're not excitin' your mama. She's just started comin' out of her slump," he tells me. Then he walks behind a bar in the cabana and opens a refrigerator. Meanwhile, a nurse dressed in white comes out of the house with a wheelchair. "Time for your nap, Miss Mollie," the woman says, and my mother sits obediently down in the chair, but before they leave she pulls me close and whispers, "Next time you see him, tell him . . ." She suddenly looks away as if she's changed her mind.

"Tell him what?" I imagine she wants to say she never stopped loving him, but I want to hear it from her.

"Tell him I never had the nerve to make the big time, but it was easier to blame him than to admit I was afraid. Tell him . . . I'm sorry. Tell him it wasn't all his fault."

"What wasn't all his fault?" I ask, but by then she is being wheeled away.

I walk over to Uncle Mitch, ready for a fight. He opens two Coronas, keeps one for himself and slides the other to me across the bar. Thirsty as I am, I cannot bring myself to touch it. Partly because I remember the last time I started with beer and woke up in a dumpster clutching an empty whiskey bottle. Partly because accepting any gift from him feels like I'm betraying my father. "Guess we got a few things to talk about," he says. "From what I understand, you're gonna need a good lawyer."

"Why didn't you ever tell us my father gave you money to take care of us? Why did you keep it for yourself when you knew he wanted us to have it?" My throat is so dry I can hear the words cracking like sandpaper against brittle wood.

"Whoa, boy. That's a mouthful of accusations for a kid on the run from the law."

"Don't act high and mighty with me," I say. "You're the one who got me that job with Jake. He's the one who hooked me up with Eight Ball and had me chopping cars. You knew he was dirty the whole time, didn't you? What was I supposed to do when Wade robbed a liquor store to get into their gang and then Two Tone came after him with a blade?"

"Is that really the way it happened?" he asks.

"Yeah," I say, and realize that even though I started out with all the questions, I'm the only one giving any answers.

"Let me see what I can do," he says, winking like he's about to do me some huge favor, but I'm sick of Mitch and his favors.

"Why did you keep the money my father gave you?" I ask again.

"Sit down," he tells me, pointing to a bar stool.

"I'll stand."

He shrugs, pushes the beer a little closer to me. "Go on. I didn't poison it," he tells me.

I've been driving around all day in a truck without any air-conditioning. My head is spinning, and I know I'm dangerously dehydrated. "Do you have any Coca-Cola?"

"You know me better than that," he says with a grin. "Go on. One beer won't kill you."

I put the bottle to my mouth, and it feels so good against my parched lips that once I start drinking it I can't stop, until the entire bottle has been emptied. The familiar alcohol buzz starts to settle me, taking off the edge, turning down the tension that's been threatening to explode inside of me.

And I realize that a little alcohol might be just what I've needed.

"Feel better?" he asks.

"The state of Texas is getting ready to kill my father. How the hell do you think I feel?"

Mitch looks at his Corona, shakes his head, and puts the beer back in the refrigerator. Then he opens a cabinet and takes out a bottle of tequila. "I think this conversation calls for something a little stronger. Want a shot?"

He's not going to drug me and dumb me up like he's done to my mother. "I want answers."

"Suit yourself," he says, taking out a shot glass and filling it with liquor. Then downs the tequila. "That's better."

"Travis Seagraves told me you were my father's border connection," I say, figuring I'll get more of the truth if I pretend like I already know what it is. Already feeling confidence working its way through my bloodstream.

"Guess he wasn't as stupid as I thought," says Mitch.

So it was true. Mitch was involved.

"He said you were the one who set up the deals."

"I happened to have low friends in high places."

"What about the money my father gave you to take care of us?"

"Your grandma brought me some cash after the trial," he allowed. "It was supposed to be my cut from the Colombian deal, but she informed me it was blood money. Told me your father wanted me to use it to take care of you and your mama. Said if I kept it for myself I'd burn in hell."

"But you *did* keep it for yourself!"

"Hell never scared me." He smiles at me and downs another shot of tequila.

"What about your obligation to my mother, your sister. How could you let us live like we been living, scraping by for all these years?"

"That money was mine, and I've been damn generous over the years with the two of you. Your mama could have got a real job, but all her life she's been expectin' people to take care of her. Buy her fancy things. Make a big fuss over her. She can't hold on to a dime and you know it. You've seen that room of hers full of crap that she never even uses. I invested the money in my car business, and now there's enough to take care of all of us, and it's all clean cash. You ever stop to consider how it would have looked for your mama, wife of a convicted murderer and drug dealer, to suddenly come into money?"

He's made a good point. He's made several good points, actually, but that doesn't put him in the right. "In the meantime, you're living in a mansion while we live in a piece of crap rent house in Downey."

"Your mama lives exactly the way she wants to live. She talks a lot about her big dreams, but she's never had any action to back them up."

"Too bad we can't all be like you . . . full of action."

"Life is a head game, kid. Blame who you want, but what you believe determines who you become. Pure and simple. My father, your granddaddy, lost all his money in the oil business, so he shot himself in the head when Mollie and me was away at UT. My mother, your grandmother, didn't know what to do with herself after that, and six months later she was dead of cancer. My sister always had lots of talent but no spine to back it up. Didn't believe she deserved happiness after what happened to our folks."

Wow. Mitch has just revealed more family history in ten seconds than my mother has shared in seventeen years. "What do you believe in, Mitch . . . money?"

"Yep, and I got loads of it. But I ain't the bastard you think I am. For your information, when I bought that house in Downey, I put your name on the title. I also started you a college fund about ten years ago. A lot of good that did," he says, shaking his head. Then he tosses the empty tequila bottle in the trash and walks back into the house, leaving me alone, confused, and thirsty.

32

I WAKE UP FACEDOWN ON A BALE OF HAY, TURN OVER, AND find myself looking up into the butt of a donkey. Sunlight streams down through the cracks in the ceiling and I realize I'm in a barn, but my grandmother's barn no longer has a ceiling, so I wonder where the heck I am. I start to stand and collapse back down onto the hay, feeling like I've been worked over with a baseball bat. Every part of my body aches. My heart is beating in my head, and as I put it between my knees to try to relieve the pain, I puke on my boots.

The donkey brays and kicks dust in my face.

A woman in a cotton dress comes out of nowhere, cussing at me in Spanish, chasing me out of the barn with a pitchfork.

I run outside onto a dirt street, where children dressed in rags hold up their hands to me. *"Dinero, señor, dinero por favor!"* Looking up into the scorching light of morning, I see a sign shaped like a bottle of beer. It's in front of a cantina where I vaguely recall consuming large amounts of cheap liquor the night before. The only other thing I remember is leaving my uncle Mitch's place feeling very, very thirsty and asking the man who guarded his house for directions to the nearest bar.

Somehow I've ended up in Mexico.

I walk the streets for half an hour before I find the Ford, then drive to the nearest café, where I order coffee and eggs. Mostly coffee.

I can't believe I woke up from a blackout in Mexico. I'd like to tell myself that my uncle drugged me and dragged me across the border, but I've had enough experience with blackouts to know that the pounding sensation pulsing between my ears is my own fault.

I will *never* do that again.

Maybe I should just stay in Mexico. Doubt anyone could find me here. I'd be safe from the law and from Eight Ball's crew. Besides, nobody would miss me. My mother is drugged out and seems happy to stay that way. My father will either be dead soon or will spend the rest of his life in prison. My uncle is an ass. Wade is happy with Dorie, and my grandmother cares more about her pig than me. The only person who gives a damn is Jess.

Would she come to Mexico?

I take her note out of my back pocket and carefully unfold it, spreading it out on the checkered tablecloth, hands still shaking from the toxins in my body. I could probably make out what she'd written if I had the time. Not much of that lately, but today it feels like that's all I've got.

I am not stupid. My problem is not that I can't read, it's just that the process is so painfully slow, the letters so hard to manage as they skip across the white space, the words so burdensome to decipher, that by the time I get to the end of a paragraph, I've forgotten what was at the beginning. But I will never forget what I read on that page:

> People look at me and say I've got it all,
> But when you're standing at the top you've got
> A long, long way to fall.
> And tell me, if I do
> Can I depend on you?
> Will you be the man
> Who will catch me if you can?
> 'Cause I'm fallin' hard,
> I'm fallin' fast,
> And I gotta know
> If it's gonna last.
> You're the one I need
> To teach me to believe.

I read it again, and then a third time, and then I trace each letter with my fingers and commit each phrase to memory.

Jess thinks I'm somebody she can depend on. God, how I want to be that person, but I'm not sure I can anymore. My life is such a mess.

I ask the waitress for a pencil, and then I turn over the paper place mat stained with coffee and bacon grease and slowly, painstakingly write my response:

> Peeple luk at me and wok akros the street.
> So tired of the suspishus eyes
> On all the faces that I meet
> And tell me, if I try
> To be a difrent guy,
> Will you be the girl
> To rearrange my wirld?

You take me up,
You take me down.
Take me to the sky,
Take me to the ground.
I'd go anywhere
If you would take me there.

I carefully fold the paper place mat and put it in my pocket
next to Jess's note. I will go back to Livingston and see my father
and ask him if people like me can start over. I believe he is the
one person who would know.

33

"YOU LOOK LIKE HELL!" MY FATHER TELLS ME.

It has taken me four hours and two gallons of coffee along with the pointing and gesturing of at least five different Mexican nationals, but I have finally made it back to Livingston.

"Looks like the same clothes you wore yesterday."

"Didn't have time to go back to the farm and change."

"Where have you been?"

"La Puerta."

"Why?" His jaw tightens.

"Went to see Uncle Mitch . . . and Mom."

My father's face grows as pale as his white prison shirt. "What's she doin' back in Texas?"

"She's been depressed. Uncle Mitch wanted to take care of her."

"That so?"

"She's a good woman."

"I know."

"Why do women like her and Jess fall for guys like me and you?"

"Only God can answer that question, son."

"Do people like me . . . like you . . ." Suddenly I don't know how to phrase my question. "How far can you go down the wrong path before you can't get back on the right one?" I finally ask.

He leans forward, studying me. Looks at the guard. Looks back at me. Knows I can't give any details. "Well," he replies, "I always say that as long as you're breathing, there's still hope."

I nod, but inside I cringe. If the State of Texas has its way, my father will be without a shred of hope in five short days. I can't believe he's a cold-blooded killer. Maybe what happened to Jack Golden was an accident. Like what happened to Two Tone.

Or maybe somebody else did the murder. "Do you think Seagraves could have killed Jack Golden?" I ask.

"Have you read any of my book? Cartwright gave it to you three days ago."

"Do you think Seagraves tipped the cops?"

"Why don't you read chapter five and find out?"

"Why won't you just answer my questions?"

He leans toward the glass, eyes looking right through me. "Why won't you answer *mine*?"

A silence as wide as an ocean passes between us.

"You can't read it, can you?"

I feel myself take in a sharp breath before consciously realizing what I'm doing. "I lost my glasses."

"Don't try to bullshit a bullshitter, son."

"Don't you care at all that they're planning to kill you in five days?"

"That isn't going to happen."

"But what if it does? Don't you want to see Mom one last time?"

"She left me, Dylan."

"What do you mean?"

"She found out about the drugs. She left, and she took you with her," he says, and I see that the pain is still fresh for him, even after all these years. "When Jack died, you were in La Puerta with your mother, staying with your uncle Mitch."

"No, I wasn't. I was at the trailer."

"You weren't there!"

"I was there!" I yell, pounding on the counter between us. "Don't mess with me, Dad. Not about this." I lean toward him and feel my fists clenching. "I remember that night. I dream about it. Ever since I was little. The clock. The blood on the curtains. I was there!"

My father leans back, rubs his chin, seems to grow ten years older in the span of five seconds. Whispers, "How much do you remember?"

"Not much," I say, wondering why me being there is such a big secret. Wondering why everything has to be a secret. "I remember a bird coming out of the clock and a voice saying, 'You killed him!'"

"Whose voice?" he asks.

"I don't know."

He nods his head slowly. "Okay." He sighs. "I guess I owe you an explanation. Your mother left me, takin' you with her, and your grandma was fit to be tied. She never liked your mama. Claimed she stole you from us. So Levida went down to La Puerta to get you. Said she was entitled to bring you home for a weekend visit, but then she wouldn't take you back. You were stayin' with her down at the farmhouse. I don't know how you ended up back at the trailer. Things got real crazy that night. I was setting something up. Trying to get out of that crazy business I was in. The Colombians found out. This guy, Zorro, broke in and tied up your grandma. Tried to make her tell him where I was, but she didn't know. Guess you ran. Zorro went up to the trailer, and somewhere in the middle of it all, Jack Golden showed up and got himself shot by the Colombian. After it was all over I found you hiding in the pantry. You were so shook up you couldn't even talk. I took you to Travis Seagraves's house and asked his wife to take you to La Puerta the next day."

"Travis Seagraves's house?" I can't believe it.

"It's up the road from your grandma's place. I didn't see a need to tell anybody you'd been there. Havin' policemen ask you all sorts of questions. You were already scared enough."

"Maybe I would have remembered something that would have helped your case."

"You were six years old. You couldn't have helped my case. You still don't understand, do you?"

"I guess not," I say in total frustration. "Why don't you explain it to me?"

"I didn't want any *help* with my case."

"Why not?"

"Do you remember your grandfather?"

"Quit trying to change the subject."

"I'm not! Just tell me if you remember him."

I can't bring up a single image of the man. "He didn't talk much. That's about all I recall."

"The Colombians killed him, about a month before they killed Jack Golden."

"How?" I ask.

"They stole his dreams."

"What do you mean?"

"They killed his prize pigs, and five days later he had a heart attack."

"Is that why Levida won't come see you?"

"That and a long list of other things. A man's beliefs are his destiny. As soon as my father believed his life was over, it was."

I shudder as I remember what Uncle Mitch told me about his family just the day before. "What do you believe?" I ask my father.

"I believe there's a lot of ways to kill a man besides pullin' the trigger of a gun. And I believe a lot of innocent people have suffered as a result of piss-poor decisions I have made." He covers his eyes with his hand, and I can see that he's shaking.

"Dad?"

"I'm gettin' a little tired," he says, looking up at me. "You come back tomorrow. But tomorrow it's my turn to ask the questions." He takes a deep breath, and his hand finally stops shaking. "Tomorrow we talk about you. Guard," he calls to an armed man in gray on his side of the glass. "I'm ready to go back to my cell."

When I return to the farm, I'm surprised to see there isn't a board of the barn left standing. Wade, who is busy digging up the floor, drops his shovel when he sees me and runs up to the truck. "Dylan, where ya been? Your grandma is fit to be tied. Pew-wee! You stink, dude," he informs me as I get out of the truck. "Where did you go?"

"Mexico," I say as I walk over to the hose and start cleaning the dried vomit from my boots. "Why are you digging up the barn floor? Haven't you demolished it enough?"

"Your grandma said she wants the whole thing dug up so she can build a new swimming pool for that dang pig, but I think she's really after that box."

"What box?"

"The old metal box with the padlock that was buried by the pig trough. Oh, I forgot. You haven't seen it yet. I found it yesterday morning."

I throw down the hose. "Where is it?"

"I took it up to the trailer and hid it under the couch."

"Wade, I could kiss you."

"I wish you wouldn't. I'm kinda partial to girls. Besides, you don't smell too good."

I grab him and kiss his forehead anyway. "C'mon, let's go have a look."

"Not so fast," Levida says, huffing and puffing toward me with Charlotte at her heels. "Where have you been, boy?"

"I went down to La Puerta to talk to my uncle Mitch."

"I'm not runnin' a hotel. You don't just saunter in and saunter out at your leisure. If that's the way you feel, you can collect your junk and find a Holiday Inn."

"What did I do?" I ask. My mother never kept tabs on me, and I see no reason why this old woman should.

"I think she was worried about you," whispers Wade, and Levida shoots him a look.

"You missed Wednesday night church," Levida says. Her bottom lip is quivering, and I can see that Wade is right, but she's not about to admit it. "You can make it up tonight, though," she informs me. "There's gonna be a special prayer vigil."

"I got some stuff to do tonight," I tell her, thinking of the rusted box waiting for me up at the trailer.

"Yeah, you've had a lot of 'stuff' to do. You keep runnin' here and there all over the darn state, but you won't sit still long enough to face anything."

"Sit still!" I say. "You really expect me to sit still while they get ready to kill my father?"

She glares at me, the wheels of her brain working on some plan. Then she turns to Wade. "Go get the diesel. We're goin' to town."

"Town?"

"Brenham."

"What are we gonna do in Brenham?" he asks.

"I don't know. Buy a hat. Get some ice cream. I believe Dylan needs to spend some time alone."

"Fine. That's what I was planning to do anyway," I say.

"And be sure you meet us at the church at seven o'clock."

"Levida . . ."

"Don't even think about missing it. They're having a prayer meeting. If you miss it and your father dies, you'll have to live with that guilt for the rest of your life."

I could tell her I don't think that's the way God works, but why waste the breath? "Fine!" I say.

"Fine!" she snaps right back. "C'mon, Wade."

I go up to the trailer and find the rusted box Wade hid under the couch. It's about the size of a school binder, only deeper, and I wonder what's inside. Maybe money for a fresh start in Mexico, but when I shake the box I hear something solid and hard inside. My hand trembles as I twist the knob, this way and that, trying to listen for any variation in the tumblers so I can figure out the combination. I try my father's birthday, 5-15-72, but the numbers don't go that high, so I try 5-15-7, but that doesn't work. Then I try my mother's birthday, 4-18-71, but that doesn't work either because the highest number on the lock is 39. I consider that I will run into the same problem with my own birthday, when I realize I will be turning eighteen in two days. "Happy birthday," I tell myself, knowing that if I didn't remember, nobody else is going to. I wonder if whatever is inside this box will free my father. That would be the best present in the world.

After ten minutes I give up on the numbers game and go down to the workshop. I sort through Levida's tools until I find what I think might help me, a file, two screwdrivers, and a hammer.

Setting the metal box on the floor, I try to jimmy the lock, but it's no use. Next I try to loosen the hinges, but the box is sturdier than it looks. Finally I bang on the thing with the hammer, but I don't even leave a dent. I throw the box against the wall in frustration, finally shoving it back under the couch.

Then it's just me and the clock and the blood-stained curtains. What Levida thinks I'll gain from sitting here staring at the walls is beyond me. The silence of the place is louder than a jet engine and builds between my ears, bringing back the alcohol headache of that morning.

I go to the back of the trailer and take a shower, in a bathroom covered in rose-colored tile that makes me want to vomit again. I wonder if it's possible for a kid of seventeen to be an alcoholic.

I dry off and think about calling Jess and asking her to run away with me to Mexico. No, that wouldn't be right. I can't ask her to drop out of school just to be with me.

I feel like I'll go crazy if I sit here staring at the walls and thinking about Jess. Then a thought occurs to me. I have my father's book. I could try reading it.

I go out to the Ford and grab it, thankful for any diversion. Taking it back into the living room, I open to the first page and am startled to see my name printed there. It's a dedication. A note to me, published right in the book.

To my son Dylan.

I've written this book for you.

It's a guide for how not to live your life.

I'm sending it out into the world in the hopes

that someday it will find you.

Even if I never do.

All my love,

Dad

Wow! My father wrote a book for me, to tell me all the things he couldn't say in person. I thumb through the pages, amazed that someone would go to all this trouble for me. I already know how *not* to live my life. What I desperately want to know is how to live it. So I keep on reading, hoping I'll find some answers. It's a slow, painful process, but I don't have anything else to do.

I wake up to the sound of the cuckoo clock clucking out seven annoying chirps and realize I've drifted off to sleep, clutching my father's book. I'm sure Levida wound up that stupid clock just to terrorize me. I check the time again. Realize the prayer meeting is starting.

I splash water on my face, get into the truck, and drive to the redbrick church on Main Street. As I go inside and sit in the back row, I hear angry voices grumbling among themselves while the preacher tries to talk.

"All I said was that we should pray for God to have mercy on D.J.'s soul," says the preacher.

A man sitting next to Red in the second row stands up. "Well, in that case, why don't we just open up all the prisons and let out those killers and rapists and child molesters? If we're gonna practice mercy and forgiveness, I say let's get after it."

"I didn't say that," the preacher replies.

"You might as well have," a woman yells from the back of the church.

"You're forgettin' that the Goldens are our friends," says another man. "Just because they aren't Baptists doesn't mean we're gonna pray that the law lets Jack's killer get off easy."

"That's not what I'm suggesting," the preacher says, but the crowd doesn't hear him. They're all grumbling too loudly among themselves. My grandmother sits up front at the church organ, glaring out at them like a flashing neon sign no one notices. *Hey, remember me. That man you're talking about is my son.*

"Please, brothers and sisters, let's try to remember why we're all here," says the preacher. "It's a prayer service for everyone affected by this tragedy."

"You weren't here back when it happened," says the first man. "You don't remember how it tore this town apart, but we do."

The crowd cheers.

"All I suggested," says the preacher, "was a prayer vigil for *both* of the families. I'm not advocating public policy."

"I agree with the preacher," says a pretty blond woman about my mother's age. "Not only that, but I think the governor should let D.J. go for time served."

Voices rise up from the crowd, but the woman keeps talking above them all. "You all know that trial was a mockery. D.J. has paid his debt to society. I say they let him go."

"That's because you had the hots for him all through high school. Everybody knows you wrote all his papers. But in case you didn't notice, he went off to play for the Longhorns and left you in the dust," someone shouts.

"I know the wounds go deep," says the preacher. "Which is precisely the reason we need to turn to Our Father in prayer to guide us peaceably through these dark times."

"May I say a word?" asks Levida, and only then do the people in the church seem to notice her.

"All right, Mrs. Dawson." The preacher steps aside, and my grandmother walks up to the podium.

Levida stares at the crowd for a long minute until she has everyone's undivided attention. "My son was tried and convicted and sentenced to death by a jury of his peers."

This hardly seems helpful, but at least no one can argue with her, and so she continues, unchallenged. "This town was left in turmoil, a woman was left without a husband, and a child was left without a father." The crowd thinks she's talking about Tornado T., but she's looking right at me. "D.J. made some bad decisions. Some real bad decisions. And he's payin' for 'em. I ain't here to argue about that. I just wonder if we can be honest with ourselves long enough to admit why we're really angry. Is it because we *think* the Dozer killed Jack Golden, or because we *know* he killed our dreams?

"If you don't want to take a moment of silence to pray for D.J., maybe you can take that moment to pray for yourselves. What you feel about my son says more about you than it does about him. So take a moment. Figure out what truth you're hidin' that you can't admit even to yourself. We all got a secret. I'll tell you mine. I was nothin' in this town but a poor pig farmer's wife until my son became the school football star. Then I became the Dozer's mama. He stole that from me, and it's taken me eleven long, lonely years to forgive him . . . and myself."

With that my grandmother steps down from the podium and walks out of the church into the light of the summer night. As I watch her go I whisper a silent prayer. "Dear God, please show me the truth. Let the truth set me and my father free."

That night I dream again of the room with the pale blue curtains.

There are angry voices.

Gunfire.

Screaming.

Everything is darkness and confusion.

One thing I know.

Something evil has come to hurt us.

Kill us.

I remember a gun my father hid in the pantry, in a peanut sack.

I find it.

It fits in my hand, and I'm not so afraid as I hold it.

The door to the clock flies open, only it's not the door to the clock, it's the door to the house. Then the bird pops through the door. Only it's not the bird. It's my father. And it's his voice that screams, "My God! What have you done? You've killed Jack."

And he's looking straight at me.

But he doesn't see me. At least not at first.

Where is he looking?

Over me?

Through me?

Then his arms are around me and he's holding me very tightly.

He's crying as he says, "It'll be all right. I'll fix it so everything is all right."

34

I HAVE NEVER BELIEVED IN DAYS OF BAD LUCK OR OMENS OF bad fortune. But I wake up on Friday the thirteenth feeling like nothing will ever be right again.

My dream from the night before haunts me. It is no longer a fuzzy vision but has become a crystal clear memory. The man storming into our trailer, yelling in a language I didn't understand. The gun hidden in the pantry. Finding it and holding it in my hand. Jack Golden lying dead on the floor and my father carrying me away.

I must have been the one who shot Jack. I must have been scared and confused and trying to defend myself, and now my father is rotting away in prison, about to die, because of me.

Maybe I didn't inherit bad blood from my father. Maybe all the bad blood belongs to me. Maybe everybody would be better off if I'd never been born.

I can't remember actually pulling the trigger, but maybe it's like Levida says. The mind can only remember what it's willing to remember—because if you are guilty, then the truth is not the thing that sets you free. It's the thing that gets you locked away.

I showered last night, but I shower again when I wake up. I scrub myself for nearly half an hour, but I still don't feel clean, and I'm afraid I will never feel clean again.

"I know you didn't kill Jack Golden," I tell my father.

"I'm glad you believe that." He looks tired, like maybe he didn't sleep last night, and I wonder what it's like at night in this place. In juvie they dimmed the lights but never turned them all the way off.

"I killed him," I say.

"What?"

"I remember."

"You can't possibly remember a thing like that, because it didn't happen." He looks like he's telling the truth, but how can I know for sure when he's so good at lying?

"I was the one who knew where the gun was hidden," I whisper into the phone. "You showed me when you put it in the peanut sack. Why did you take the blame? The law wouldn't have done anything to me. I was six years old."

"That is *not* the way it happened, and that is the end of the story." My father looks straight at me. "I don't want to discuss it anymore. I already told you that today I'm the one who's going to get some answers. Now I want to know why you didn't get help with your reading. Things aren't like they were when I was a kid. There are lots of programs to help kids with learning problems."

"What happened to the gun?" I ask.

"Zorro took it. He found it while he was casing the house.

Jack surprised him and Zorro shot him with it. Then he fled and took the gun with him. Now it's my turn to ask the questions. Does your mother know you have trouble reading?"

"Will you stop it! Just stop!" I yell. "They're fixing to kill you. Do you really think my English grade has anything to do with that?"

"It has everything to do with that," he tells me. "Do you have any idea how close you are to bein' where I am?"

I think of the night I killed Two Tone. How I hit him and he fell and then he didn't get up. "I got a pretty good idea," I reply.

"But you got no idea why?"

"I got in with the wrong crowd."

"But why?"

"I don't know. For the regular reasons, I guess. What does that matter?"

"Don't you understand what I'm trying to tell you? These walls are filled with men who can't read or write. That wasn't their crime, but it's no coincidence they turned up here. Did you know there are studies linking literacy skills to juvenile delinquency?"

"So you're saying that a kid's future is pretty much set if he can't read."

"Not set in stone. There are a lot of factors, but that's a big one."

"And what if he kills somebody when he's six, is that a factor?"

I leave the prison driving a hundred miles an hour. It's not because I have any place to go. I just don't care anymore. Don't care if the police catch me. Don't care if they lock me away. Don't care if I total Levida's truck and die.

All I can think about is how in four days the state of Texas is going to kill my father for something I did.

I look in the rearview mirror, half hoping to see the black Jeep. Willing it to run over me. But I don't see it. Until I get back to the farm and find it parked in front of Levida's house, next to Dorie's Ford Explorer.

I park around back, wondering if Eight Ball is inside the house, holding Levida and Wade and Dorie hostage.

Getting out of the truck, I shut the door as quietly as I can, praying that whoever is inside didn't see me coming up the road, knowing I could never be that lucky. Baby Face greets me, wagging her tail, whining in agitation.

"Shhh!" I tell her, scratching her neck to calm her so she won't make any noise. Then I go into the workshop, looking for something I might use as a weapon. I sort through the various tools and find a long-handled screwdriver. It won't do much against guns and switchblades, but it's all I've got.

Walking silently out of the workshop, I enter the house through the back door, thinking maybe I can surprise whoever is inside.

There are voices coming from the living room. Women's voices. I inch my way through the kitchen, past the refrigerator and the butcher block. I open a drawer. Take out a knife and hold it out in front of me, along with the screwdriver. Then the living room comes into view and I see . . .

Jess.

I quickly set down the weapons on the bar.

She looks up. Sees me. Jumps up from the couch. Runs into my arms. Wraps herself around me. Holds me so tight I feel all the scattered pieces of myself coming back together. Feel myself becoming solid again. Her hair is silk and she smells like fresh rain.

"How did you get here?" I ask.

"My emergency credit card. I flew to Houston and rented a car. Dylan, I've been so worried about you."

Levida, who is standing now, crosses her arms against her chest and glares at me. "Wanted by the law for armed robbery. I guess the apple don't fall far from the tree."

"How did you find me?" I ask Jess.

"When you told me you were in Texas, I knew you'd come looking for your father. Livingston is where they keep the men on death row, so I figured if I hung out there, I would eventually find you."

"You were the one who followed me the other day."

"Yes, but then I lost you."

If Jess could find me, so could anybody else who might be looking.

"If there's one thing I won't abide, it's a liar," says Levida.

"What happened that night, Dylan? What really happened?"

I look at Wade, sitting on the couch holding hands with Dorie, and my friend looks down at the carpet, as if the pattern of the old braided rug is taking all his concentration.

"You been runnin' from the law this whole time," Levida says. "Bringin' more shame and humiliation to this family."

"I didn't rob that liquor store," I say, feeling like I'm at the bottom of a swimming pool, unable to breathe. I glare at Wade, who looks up at me, then looks away just as quickly.

"Why should I believe you when your entire life is a lie?" Levida fumes. "Pretending to need glasses because you don't know how to read."

"Don't talk to him that way," Jess says. "You don't know anything about him. He's not a bad person. And of course he can read. He's a poet." Jess looks up at me and smiles.

She must have read the poems in my leather journal, printed there by my reading teacher. She must have seen her name above that sappy love poem. Now my humiliation is utter, complete, and final.

"Go ahead and tell your girlfriend the truth," says Levida. "If it's possible for anything honest to come out of your lyin', filthy mouth. It's all just lies upon lies upon lies, ain't it?"

I look from Jess to Levida to Wade and Dorie, who are all staring at me expectantly.

Levida reaches down to grab her black leather Bible off the coffee table. She opens it and thrusts it at me. "Go on and read it. Prove me wrong. And don't give me that lame excuse about needin' glasses."

"I can't read it." I admit to her, to them all. "I mean, I could, if I had long enough. I could make out the words, but I probably wouldn't understand them."

"But . . . your poems," says Jess, a look on her face of total betrayal. And I feel myself slipping away again.

"I think it's about time for you to be movin' on, boy," my grandmother says, snapping shut the Bible.

"I didn't rob that liquor store," I tell Jess.

She takes a step away from me, still looking confused and hurt. "You were the one person I thought was genuine. I don't know what to believe. I don't even know who you are."

"Tell them, Wade," I plead to my friend.

"He's tellin' the truth," Wade says. "He didn't have nothin' to do with that robbery."

"I doubt Dylan even knows what the truth is," says Levida. "You got thirty minutes to get your gear and clear out. I don't want to see your face on this farm or in this town ever again. Do you understand me?"

"I understand." I'll get my car and I'll leave. That will be better for everyone.

"No, wait, please," Wade says, looking at Dorie and then Levida. "It was me. It was all my doing. I robbed the liquor store. Dylan didn't know what I was planning. He was just driving the car." Wade goes on to tell all the details of how he was trying to become a member of the BSB. How they wouldn't take him unless I joined up too. How they cornered us in the park and pulled a knife on him. How I punched Two Tone and saved him. But he leaves out the part about Two Tone dying.

When he is finished, both Jess and Levida are looking at him in total disgust. Dorie seems confused, like she can't decide what to think.

"You're one helluva friend, aren't you?" says Levida.

"I've found the Lord and changed my ways. I'm saved now." Wade smiles pathetically.

"And the good Lord forgives you, baby," Dorie says, clutching his hand ever tighter. "I forgive you too."

"The good Lord may forgive you, and the preacher's daughter may forgive you, but don't expect the same from me, boy," Levida tells him. "All y'all can just hightail it off my property!" she yells at the lot of us. Then she storms out the back door.

I follow her outside to the workshop, where she grabs a shovel hanging on the wall. She spins around to face me so fast she almost hits me with it. "You don't back down, do you?" she yells.

"I'm the one who shot Jack," I say, and the words stick in my throat like a pill that won't go down. "My father says it was a Colombian, but he's lying. I remember I was there. I remember getting the gun."

Levida looks me up and down, and then rests the shovel against the wall. "You didn't shoot him."

"There was a lot of confusion. It was dark, and I was scared out of my mind. I didn't know he was a cop."

She shakes her head. "The authorities never would have prosecuted you. There was no need for D.J. to lie to protect you if you were the shooter."

"My father was trying to save me."

"From what?"

"I don't know. From being emotionally scarred."

"Oh, like you haven't been emotionally scarred by havin' a daddy locked up in prison."

I have to think about this. She's right, of course. I was a little kid. They wouldn't have put me in jail, but I can't shake the feeling that my father was trying to protect someone. "I don't know. I guess he had his reasons."

"I'm sure he had his reasons. I just don't believe you've figured them out yet."

I should feel relieved, I guess, but I don't. Just more confused.

"A .22 might stop a man," says Levida, "but it won't kill him, unless the bullet hits him in a vital organ. The heart. The head. You think in all that *confusion* you had the presence of mind to shoot to kill?"

"It could have been a fluke."

"Yeah, a fluke," says Levida, nodding. "That's exactly what it was."

"Why can't you tell me what you know?"

"Because I don't *know* anything." She picks up the shovel and heads toward the door. "I'll give you four days. If you don't figure it out by then, it won't matter. After that you can go back to where you came from and settle your troubles with the law."

"What about Wade?"

"You test the edges of my patience, boy," she says. "Why would you even want to keep a friend like that around?"

"He saved my life in juvie."

She shakes her head. "Juvie. Should have known. Some people just draw trouble. Fine. Keep him around. But thinkin' you owe people is dangerous business. Like your daddy discovered."

I go back to the house and see Jess getting into the black Jeep. I run out to stop her, but she's already pulling out of the driveway. I run up alongside her, pounding on the window, begging her to stop.

She brakes and rolls down the window, but won't look at me. "What?" she says, and I can see that this time, I've really lost her.

There's nothing for me to say, so I just pull the crumpled poem written on the greasy paper place mat from my back pocket and try to hand it to her.

She makes no move to take it, so I reach inside the window and set it on her lap. "It wasn't all a lie," I tell her.

She bites her lower lip to keep from crying, then steps on the gas, and as she speeds away her last words to me echo in my ears. *I don't even know who you are.*

That makes two of us.

* * *

That night as I sit in the front room of the trailer, listening to Wade and Dorie giggling and laughing in the back bedroom, all I can think about is Jess. Jess loved me. She came all the way from California to find me, even after she knew I was wanted by the law. I could have told her the truth, but I lied about who I was. I search my pockets for the poem she wrote for me, but it is gone—just like she is gone. There will never be another girl like Jess, and the weight of this truth settles on me like a foot on the back of a drowning boy.

THE GIRL WHO LOVED ME

There was a girl who loved me,
her eyes aquamarine.
I used to dream I'd swim in them,
that sea of blue and green.
She didn't care about my past,
or the trouble I had seen.
But in the end she walked away,
one lonely, desperate summer day.
There was nothing more for her to say,
once she knew I had betrayed
her with my pitiful disguise.
There were just too many lies.
Too much deceit had come between
me and the girl who loved me,
when
     I was
          seventeen.

35

MY BIRTHDAY. I CAN'T GO TO SEE MY FATHER UNTIL FIVE o'clock, when death row visitation time begins. The rest of Saturday is reserved for the general prison population. I should be doing something, but I'm not sure what. I open my father's book and read chapter five. It's only three pages long, and it takes me the better part of two hours to muddle through it, but in the end I feel proud, as if by this one small gesture I have disproved everything my grandmother said about me yesterday.

It helps that most of it is information I already know, his version of what went down in the trailer the night Jack Golden got shot. The version where my presence is not mentioned.

I set down my father's book and pick up *Poetry Through the Ages*, wondering if what my reading tutor told me might actually work, if I really could learn to read by deciphering the poems I've already memorized.

"Fourteen, thirty-eight, twenty-two," I say, absentmindedly, turning to page twenty-two, "The Stolen Child."

"Why do you always say it like that?" Wade asks, coming out of the shower, towel drying his hair.

"Like what?" I reply, snapping the book shut. I didn't get much sleep last night, because he and Dorie didn't stop laughing and carrying on until she left at midnight.

"Why do you always say them page numbers out of sequence?"

"I don't know, Wade. That's the way my mother always says them. Is there some law about saying page numbers in order?"

"No. It just sounds weird. Like a combination to somebody's gym locker or something."

I jump off the couch, and the book falls to the floor. "Wade, you're a genius."

"I am?"

"'The key is in Yeats.' My mother always used to tell me that." I crawl under the couch and pull out the metal box with trembling hands.

"Fourteen," I say out loud as I turn the dial to the right. "Thirty-eight," I say, turning the dial to the left. "Twenty-two." I turn the dial to the right, holding my breath as I hear the tumblers clicking into place, and the latch slipping open.

"Who woulda figured," says Wade, who has come to stand beside me. Suddenly I can't move. I can't help feeling that whatever is in this box will change everything forever.

"Go on," Wade says.

I ease open the top of the box and see a tiny revolver sitting inside. A snub-nose .22. The gun that killed Jack Golden.

I slam the lid shut, as if this will make the contents disappear. "He lied to me," I say, shaking all the way down to my bones. "He told me the Colombian got away with the gun, but it's been here all this time. What if . . ."

"What?"

"Nothing." I can't finish the thought out loud. What if the person my father has been trying to protect all these years is himself?

My head starts to spin, like I'm being sucked backward in time. I remember finding the gun in the peanut sack. I remember seeing Jack Golden dead on the floor. I remember seeing my father standing over Jack's body, holding the gun in his hand. He put the gun in his back pocket and then picked me up and ran with me out of the trailer. "Everything's going to be all right," he told me. "Don't you worry. Everything is going to be all right." The next thing I knew, he was banging on the door of our neighbor's house. A woman answered in a nightgown. A man was standing behind her. My father left me there and ran away into the darkness, and I could see the bulge of the gun in his back pocket.

"Dylan, are you okay?" Wade's voice brings me back to reality.

"I can't breathe," I say. "I can't . . ." I run out to the truck, start the engine, and drive as fast as I can, leaving behind Wade and the trailer full of memories. I don't know where I'm going, or what I will do when I get there, but I have to put some distance between me and that place.

When I get out to the highway, I go south toward Brenham. I drive for over an hour before my head begins to clear and I start thinking straight again. I see a sign for Victoria, and that's when I realize I'm on my way to La Puerta. To my mother. I pull over to the side of the road and try to figure out what I'm going to do.

It doesn't matter, I tell myself. If my father killed Jack Golden, it doesn't matter. It had to be an accident.

I bang my head on the steering wheel. My mother knew

that combination. She must know other things as well. I need to talk to her, but if I drive all the way down to La Puerta, I'll never make it back to Livingston in time to visit my father. I can't see him tomorrow because it's Sunday, and they're scheduled to kill him on Tuesday.

I stop at a gas station in Hope, fill up, and then call my uncle's house from a pay phone.

"I need to talk to my mother," I say when Mitch picks up the phone.

"Hello to you, too."

"I don't have time to jack around with you, Mitch. Put my mother on the phone."

"She's asleep."

"Wake her up."

"You're not in a position to be orderin' me around, boy."

"I'm going to talk to her one way or another, so put her on the phone, or else I'm going to drive down there and talk to her face-to-face, and by the time I get there I'm gonna be pretty damn agitated, so maybe I'll just mention how you've been weaseling her out of her money all these years."

"Fine!" Uncle Mitch leaves, and a voice comes over the phone telling me to deposit more money. I search my pocket for quarters and just about decide Mitch has left me standing there, when I hear my mother's voice.

"Dylan?"

"Mom, I found the gun."

"What?" Her voice is a hairline crack in a sheet of glass about to shatter.

"Fourteen, thirty-eight, twenty-two. The combination to the lock. You knew it all this time. How did you know?"

There is a long silence, and I can't be sure, but I think my mother is crying. "They won't kill your father. It won't come to that."

"How can you be sure?"

"He promised me."

"Who promised you?"

"Your father."

"When?"

More silence.

"Mom?"

"D.J. had a box hidden in the barn. He told me about it right before—"

"Before you left," I say, so she doesn't have to.

"He told me the combination and said that if anything happened to him, I should find the box. There were certificates of deposit, stocks, bonds, numbers for foreign bank accounts. Enough money to take care of us, he said. I told him I didn't want any of his drug money. Then I called your uncle Mitch to come get us. I took you away from that awful place and I left him."

At least that part of my father's story was true. I take a deep breath before I ask my next question. "Mom, what do you think really happened that night?"

It is a long time before she answers, and the voice comes on the line again. *"Your time is about to expire,"* it says. I search my pockets but I'm out of change. "Mom, I gotta go," I tell her.

"He didn't kill that cop," she says.

"How can you be sure?"

"Your time is about to expire."

"Just a minute," I tell my mother, spotting a quarter lying on the ground. "Mom . . ."

"He said he wanted me to forget about him and go on with my life. If only I could have forgotten." She's crying again, and I realize that she may have left my father, but she has never stopped loving him.

"If I talk to him and get him to agree to see you, could you meet me there Monday morning?"

"He'll never allow that."

"Maybe I can get him to change his mind."

"He won't."

"Please, Mom," I beg.

"All right then," she says with a sigh filled with regret and loss and a hundred other emotions I can't begin to understand. "If you can get him to put my name on his list, I'll meet you up there Monday morning."

"Thank you."

"Dylan."

"Yes."

"Happy birthday, honey," she says right before my time elapses.

I get into the truck, turn around, and head to Livingston. By the time I get there, it's already six o'clock and I've been driving for nearly five solid hours.

"I thought you weren't coming," my father says when I see him.

"I had some stuff to sort out."

"Like what?"

"I figured out the combination to that box, and I found out what was inside."

He studies me to see if I'm bluffing. So to prove my point

I say, "Fourteen, thirty-eight, twenty-two."

His expression doesn't change, and yet a total transformation comes over him. Like in those old Westerns where the cowboy's face suddenly goes slack, and the camera angle widens to show that the Indian up on the mesa has just shot an arrow through his heart.

My father takes a deep breath and lets it out slowly. "Well then," he says.

"Stop jacking with me, Dad. All I ever wanted was the truth."

"That's the problem. People think if they can add up all the facts, they'll end up with the truth, but that's like sewin' body parts together in the hopes you'll get a man."

"Mom is coming Monday morning to see you. You gotta put her name on the list."

His whole body goes stiff. "You leave your mother out of this." He lowers his voice to almost a whisper. "I won't see her and she knows it."

"Please," I beg him. "Just talk to her. One time. She really wants to see you."

"Did she say that?" he asks, softening ever so slightly.

"She still loves you."

He shakes his head and runs his hands through his graying hair. "Why?" he asks, but not like he expects an answer.

"Please."

He pounds his fist against his head. "Why, why, why? After everything I've done to . . ."

"Dad?"

He looks up at me as if suddenly realizing I'm sitting there. "I'll think about it."

"Come on . . ."

"That's the best I can do," he tells me in a voice that warns I shouldn't push him too far.

"Okay."

"Tomorrow's Sunday. I'll have Mr. Cartwright call you at Levida's house and give you my answer."

"I can live with that," I say, realizing I don't have any choice.

"Good." He suddenly seems at peace, and I know he's already decided what he's going to do, though he won't tell me.

I don't ask him any more questions. Instead we talk about everything else, and it's just like that first day I came to visit him. I tell him all about Levida and that stupid pig of hers. I describe how Jess found me, only to leave me again. I report how Wade has hooked up with the preacher's daughter. And I forget, for a while, that I'm talking to a man on death row, until the guard's voice comes over the speaker and says it's almost time for me to leave.

"I started reading your book," I say.

"That's good."

"There's a letter in it to me."

He smiles. "A teacher of mine once told me that when you write something, you should think about who you're writing it for. Picture in your mind the one person you most want to read it and why."

"Me?"

"Yes. She said if it means something to that one person, it will mean something to others as well."

"Your time is up," the guard says over the intercom.

I stand to leave, but my father says, "Wait!" over the red telephone. "Let me just look at you a minute." He smiles at me proudly. "I know you been in some trouble, son, but you turned out good. That's all I ever wanted," he tells me. Then he puts his hand against the glass and I put my hand against the glass. "I love you," he says.

"I love you, too," I say back.

And then I leave.

It's nine o'clock at night before I get back to the farm. I walk into the house and smell apple pie baking. Wade is standing at the sink, washing the dirt off a huge zucchini squash from Levida's garden. "Hey, you okay? You left kinda fast this afternoon."

"I talked to my mom. She's going to meet me in Livingston Monday morning."

"That so?" Levida says, walking into the kitchen with an armload of zucchinis from the garden and Baby Face sniffing at her heels.

"Yeah," I say.

"Your daddy said he'd see her?" she asks, plopping the long green vegetables on the counter next to Wade.

"He said he'd consider it."

"Humph," she replies, like she doesn't believe it. She seems more irritated than usual, which I didn't know was possible. Then she looks over at the dining table, and I understand why. The box holding the .22 is sitting open on the table. My grandmother glares at me, so angry that she's shaking. "About time to get dinner on the table," she tells Wade, then storms into her bedroom and slams the door.

I turn on Wade. "You showed her the gun?"

"Nah. She came up to the trailer after you left and saw the box."

Levida storms back into the kitchen, having taken off her dirty overalls and slipped into a pair of jeans and a man's white cotton shirt. She opens and slams cupboards, setting various serving dishes on the counter with notable thuds. Taking a meat loaf out of the oven, she throws it onto a serving dish, then surrounds it with boiled potatoes she hasn't bothered to mash. Next she pours green beans and gravy into bowls. She carries the dishes over to the table and sets them around the rusted metal box, like it isn't even there. Then she walks past me over to the stove, like I'm not there either, fills a basket with rolls from the oven, and hands it to Wade. "Go put these next to the gravy," she tells him. We all sit down, Wade and I sharing awkward glances while Levida passes the serving dishes.

We fill our plates and eat in silence with the strange centerpiece staring up at us. "Do you want to talk about the gun?" I ask.

"What gun?" she says, stabbing her dinner roll with a butter knife.

"I'm sorry. I was wrong not to tell you about finding the box."

"What box?" It's obvious she isn't going to make this easy for me, but I guess I deserve that.

"I didn't know what was in it until this morning."

"More gravy, anyone?" she says, picking up a bowl.

"You haven't been to see my father in eleven years. Why do you care what's in that box when you don't give a damn about him?" My anger and frustration are mounting. "Why haven't you seen him in all this time? Why won't you go to him? And don't give me that bullshit about him destroying all your dreams. He's your son!"

Levida places her fork on the edge of her plate, coolly and deliberately. Her voice is ice. "He asked me to do something that went against my nature."

"What?"

"Keep my mouth shut. And I been keepin' it shut for over a decade. So here's what we're gonna do," Levida tells me, her voice beginning to rise. "We'll keep this gun sitting here between us in the middle of the table for the next eleven years with the understanding that we will never, ever talk about it. The word will not pass our lips. What happened out there"—she jumps to her feet and points up the hill—"will never be spoken of again, and if it is . . . you will not see my face again." She holds her fist up to her mouth to hide the fact that she's crying, and then she runs out the back door.

And I realize: The silence and separation wasn't her doing. It was my father's. He has shut out everyone but me.

"Maybe you should go talk to her," Wade says.

"I know," I reply, even though I have no idea what to say or do. I didn't even know the old bag was capable of tears.

I walk out the back door and don't have to go far. Levida is standing out in the grass, hosing off Charlotte, whose pitiful face and entire right side is covered in mud.

I walk over and stand nearby, my hands in my pockets.

"I'm sorry, baby," she says to the pig, as if she's betrayed a child. "I didn't realize you been standin' outside in the heat for so long." She rubs her hands across Charlotte's body, wiping away the filth.

"You don't have to keep quiet anymore," I tell her.

Levida drops the hose, reaches me in three long strides, and starts to weep all over again.

I put my arms around her, and she feels tiny. She cries and cries and cries, and when she is all cried out, she takes a bandana out of her pocket and blows her nose into it. "Your daddy and that ambulance chaser he calls a lawyer wouldn't put me on the witness stand," she says.

"What would you have said if they'd let you testify?" I ask.

"The truth. I would have told the jury that a man in a mask broke into my house, tied me up, and demanded to know where your father was. I would have said that shortly beforehand I'd been awoken by the headlights of a Cadillac making its way up the road to your trailer. I would have said that the masked man left as I saw your father coming toward the house from the workshop with your granddaddy's shotgun. I would have said I heard gunshots from up on the hill and then your daddy turned and ran toward the trailer. But afterward I didn't hear any more gunshots."

I consider what she has told me. "So by the time my father got up to the trailer, Jack had already been shot."

"As far as I can figure. I was sittin' there, tied up, not able to do anything. Not even able to get to the phone to call the police. I started yellin' for you. 'Dylan,' I called. You were supposed to be asleep in the front bedroom. I kept callin' for you, but you didn't call back. I didn't know where you were. I was out of my mind. Didn't know what had happened to you or your daddy. Then I saw him in the moonlight, down by the barn, takin' something out of his back pocket that looked like a gun. He went into the barn, and a few minutes later he came out. Came up to the house. Untied me. He was cryin'. Told me he had some plan to get out of that awful business he was in, but it backfired and Jack was dead. I told him to find you. He said he already did. Said you done run up to the trailer for some fool reason and he'd taken you to Travis Seagraves's place. Then he gave me a big brown envelope filled with certificates of deposit and bank account numbers. He said there was enough money in there to take care of all of us. He told me to give a third of it to Jack's widow, keep a third for myself, and use a third to take care of you and your mama.

"After he gave me the money, he hugged me and told me to call the police. Then he left. I figured he'd run off to Mexico or at least flee the state. I had no idea he'd gone back up to the trailer to wait for the authorities."

"He didn't run?"

"Didn't even try."

"Why?"

"I don't know," she says, shaking her head. "After he went to jail, I put my share with the money I left for the Goldens."

"You didn't keep any of it?"

"Just enough to hire that ambulance chaser he found to represent him, along with a private detective to try to locate you and your mama. But by then you were long gone. That uncle of yours knew where you were, but he wouldn't tell me. Against my better judgment, I gave him the third your daddy intended for you and Mollie. I never trusted that man, but I didn't have much choice except to hope he'd do the right thing."

I try to process all she has said. "If the shots were fired before my father went up the hill, he couldn't have been the one who killed Jack."

"I know."

"But he wouldn't let you testify to that effect."

"His lawyer told me they decided I was an unreliable witness. The jury would just think I was tryin' to protect my son, and if the DA cross-examined me, I might fall apart on the stand."

"And you never told the newspapers or the TV reporters what you knew?"

"No."

"Why?"

"They wouldn't have believed me. Besides . . ." She looks down at the dirt. "The day you take away a man's right to choose his fate, he starts to die. I saw it happen to your granddaddy."

"You can't possibly think my father chose to be where he is."

"I believe he looked at his options and did what he thought was best. Who am I to say? Maybe he was right."

36

I WAKE TO THE SOUND OF A HONKING HORN AND LOOK OUT
the window to see Levida sitting in the diesel pickup. I slip on
my pants and am surprised when Wade and Dorie both come
out of the back bedroom, half-dressed. I slept so soundly I
never even heard them come in last night.

"What time is it?" Dorie asks in alarm.

I look up at the cuckoo clock. "Eight thirty," I tell her.

"My daddy is gonna kill me," she says, buttoning her blouse.

I walk out the front door, while Dorie crawls out a back
window. "What's going on?" I ask Levida, surprised to see her
in her black dress.

"It's Sunday. Time for church," she says.

"After what happened there last Thursday night?"

"Put a shirt on, and tell lover boy to do the same."

There's no use arguing, so I go back to the house and put on
one of my father's cotton shirts. It feels good to wear it today.

"Put a shirt on," I tell Wade. "We're going to church."

"Do you think Dorie's father will shoot me?" he asks.

"He's a preacher, Wade."

"He's gonna know what we've been doing. He owns a twelve-gauge, you know."

"Everybody in this town owns a twelve-gauge. Besides, don't you think he'll get more suspicious if you *don't* show up?"

"Good point. He might come lookin' for me."

Wade throws on a shirt, and we get into the backseat of the extended cab diesel.

When we get to the church, no one will talk to us. People walk right past us. Like the gun in the middle of the table.

The exception, of course, is Pastor Bob. He hugs Levida before she goes off to sort through her music. Then he shakes my hand and slaps Wade on the back. "I want to thank you for what you did with Dorie last night."

"Uh," replies Wade, his jaw hanging open like it's become unhinged.

"She told me how the two of you stayed up all night with Widow Spencer. I'm sorry to hear her rheumatism is giving her so much trouble that she can't sleep. You're a fine example of Christian charity, Wade. Thank you."

"You're welcome," he manages to say.

For my friend's sake, I'm glad the preacher is so stupid and naive.

"I know it isn't easy being the preacher's daughter. Living next door to the church. You're the first boy who's shown any real interest in her."

"I should probably find her," Wade says, awkwardly backing away.

"You go right ahead. She's in the fellowship hall setting up for the potluck."

When he leaves, the preacher turns to me. "Would you consider Wade a loyal friend?"

"Loyal?" I say, not sure what the preacher is after.

"Does he stick by people, keep his promises?"

"To the death," I say truthfully.

The preacher nods his head. "I'm glad to hear that." And I realize he's neither stupid nor naive.

Levida plays the church organ like there's no tomorrow, and I think about how brave she is to show her face here every Sunday. She hasn't just lost her husband and her son, she's lost her friends. Her place in the world. Maybe she has a right to be bitter.

Pastor Bob gets up in front of the congregation and opens his Bible. "Matthew, chapter five," he announces. Then he looks straight at Wade, who sits next to Dorie in the front row. "Blessed are the poor in spirit, for theirs is the kingdom of heaven." Then he looks at my grandmother, sitting at the organ in her black dress. "Blessed are those who mourn, for they shall be comforted." He looks at his daughter. "Blessed are the gentle, for they shall inherit the earth."

Then he looks at me, his dark eyes boring their way through my soul. "Blessed are those who hunger and thirst for righteousness, for they SHALL BE SATISFIED."

It's like he's made a prophecy right then and there. Justice will win. I know it has to be true. The preacher read it from the Bible.

"And blessed are the merciful," says Pastor Bob, looking up and down the aisles until people start squirming in their seats. "For they shall receive mercy."

He goes on to spend half an hour talking about the pure

in heart and finishes with a prayer, while carefully avoiding the subject of my father, but by avoiding it, he seems to drive it home even more.

The preacher has nerve. I'll give him that. It takes a lot to stand up to people. Especially if they sign your paycheck. Even if it is only by what you don't say.

An easy peace settles over me. The peace that comes from knowing there is nothing you can do, that decisions are out of your hands. I look at the cross hanging above the preacher, rub the cross on my hand. I pray for myself, for my father, for my mother, for Jess and Wade and Dorie and Levida.

After church everybody starts heading downstairs to the basement for the potluck. Red and Dakota glare at me as if they don't care a rat's ass for the part of the reading about mercy.

"I think I'll go on back to the farm," I tell Levida.

"You run now, boy, and you'll spend your whole life runnin'."

"I'm not running. I'm just avoiding trouble."

"In my experience, it always finds you."

"Maybe. But there's no reason to go looking for it," I say.

"Suit yourself, but I'm not cooking for you when there's free food at church," she says, then goes downstairs, followed by Wade and Dorie, whose arms are intertwined.

I walk outside into the wet Texas summer. A storm cloud has gathered overhead, cooling things off slightly, but if anything, it's even more humid than usual. It's about a two-mile walk from Main Street to the country road where the farm sits, but I can see that I can cut my time in half if I go through the pasture behind the church. I start walking but am stopped by a voice in the church parking lot.

"Dylan, I have to talk to you."

It's Jess.

She's wearing a white cotton T-shirt and a skirt that billows in the hot wind. I have to pinch myself to make sure I'm not dreaming.

"What are you doing here?" I ask as she approaches, green eyes smoldering. I wonder if she's come back to finish telling me off.

"I went looking for you up at your grandmother's place. You weren't there, and nothing else is open in this town on Sunday morning but this place and the Catholic Church."

"Why aren't you in California?"

"Can we take a walk or something?" she asks, and I realize we're still standing in the middle of the church parking lot.

"Sure. There's a tree," I say, pointing to an oak sitting by a pond out in the middle of the pasture. "Maybe we can find some shade." There is a stone house in the distance, but I'm not worried. Everybody in this town is at one church or another.

"I tried to leave," she tells me as we cut across the grass.

"Why didn't you?" I ask, still unable to believe she's here. My legs are shaking so badly I'm not sure I'll make it across the pasture.

"I was standing in line at the airport with my boarding pass, but I just couldn't get on the plane."

"Why not?"

She stops and shows me the poem I scribbled on the greasy paper place mat.

My heart skips a beat.

She looks up at me grimly. "If you wrote this, then who wrote the poems in your journal?"

"I did."

"Liar! The handwriting is completely different."

How can I explain to her the words that came into my head when I didn't expect them? How could I confess that I was reciting love poems about Jess to another woman, who wrote them down for me in the leather book? How can I ever make her believe that I love her after the way I acted? "Somebody else wrote them down for me."

"Who?"

"It doesn't matter."

"It matters to me!" She covers her face with her hands and starts to cry.

I feel like someone has stabbed me in the heart. I never meant to hurt her like this. "Jess, the best thing you could do right now is to turn around, go back to Houston, get on a plane for California, and forget about me."

The tears keep pouring down her face. "Who wrote the poems in your journal?" she demands.

"My reading teacher."

"Why?"

"Because I couldn't do it myself."

"Are you telling me they really were your poems?"

"I got words in me, Jess, fighting to find a way out. Sometimes there's so many words and they get so crowded in my skull I think my head is gonna explode. I want to write them down. I've tried, but most of the time my thoughts and my feelings are bigger than what I can get on the paper."

She wipes her eyes. "Those poems about me. Did you really mean them?"

"Yes."

"When I read that first one, I knew I was never going to

find anybody like you again." She moves toward me. Takes my hand in hers and traces her silk-soft finger across the tattoo on my right hand. "Things moved kind of fast last time. Maybe we could start over."

"Are you sure?" I ask, unable to believe she's even willing to talk to me.

She puts her hands on my face, pulls my lips to hers, and kisses me so deeply I forget where I am.

Who I am.

I wrap my arms around her, holding on for dear life, and I decide if she can believe in me, then maybe—just maybe—I can believe in me too.

OCEAN BLUE

I was
holding her
and she was
holding me.
Couldn't see
we both were
going down.
When holding on
is the only thing
you've got,
how can you know
this is how lovers drown?

37

I DON'T KNOW HOW LONG WE SLEEP, INTERTWINED IN THE grass beneath the oak tree. I open my eyes every now and then, see Jess beside me, and then immediately close them, afraid to disrupt the dream. I am finally awoken by someone kicking me in the back with a boot. "You got any idea where you are, boy?"

I look up to find Arnie Golden standing over us with his nephew, Tornado Tim. I sit up, see that the sun has moved far into the west, realize that we were here talking most of the afternoon, until we fell asleep, exhausted, under the oak tree. I take a closer look at the house up on the hill and realize I am on the Goldens' property.

Jess opens her eyes, sees Arnie and Tornado standing there, and quickly sits up, straightening her clothes.

"Have a nice afternoon?" Arnie asks us.

"We were just about to leave," Jess says, slipping into her sandals.

"Yes, you are," he tells her. Then he turns to his nephew, who looks like he'd enjoy shooting us and burying us right here on his property. "You drive the girl home. I got a few things to say to Mr. Dawson here."

"But—," Tornado says, but Arnie cuts him off.

"Do what I say."

"No, please!" I stand up, imagining all the horrible things Tornado might do to Jess to get back at me. "She hasn't done anything. Please leave her out of this."

"I am leaving her out of this," Arnie tells me. "That's why Tornado is taking her home." He turns to Tornado. "And the boy is right. Don't bother her."

"Yes, sir," Tornado says. Jess looks at me questioningly.

"Go on," I tell her, figuring it's better for her to take her chances with Tornado than to stay here and watch what is going to happen to me.

Tornado walks her up the hill, and Arnie starts talking. "How long do you think it took me to find out you were wanted by the law in California?"

So this is how it will end. He's going to turn me in. I should have known this was the way he would handle it. "I imagine you figured it out pretty fast," I say.

"One phone call and I could have had you locked up last week."

"Why didn't you?" I ask, wondering if he's planning to shoot me and claim I was resisting arrest.

"You've got until Tuesday night, and then the law will be on your ass like hemorrhoid cream."

All I can say is, "Yes, sir." Don't know why he hasn't already turned me in, but I don't dare ask him.

He starts to walk back up to the house, and then turns around. "My brother, Jack, loved your father like a second brother. The three of us grew up playin' ball together. I don't think your father would have ever hurt Jack intentionally, but it doesn't really matter. A good man died, and justice demands that somebody pay for it. Not me, not my family, not even the people on that jury. It's justice demands it, and justice doesn't always care who it is who pays. Even if your father didn't pull the trigger, it's his fault my brother is dead. And D.J. Dawson knows it."

And with that, he is gone.

I run as fast as I can all the way to Levida's house and am surprised to see a pink Cadillac the color of Pepto-Bismol parked out front. I hope maybe it's the lawyer or one of his associates, come to bring us good news, but when I walk inside, I find Jess anxiously pacing the kitchen. My mother and grandmother are sitting at the dining table, facing each other in stony silence—the rusty box with the gun sitting between them.

"Thank God you're okay," Jess says, running up and hugging me. "I thought that man was going to kill you."

"Me too," I confess. "Tornado didn't bother you, did he?"

"No. He didn't say a word," Jess tells me.

"Have a nice nap?" my grandmother asks. I wonder how she knows these things, but I don't bother to ask. It's obvious that seeing my mother has put her in a bad mood.

"What are you doing *here*?" I ask my mother.

"That's what we're all tryin' to figure out," Levida says.

"I've come to see D.J. and to bring Dylan his birthday present. He turned eighteen yesterday, in case you didn't know."

"It was your birthday?" Jess asks.

"It's not important," I tell her.

If my mother's comment is supposed to make Levida feel guilty, it doesn't work. "If you're lookin' for a free place to stay, you can keep on lookin'," Levida says. "I ain't runnin' a Motel 6."

"Staying with you was never *free*," my mother retorts. "I paid for that experience in more ways than one. But for your information, I'm staying at the Home Suite Inn in Huntsville with my brother."

"Mitch is here?" I ask.

"He wanted you to have something special for your birthday," she says, holding up a car key.

"You can't be serious," I say, looking out the window at a car only a cosmetics dealer should drive.

"No, not the Caddie. He found you a brand-new Chrysler convertible."

"I don't want any more of Mitch's presents."

"But why not?"

"The boy don't care about a car when the state is fixin' to kill his daddy," Levida says. "But as usual, you think you can fix all your problems with some shiny new gadget. You were always worthless, Mollie. The only thing you were good for was spendin' D.J.'s hard-earned paycheck."

"This really isn't the time—," I try to interject.

"Well we all had our little addictions, didn't we?" my mother says. "Did you tell Dylan about the bottle you keep hidden under the kitchen sink?"

A bright crimson flush begins at my grandmother's neck and moves quickly up her face. "My husband had died. I've made my peace with the bottle since then."

"Have you made your peace with anything else?"

I know my mother is playing the hypocrite. She hasn't made

her own peace with the bottle. But I'm also impressed that she can stand up to Levida as easily as she does. Levida has a lot more secrets than I realize.

I wonder if she was drunk that night. I wonder if *she* could have shot Jack Golden. If she was drinking, she might have gotten it all mixed up in her mind. Has my father spent all this time in prison protecting her?

"If living with us was so god-awful," Levida hisses at my mother, "then why did you stay here all those years?"

Suddenly all the fight seems to leave my mother. She sinks into herself and says, so quietly I almost don't hear her, "Because I loved your son."

Levida heaves a great sigh and closes her eyes, like someone who has lost the battle, but suddenly doesn't care.

The phone rings, but Levida makes no move to answer it, and so I walk into the kitchen and pick it up. "Hello, this is the Dawson residence."

"Hello, Dylan. This is Buster Cartwright."

"It's Dad's lawyer," I say.

"Is D.J. going to let me see him?" my mother asks.

"Will my dad talk to my mother tomorrow?" I ask the lawyer.

"No, I'm afraid not."

"What do you mean? He has to."

"Your father doesn't have many choices, but who he will or will not see is one of them."

"No. This isn't right." The look of hope fades from my mother's face as she listens to my side of the conversation. "Somebody has to make him understand. If you can't make him understand, then I will."

"I'm afraid that won't be possible," he says.

"Why not?"

"He's taken your name off his visitation list."

It takes a minute for what he is saying to hit me. "What? Why? What have I done? What is so horrible that my own father won't see me?"

"Oh, Dylan," my mother says, and she starts to cry.

"I hate to be the bearer of bad tidings," says Cartwright, "but you might want to turn on your television and watch the news."

"Why?"

"I'm sorry I couldn't be more help. I truly am," he says, and then he hangs up.

I set down the phone, walk into the living room, and turn on the television, with my mother, grandmother, and Jess following behind me.

"Breaking news today in the case of convicted cop killer D.J. Dawson," says a newswoman. "But first a look at the local weather. Record temperatures continue throughout the hill country...."

There is a report about a power outage in San Antonio, an oil spill near Galveston Island, and a fire in Houston before the newswoman returns to the story about my father.

"And now here's our breaking story," she tells her viewers, and my father's face appears on the TV screen.

"My God! He looks just like you," Jess tells me.

My mother kneels in front of the television screen and reaches out to my father's picture as if she can touch him. "I almost forgot how beautiful he was."

Wade walks in, sees us all staring at the television, and says, "What's going on?"

"Dylan's dad is on TV," Jess informs him.

The anchorwoman continues, "After eleven years on death

row, just forty-eight hours before he is scheduled to die, D.J. Dawson, the man convicted of killing border patrol officer Jack Golden, has come clean with a confession."

"No!" my mother cries, covering her mouth with her hands.

"In an open letter to the governor, Mr. Dawson wrote, 'I'm getting ready to meet my maker, and I wanted to do it with a clear conscience. Jack Golden was a good man and a good cop. He comes from a good family. They've suffered enough over me. So has my own family, for that matter. I just want everyone to be able to put this behind them.'"

I can't believe this is happening. This is *not* how things are supposed to turn out. My father is giving up. "Why?" I shout at the television.

"D.J., please don't do this!" my mother says, crying, then flees the room.

The newscaster continues reading my father's letter. "'I deeply regret the pain and suffering I caused by the death of Jack Golden. I offer my apologies to the people of Texas, who lost a hero, and I withdraw my petition for clemency.'"

My father's photo fades to black, and the news anchor is back on the screen. "And now we go to the capitol building, where we'll get a response to these new developments from Governor Billy Banks."

The governor stands on the capitol steps with another reporter. "Governor," she says, "what is your reaction to the confession made by D.J. Dawson earlier today?"

"I respect what he's trying to do."

"You got no idea what he's tryin' to do, you snake-livered mama's boy," Levida yells, throwing a shoe at the television screen.

"What makes us a civilized society," the governor continues, "is our desire to make right our wrongs."

A scene appears on the television of protesters outside the
Walls Unit in Huntsville, and we are all suddenly surprised by
the sound of someone pounding on the front door.

Wade looks out the window and says, "It's a cop!"

I remember what Arnie Golden told me about sending the
authorities after me, and I tremble as my entire body breaks out
in a cold sweat.

"They're comin' for us," Wade says, standing up and backing into the kitchen like a cornered animal, grabbing a knife out
of one of the drawers.

"Wade, don't be crazy!" says Jess.

"I can't go back to jail," he says.

The cop knocks again.

"I *won't* go back to jail," says Wade.

"I'm comin'," Levida yells, though she makes no move
toward the door. "Maybe they've come lookin' for the gun,"
she says. She and I both look at the table at the same time, but
the gun and the rusted box are gone.

"What happened to it?" I ask.

"I don't know."

"Maybe your mother took it," says Jess. "She's gone too."

Levida and I both look at each other.

"You gotta find her," Levida tells me. "No tellin' what she
might do. You and Wade go out my bedroom window. There's
a storm cellar out by the workshop. Hide there till it's safe to get
away."

"Come on," I tell Wade, but he just stands there frozen like
a statue.

"Go!" Levida tells us. "And put that knife down, Wade, before you hurt yourself."

"Be careful," says Jess.

I grab Wade and shake his arm till he drops the knife. Then we run for the bedroom, while Levida opens the door for the cop. We scramble out the window, but I run right past the storm cellar on my way to the truck. "Where you goin'?" says Wade.

"I gotta find my mom."

"Levida said to wait in the cellar."

"I can't wait, Wade. I gotta go look for her now."

"What if the cops hear you tryin' to get away?"

"That's a chance I have to take."

"I can't go with you," he says. He's trembling from head to foot, and I know he's thinking of juvie. "I can't ever go back to that place."

"I understand. You wait here. I'll be back."

I run to the truck, and I realize Wade is right. If the cops hear me starting the engine, they'll come after me. I put the truck into neutral and start pushing it down the dirt road until I think it's safe enough to turn on the engine, and then I drive through town until I get to the highway. But I don't know where to go. The only thing I can think of is my uncle Mitch and the Home Suite Inn in Huntsville.

Every time I pass a car, I check to see if it's my mother, but she's nowhere in sight. I get to Huntsville and start looking for the Home Suite Inn.

I find it, but there is no sign of the pink eyesore my mother was driving. I do see a Chrysler convertible with a frame around the rear license plate that says MITCH'S MOTORS. I park next to it and go inside. I'm about to ask for his room number at the front desk when I hear his loud, obnoxious voice coming from the bar. I find my uncle Mitch drinking tequila shots and talking to the bartender. "Those were the days," Mitch brags. "When me and Dozer Dawson played for the Texas Longhorns. I remember this game against A&M—"

"Uncle Mitch!" I say, hurrying up to the bar. "Have you seen Mom?"

"There he is," Mitch tells the bartender, a definite slur to his words. "Dozer Junior. Wanna drink, kid? It's a helluva night for a drink. Did you see your daddy's picture on TV? Never thought I'd see the day. Pour my nephew a shot, bartender."

"I'll have to see some ID."

"Forget the liquor," I say, even as I imagine the tequila on my tongue and burning through my veins. "I've got to find Mom. Did she come back here?"

"Thought she was with you," he says, motioning for the man behind the bar to refill his glass. I've never seen my uncle visibly drunk before. He can usually consume great quantities of liquor with no visible effects. I wonder how much he's been drinking and when he started.

"Mitch, I gotta find her." The bartender has turned away, to dry some glasses. I lower my voice to a whisper. "She has the gun."

"What gun?"

"The one that killed Jack Golden."

Mitch pauses mid-gulp and puts down his glass, his eyes becoming steady and hard. "Where the hell did she find that?"

"It was hidden in a box buried in the barn. Mitch, I'm afraid she's going to . . ." I can't finish my thought. "She was really upset. What if she hurts herself?"

"You afraid she's gonna go shoot herself in the head like our daddy did?" he says too loudly.

"Please, you gotta help me find her."

"You worry too much, kid. Your mama doesn't have the gumption to kill herself. She hates pain too much." He says this with a coolness that makes me want to shove that shot glass down his throat.

"Then why did she take the gun?"

"How the hell would I know?" He picks up the glass again and tries to act like this isn't a big deal, but I notice his hand is shaking.

Something suddenly clicks into place in my mind, like when you're looking all over the floor for the last piece of a puzzle, only to realize you're already holding it in your hand. "The Cadillac Levida saw . . . You were there that night!"

"Don't be ridiculous," he says, motioning for the bartender to pour him yet another shot. "I was in Vegas at a blackjack table with at least twelve witnesses."

"You're lying."

"One of them was the manager of the casino."

"A friend of yours?"

"Yep, and he'd testify as to my whereabouts."

"Would he lie on the stand to help you?"

"You're sniffin' up the wrong pant leg, kid."

A smile starts to spread across my face. "I know why my mother took the gun. She's going to bring it to the police and tell them what really happened that night."

Mitch's grip around the shot glass tightens. He tries to smile, but his lips can't quite make the effort. "Let's hope it doesn't come to that." He stands to leave. "I'm finished," he tells the bartender.

"Yes, you are!" I say before I go. He's wrong about my mother. She has a lot more gumption than he realizes.

I drive to the Huntsville police station, looking for the hideous pink car. I'd love to hear what she has to say to the police. I know I can't go inside and risk getting arrested, but I could wait for her to come out and tell me the story. Tell me how she's cleared my father's name. But the car isn't there. Maybe she's gone to Livingston, straight to the prison warden, I tell myself. And so I get on the road that has now become so familiar to me I could drive it with my eyes closed.

When I get to the Polunsky Unit I still don't see the pink car, but it doesn't matter. My mother could have gone to the police in Brenham or Austin. I get out of my truck and smile as I look through the razor wire at the front door and imagine my father walking outside, a free man. "Soon, Dad," I say out loud.

As I get back on the road I pass a black van, and my heart nearly stops beating. I look in the rearview mirror and am relieved that it doesn't turn around to follow me. "Don't let your mind play tricks on you," I say. It was just a black van. It doesn't mean anything. Even so, I keep checking my mirror the whole way back home.

When I finally arrive, it's late and the farmhouse is dark. I drive up to the trailer, and there is Wade, sitting on the steps waiting for me. Good old dependable Wade. As I get closer, I see that he is shaking. I hurry out of the truck, afraid something has gone wrong.

"Where's Jess?"

"Down at the farmhouse with your grandmother. Levida put her in the guest room with Charlotte."

"Are you okay, Wade? Did something happen?"

"Hell yes, something happened. I was stuck in that cellar for an hour, till your grandma came and got me."

"What did the cop want?"

"Turned out he just came by to make sure Levida was okay, but I didn't know that. Got so scared down in that cellar I pissed on myself. I can't go back to jail, Dylan."

"I know."

"Next time they come, they'll be comin' for us."

"I know." A victory for my father doesn't mean I'm out of the woods. I'll probably be going into prison just as he's getting out. If the police don't catch up to me, Eight Ball eventually will.

Wade looks up at the stars. "Sure is pretty here," he says. "Would have made a nice place to settle down."

"Yeah," I say. I'd never be caught dead living in a town like Quincy. I can see its appeal for Wade, though.

"I can't stay here no more."

I nod. "Do you want my car?"

"Nah, we're takin' Dorie's truck."

"She's going with you?"

"Something I been meaning to tell you . . . we got married a couple of days ago!"

"You got married? How? When? You haven't even been here long enough to get a marriage license."

"Dorie has a friend at the county clerk's office."

"Oh, Wade, why would you want to do something like that?"

"It ain't a crime to try to do the right thing," he snaps.

"You didn't give them this farm as an address, did you?"

"Yeah, why?"

"Wade . . ." I start to tell him how he's led the cops straight to our doorstep, but then I realize they've already been here, and sooner or later Arnie Golden is going to tell the police we're wanted in California. "Nothing. It doesn't matter. I'm sorry, Wade. You're right. I'm glad you're trying to finally go legit. Congratulations."

"Thank you," he says, his anger going as quickly as it came. "Dorie said we had to be married before we consummated our love or else we'd go to hell. I just couldn't stand the thought of her in hell."

"What about you?"

"I wasn't so worried about myself. I been in worse places."

"When is she coming for you?" I ask.

"Any minute now. Dylan, I'm sorry to run out on you like this, but I just can't cover your back no more."

"You think you're covering my back?" I ask, unable to hide my disbelief. He's done nothing but cause me trouble since we left juvie.

"We been goin' in different directions for a long time. We don't want the same things."

"Really?" I say, a little indignant. "What do you want, Wade?"

"I just need to find a place where I belong."

"Like with the Aryans who almost killed you? Or the BSB who almost killed you?" Wade is leaving any minute and I don't want to argue with him, but I can't seem to stop myself. The stress of the last week has left me frayed and raw, and part of me can't believe he's running out on me now, even though I know he has to.

"I ain't sayin' those were the best choices. They were just the best choices I seemed to have at the time. Besides, we never would have met Eight Ball or ended up in juvie if your uncle hadn't gotten us jobs with Jake Farmer."

"Uncle Mitch. He's the cause of everything bad in my life."

"I ain't blamin' you. I'm actually glad things turned out the way they did, or else I never would have found Dorie . . . or the Lord. But there's a time to say no, Dylan, and now is that time. They're coming after us, and I wish you'd leave with us, but I know you won't. But I can't be here when they come."

"I know."

"I didn't want to tell you this, but Dorie says you're draggin' me down."

"I'm dragging *you* down?"

About that time Dorie drives up in her pickup truck. "I gotta go now. Dorie left a note for her father explaining things, but if he starts asking questions, will you let him know I plan to take good care of her?"

"Sure, Wade," I say, even though he's never been able to take care of himself.

He gets into Dorie's truck, turns to me, and says, "You're the best friend I ever had." As I watch him drive away, I realize he's done something I never had the guts to do.

He has said good-bye.

38

MONDAY MORNING I LOOK THROUGH THE BOX FILLED WITH
my father's clothes, find the old cowboy boots at the bottom.
Try them on and am surprised that they fit. Then I walk down
to the farmhouse. Over breakfast I tell Jess and Levida about my
conversation with Mitch and why I think my mother took the
gun. "That could mean good news," Jess comments, but Levida
doesn't say a word and as the day wears on, her silence becomes
more and more irritating.

It is a day of waiting. Waiting for the lawyer to call. Waiting
for my mother to return. Waiting for Arnie Golden to show up
with his police friends and haul me off to jail. Waiting for Eight
Ball and Ajax and Spider. I wonder if it really was Ajax I saw last
night driving the black van. I tell Jess she should leave, for her
own safety, but she won't go. I'm secretly glad. She's all I have
left to hang on to.

I should leave too, but I just can't until I find out if my father
is going to live or die. And what about my mother? She still
hasn't returned.

"Do you believe in fate?" I ask Jess that evening after supper as we sit on the living room sofa, watching out the window, waiting for something, anything, to happen. No one has called, no one has arrived, and the tension in the house is a hair trigger.

"I think you're my fate," she says, squeezing my hand, but I pull away from her, jumping up from the couch and pacing across the braided rug that I've worn thin.

"No, I mean, do you think we choose our destiny or do you think something else chooses it for us?"

"Like God?"

"I don't know. Maybe."

"I don't think God would want anybody to end up on death row."

"Well what about karma, or bad blood, or destiny? What do you believe?"

"I think we make choices, and those choices lead to other choices."

Levida walks in from the garden with a basket full of green beans and starts washing them in the sink just like it's any other day. "How can you wash vegetables at a time like this?" I ask her, but she doesn't reply.

I walk over to the sink and turn off the water, forcing her to pay attention to me. "Why hasn't anybody called?"

"Why do ya think?" she says coolly.

"I don't know. Maybe something happened to my mother. Maybe Mitch got to her. Maybe she was in a car wreck and never made it to the cops. Maybe we should be doing something."

"Like what?" she asks, drying her hands on a towel and putting them on her hips.

"I don't know. Like going to the police. You could talk to them. You saw Uncle Mitch driving the Cadillac."

"All *I* saw was a car. That don't mean nothin'."

"Were you drunk that night?"

"Dylan!" Jess says, stepping in to stand between me and Levida. "Don't say things you can't take back."

But it's too late for that. "Is my father going to die because you were too drunk to know what happened that night?"

"Dylan, stop!"

Levida just shakes her head. "Foolish, foolish boy. You still don't understand."

"Understand what?"

"Were *you* drunk that night?" she says, pointing a wrinkled finger at me.

"Don't be stupid. I was six years old."

"Then why don't you remember?"

"I was SIX YEARS OLD!" I yell at her.

"Your father, my son, is about to die for a murder somebody else committed. Do you really think he'd do that for your uncle Mitch?"

I open my mouth to speak, but no words come out, because if she is right . . . then my mother is not at the police station turning in my uncle.

"You can't remember and your father won't talk. Who is the one person you would *both* go to the grave in silence to protect?"

"Dylan, are you okay?" asks Jess as I slump into one of the dining room chairs. My grandmother is right. My father would never die for Uncle Mitch.

Levida, kneeling in front of me, takes both of my hands in

hers. "Dylan," she says softly. "Dylan, you're the only one who knows. Tell me who shot Jack Golden."

"I don't remember."

Her grip on my hands tighten. "Who shot Jack?"

"I don't remember!" I'm shaking so badly I'm afraid I'll fall off the chair.

"You saw what happened!" she yells.

"I can't remember!"

"Leave him alone," says Jess. "Can't you see how upset he is?"

Levida lets go of my hands and slaps me hard across the face. Then she grabs my collar and starts shaking. "WHO SHOT JACK GOLDEN?"

"Stop it!" screams Jess, pulling my grandmother off of me.

"I don't remember. I don't remember! I DON'T REMEMBER!"

"Yes, you do," says my grandmother, her voice soft as a whisper.

And then I begin to cry. A flood of tears pours out of me that I can't stop. A flood of regret, of sadness, of hopelessness. Jess puts her arms around me and rocks me like a little kid.

"Who shot Jack Golden?" Levida says.

"My father."

Levida covers my hand with hers. It is warm and calloused and I grab it, holding on for dear life, as if it's the only anchor in the world. "Is that what you honestly, truly believe?"

"Yes." I still cannot see it, but it is the only explanation.

She pats my hand and nods her head. "Then your father is going to die tomorrow, and there's nothing anybody can do about it."

THE HOUSE WHERE JACK DIED

This is the house where they found Jack dead.

This is the room
of the house
where they found Jack dead.

This is the floor
in the room
of the house
where they found Jack dead.

This is the wall, splattered in red,
standing next to the floor,
in the room
of the house
where they found Jack dead.

This is the door leading into the tomb.
This is the wall splattered in red,
standing next to the floor
in the room
of the house
where they found Jack dead.

This is the clock hanging over the door.
This is the wall splattered in red
standing next to the floor
in the room
of the house
where they found Jack dead.

This is the bird coming out of the clock
hanging over the door
in the wall
by the floor

in the room
of the house
where they found Jack dead.

This is the song in the heart of the bird
coming out of the clock
hanging over the door
in the wall
by the floor
in the room
of the house
where they found Jack dead.

These are the words
to the song of the bird
coming out of the clock
hanging over the door
in the wall
by the floor
in the room
of the house
where they found Jack dead.

This is the man who sits in the cell.
Eleven years have come and gone.
Jack is dead, but he lives on.

He waits in silence, but he still can hear.
The ancient song echoes in his ears.
The sound of time with its tick tick TOCK!
The song of the bird coming out of the clock,
hanging over a door leading into a tomb,
where there stand four walls splattered all in red,
and a floor where a good man fell and bled,
in the room of the house where they found Jack dead.

These are the words of the cuckoo's song,
as he asks us who will right these wrongs.
The cuckoo sings and the cuckoo wails,
for the dead who cannot tell their tales.

Rage all you want, but at close of day,
justice is mine, and I will repay.

THE ROAD TO HUNTSVILLE
By D.J. Dawson

If you are lucky, you will never watch a man die by lethal injection, but you might be curious all the same. I know I was. So I asked my lawyer to tell me what happened in the death house down in Huntsville. He informed me there was a radio broadcast put on a few years back called "Witness to an Execution." You can listen to it on the Internet if you care to. I can't because I don't have a computer, so I had to read the transcript. You don't actually hear a man die, but you'll hear the voices of people who have watched it happen, some of them fifty or more times.

According to the transcript, a man's last day on death row goes something like this:

On the afternoon the man is to be executed, they put him in a white prison van that takes him from the Polunsky Unit in Livingston to the Walls Unit in Huntsville, where he spends what time he has left with the prison chaplain.

Around two o'clock the prisoner is allowed to make a phone call.

At four thirty he is served his last meal. He can order absolutely anything he wants, but he'll only be served what is available from the prison cafeteria. Contrary to what most people think, nobody is running down to the local Steak and Ale to buy him a sirloin.

As for me, when it comes my time to go I'm going to ask for ham steak, mashed potatoes, snap peas, and red-eye gravy.

At six o'clock the governor calls to give the final go-ahead and so does the attorney general. Shortly thereafter the man is led to a small room with a metal gurney that fills up nearly all the space inside. In about thirty seconds the tie-down team has him bound to the table with six different leather straps.

At 6:05 the medical team comes into the room and inserts needles into both of the prisoner's arms. Then they hook up the IVs through which the poison will be administered by tubes coming from a wall behind the gurney where an anonymous executioner sits waiting.

Around 6:10 the witnesses are escorted into two small rooms. One room is for the victim's family and friends, and the other room is for the family of the man about to be executed.

At that point a microphone is lowered from the ceiling, and the warden asks the condemned man if he has any final words.

When the prisoner is done talking the warden gives a signal to the executioner, who begins to administer sodium pentothal, an anesthesia like they use in operating rooms. Next he's given chromium bromide to collapse his lungs, and then a third drug is administered to stop his heart.

By 6:20 it's all over.

Those who have witnessed executions say there is no sound worse than the weeping of a mother watching her son being put to death.

They're wrong. There is one sound that is worse.

There is silence.

THE HEART OF TEXAS, 2

In the heart of Texas there's a man,
a murderer condemned to die.
They put him in a prison van,
and take him for this one last ride.
He spends the afternoon in prayer
until they bring his final bread.
Then take him to a back room where
they strap his legs, his arms, his head
down in the heart of Texas.

39

EVERY CLOCK IS A BOMB, TICKING AWAY AT THE MINUTES
of our lives, counting off the seconds one by one before we die.

All I can do all day long is to sit in the trailer, watching the second hand on the cuckoo clock going *tick, tick, tick*.

At birth a heart is given a certain number of beats. The clock is counting them off one by one and will not allow a man any more than his allotted share.

Today is the day my father's clock is to run out.

Jess brings me breakfast, then lunch. Both sit untouched on the table in front of me. The breakfast ham is a rotting pig. The meat loaf is a rotting cow. We are all rotting, making our way from womb to tomb, to the rhythm of the great clock counting downward to the grave.

When the clock strikes three and the bird comes out yet again to squawk at me in three shrill chirps, I rip it out by its spring. Then I tear its little wooden house off the wall and crush it under my boot.

"Are you coming?" says a voice, and I look up to see

my grandmother standing in the doorway, wearing her black Sunday dress.

"Where are you going?"

"Huntsville."

"To the Walls?"

"Yep."

"After all these years, you're goin' now?"

"I saw your daddy into this world. So I guess I'll see him out." She presses her lips together to keep from crying. "You coming with me or not?"

"I can't," I say, shuddering at the thought of watching the prison guards strap my father down to the metal table.

Levida nods. "I thought not."

"Will you call me when it's over?" I manage to ask.

"Of course," she tells me.

I walk down to the farmhouse. Sit on the sofa. Look at the clock hanging on the kitchen wall and resume my watching. Jess sits next to me, without a word, and folds my hand into hers. Holds it tighter when I start to cry.

This is what love is. Not the moments on the beach, or under the stars or the trees, or in the moonlight. Love is sitting together in the quiet, waiting for death to come. Knowing you're not alone.

At five o'clock, one hour before my father is scheduled to die, I hear a knock on the door. Jess and I both jump off the couch.

"Who do you think it is?" she whispers.

"I don't know," I say, but I can only imagine the cops have finally caught up with me. "You answer it."

She nods, then slowly opens the door, and I hear a voice say,

"I'm T.J. Seagraves, from up the hill. My mother wanted me to bring you this."

"T.J.?" I say, opening the door a little wider, as I see him handing Jess a basket full of food.

"My mother says she knows you all are going through a rough time. She wanted you to have this."

"Thank you." I take the basket and set it in on the coffee table. My stomach is a knot and right now I feel like I'll never eat again, but I appreciate the gesture.

"I think she knows that if things had worked out different, it coulda been my father up there in Huntsville. You've been lucky, growing up away from all this," he tells me.

"Yeah, real lucky," I say. Even so, I realize it couldn't have been easy for T.J. growing up in Quincy. "Tell your mother thanks for the food, and thanks for that night when she took me in."

"I still remember it," T.J. says with a shudder.

"You do?"

"We heard a gunshot coming from the direction of your trailer. It woke us up. We knew something terrible was happening. My dad grabbed his shotgun and started out the door. I remember my mother trying to stop him. He told her, 'I gotta go. The Dozer's in trouble.'"

"He came to our trailer that night?"

"No. He started to, but then your daddy showed up. Said Jack was dead. I'll never forget the looks on the faces of you and your mama, like you were in shock."

"What do you mean, me and my mama?"

"When your daddy brought the two of you up to our house."

"That's not possible. My mother had left. She was staying with her brother down in La Puerta."

"I guess she came back. Piss-poor timing."

"No. That's not possible. She . . ." A picture comes into my brain. A picture of my mother driving a black Cadillac. "She came back to get me," I say, and the image I have not allowed to surface plays across the screen of my memory as I see that night from so long ago.

I am six years old and I am standing at the window in a bedroom inside my grandmother's farmhouse. I am supposed to be asleep, but I'm not. I'm standing at the window crying for my mother.

My grandfather is dead. My father is gone all the time, and when he is home he is afraid. My grandmother has stolen me away from my mother, but now that she has me here, all she does is sit alone in the dark, drinking.

All I want is my mother. She is the only one who can protect me.

And then like a miracle she is there, coming for me, driving a black Cadillac past the house and up to the trailer.

I run as fast as I can, following the car up the dirt road. By the time I get up to the trailer she is already inside. I hear her calling my name. "Dylan, where are you?"

"Here I am, Mama."

I run into her arms. She holds me tight and I know I am safe.

And then come the headlights and the dark man who comes storming into the house, yelling my father's name.

"Hide!" Mom says, and we both go into the pantry.

I can hear the front door slam shut and we think he is gone, but then it opens a few minutes later and we hear footsteps. They're moving toward us.

"Don't let him get me, Mama. Don't let him get me."

"I won't let anybody hurt you, baby," she whispers, and I see a strength in her eyes I've never seen before.

And then I remember the .22. I dig through the peanut sack until I find it, and it feels good and solid in my hand. It feels safe. But I know it will feel even safer in my mother's hand. I press it into her palm.

"Where did you get this?" she asks. I point to the burlap sack.

We see the doorknob in the pantry start to turn. My mother holds the weapon up in front of her, hands trembling.

The door swings up. I see a man's hand. It's holding a gun. My mother closes her eyes. Shoots. Blood comes out of the man's mouth, splattering the blue curtains. He staggers backward and falls on the living room floor.

We step out of the pantry. It's dark except for the moonlight streaming in through the living room window.

My mother looks at the man and cries out, "Jack! Oh my God! Jack!"

The bird comes out of the clock, squawking at us so loudly I have to cover my ears. And then my father comes through the door. Looks at Jack, who has stopped moving. Feels for a pulse. Looks at my mother and says, "He's dead."

My mother drops the gun.

Starts to scream.

I start to scream.

My father puts his arms around us.

Holds us.

"Don't worry. It's going to be all right. Everything will be all right. This wasn't your fault. Listen to me. It wasn't your fault."

My mother stops screaming and starts crying. "I came back for Dylan."

"I know."

"And you."

"I know."

"All I wanted was for us all to be safe . . . and together."

"The two of you will be. Listen, you didn't kill Jack. I killed Jack."

He picks the gun up from the floor and slips it into his back pocket.

"They'll send you to prison."

"Probably."

"You can't."

"For God's sake, Mollie, think of Dylan and let me do one decent thing for our family."

I squeeze my mother's hand. I'm crying. I don't want my mother to go to jail. She is the only one who can protect me. "Mama, I'm scared. I want to leave. Take me away from here. Mama, please."

"I'm in too deep," my father tells her. "They're going to send me to prison, no matter what. We can't leave our son alone."

"What if they kill you?" she asks him, crying.

"That won't happen. I promise you."

"I won't let them kill you. I love you."

"I know."

"Dylan, are you okay?" asks Jess.

She is so beautiful, standing there in the late afternoon sun coming through the window, light illuminating her face.

I would do anything for her. I would kill to protect her. Die to protect her.

And in that moment I understand everything my father has done.

"There's something I gotta do," I tell Jess. "Somebody I gotta see."

"Who?"

"The governor of Texas."

THE HEART OF TEXAS, 3

In the heart of Texas there's a sound,
the sound of weeping in the halls.
The witnesses are drawing near
to press their faces to the glass.
Watching minutes ticking past.
Praying, crying, listening.
Waiting for fate's arm to swing.
And then the warden starts to speak,
of the sacred trust that he must keep
in this place of death and sleep,
deep, deep in the heart of Texas.

40

IT'S FIVE FORTY-FIVE BEFORE I GET TO AUSTIN AND ALMOST
six o'clock before I reach the capitol building.

I go to the front desk.

"I have to see the governor," I tell the woman wearing a security uniform.

She looks at me and smiles as if she's talking to a small child. "You can call his secretary tomorrow morning and see if he has any appointment time available. Here's the number." She writes a number on a piece of paper and hands it to me.

"I don't have time. They're going to kill my father any minute now by lethal injection."

She studies my face, pity replacing her coolness. "You're Dozer Dawson's son."

"Please. I have to talk to Governor Banks."

"I really wish I could help you."

"Just ask him," I say, grabbing the phone on the security desk and handing it to her. "It won't hurt you to ask him."

"It won't help you either."

"Please."

She stares at the phone.

"Please!"

She picks it up. Presses in a number. "This is Sally at security. There's a boy down here who wants to talk to the governor. His name is . . ." She looks at me.

"Dylan Dawson."

"Dylan Dawson," she says into the phone. "Yeah, I can wait."

While she waits, the security guard covers the mouthpiece and says, "I saw your father play for the Longhorns. He was amazing. Best linebacker that school ever had." She turns her attention back to the phone. "Really! Wow. Okay then."

She hangs up and looks at me in total disbelief. "The governor says he'll see you."

I take an elevator to the second floor, where a secretary lets me into an office with polished wood doors. "You have five minutes," she tells me.

I walk inside, march up to the governor's desk, and, without bothering with an introduction, say, "My father didn't kill Jack Golden. You have to call off the execution."

"Whoa, let's just rewind for a moment, buddy. First of all, it's a bit late to be coming forward with new evidence, if you even have any. Secondly—"

"I killed Jack Golden."

"How old were you at the time, young man?"

"Six and a half."

"So you're claiming you killed a cop when you were in elementary school?"

I look up at the clock. It's already ten past six. "My father taught me how to shoot. Please, you have to call Huntsville and tell them to call off the execution."

The governor is staring across the room at something, and when I turn to see what it is, I notice the rusted box, sitting with the lid open. I know what is inside.

The gun that killed Jack Golden.

"It's been a busy couple of days. Sunday night your father confesses to the murder. Monday night your mother confesses, and now here you are telling me you're the one who is responsible."

"They're just trying to protect me," I say.

"And who are you trying to protect?" he asks.

"Innocent people."

"You can't protect everybody, son. Believe me, I know. Innocent people die every day."

"You know my father isn't a cop killer."

"Not according to him. Besides, whether or not he pulled the trigger, he was still involved in a felony in which a law enforcement officer died, and his entire family confessing to the crime doesn't exactly exonerate him. There's no way you can convince me that a six-year-old killed a veteran cop with a .22."

I look at the clock. Wonder how long the execution process takes and how much time I have. "Okay, what if it was my mother? You can grant a stay of execution for my father and investigate. If you still think he's worthy of the death penalty, you have plenty of time to kill him."

He shakes his head. "Think about what you're saying, son. Is that really what you want?"

"If it was an accident, if she thought it was self-defense . . ."

"A jury might not see it that way."

"But what if that's what really happened?"

"What is true and what you can prove to be true aren't always the same thing. It's possible a jury would see it otherwise. We got a war on drugs going on. It's possible the DA would say your mother was in on the whole cocaine trafficking operation with your father. He might even claim premeditation. She could conceivably get the death penalty. Even if she didn't, how long do you think she'd last at the women's prison in Gatesville?"

"I don't know," I say, realizing what my father must have realized long ago. There is no way to win.

"Your father was granted one phone call today at two o'clock. Did he call you?"

"No."

"Did he call your grandmother?"

"No," I say sadly.

"No, he didn't, and I'll tell you why he didn't call you, it's because he called me. He called me and he said he was afraid someone in your family would do some fool thing to try to save him. He begged me to ignore them. He said he was ready and willing to die for what he did."

I look at the tattoo of the cross on my hand and imagine my father, strapped down as we speak. "He's dying in her place. Don't you see what my father is trying to do?"

"It's out of my hands."

"You're the fucking governor of Texas. Don't tell me it's out of your hands," I say, rushing toward the rusted box, throwing open the lid, grabbing what's inside. I don't even know I'm holding the gun until I see it in my hands. *My God*, I think, *what am I going to do now?*

"Whoa, boy, let's not get excited."

"They're about to kill my father for a murder he didn't commit. Don't tell me not to get excited," I yell.

"You're not a killer, young man. You and I both know that gun isn't even loaded."

"Really? You sure about that?" I say. The gun probably isn't loaded, and there is no way I would shoot this man, but I'm at the end of the road and desperate. "I want you to pick up that phone right now and call Huntsville. I want you to tell them you're granting a stay of execution. You have your people reopen the case. You check it out. If you can prove my father pulled the trigger, then fine, kill him, but don't let him die if there is still any question in your mind."

"The facts in this case—"

"Forget the facts," I yell, trembling now, realizing that when the cops eventually catch up to me I am going away for a very, *very* long time. "You know the facts don't always add up to the truth. Just look in your heart and tell me what you *believe* about my father. You've met him. You know him. And somewhere in your soul, I think you know the truth. When you talked about mercy on the news the other night, was it real or was it just politics?"

"It was real," he says with a sigh, and I realize that underneath the title and the suit and the name is a man who really does want to do the right thing.

"You're right. I'm not gonna shoot you," I say, slipping the gun into my back pocket and holding up my empty hands. They're shaking so badly I'm sure he can see it. "But you already know that, just like you know my father didn't shoot anybody. So think about that. Then decide what you gotta do."

He looks at me. Looks at the phone. Glances at the empty box. Looks back at the phone. Reaches for the receiver, but before he can pick it up, it rings.

We stare at each other.

It rings again.

He picks it up. "Hello."

He listens to a voice on the other side.

Looks at me.

Nods.

Hangs up.

"I'm sorry," he says, "Your father died at six twenty-one p.m."

I collapse on the couch. I would cry if there was anything left inside of me, but it's all over now. All for nothing. I've come all this way, a journey of a thousand miles through hell, and it hasn't made any difference.

Maybe one difference. I know my father was innocent. But that doesn't make him any less dead.

"Go back to Quincy," the governor tells me. "Get your mother and get out of Texas . . . as fast as you can. I'm sorry, but that's all the mercy I have to offer tonight."

I nod my head.

He looks at the empty box. "And just to make sure you don't hurt yourself, I'm going to give you an escort." He reaches for the phone, and I know he's calling security.

I run out of his office. Avoiding the elevator, I take the stairs, and then sprint as fast as I can to the truck.

Set the gun on the dash and drive. Don't know where I'm going.

It's all over now. Just a matter of time.

Time.

How much will I get now that I've threatened the governor with a weapon?

I come to a busy, noisy place called Sixth Street. It's lined with nightclubs, with live music blaring out of the opened doorways.

Park in an alley.

Open the chamber and find five bullets.

Close it.

I threatened the governor with a *loaded* weapon.

It's all over now.

I hold the barrel up to my head.

Hope it's loud enough on Sixth Street so that no one will hear the sound of the gunshot.

Imagine the police finding my body in the morning.

Picture them asking my mother and Jess to identify me and when they can't, because my face is gone, calling for my dental records in California.

"Damn it!" I say. I can't do that to them.

I put the gun in the glove box.

Get out of the truck.

Walk out of the alley, onto Sixth Street, into a nightclub called Lucky's. Catch my reflection in the mirror behind the bar. I look a hundred years old. The bartender doesn't even ask for ID when I order two shots of tequila.

I have learned there is more than one way to die.

THE HEART OF TEXAS, 4

In the heart of Texas nighttime falls,
and there is silence in the WALLS,
for there will be no mercy here.
No second chance. No words of cheer.
The prisoner says his last good-byes.
He cannot hear his mother's cries.
Then flows the sodium pentothal,
chromium bromide and his broad chest falls.
The third drug comes to end it all
from a henchman back behind the wall
who sends the deadly killing drops
that wrench and twist and squeeze and stall
and stop
                    the Heart of Texas.

41

I'M SO PATHETIC I CAN'T EVEN MANAGE TO GET DRUNK, because I end up in the alley, puking my guts out and crying. I go back to the truck. Look at the time on the dash. It's nine o'clock.

I've got to get to a phone and call the farm. Tell Jess to get out of there before the cops show up, if they haven't already, and meet me somewhere. I walk over to a pay phone at the end of the alley, dial the farmhouse, and am surprised when Jess picks up on the first ring.

"Dylan, is that you?"

"Jess, I don't have much time to explain, but I need you to leave the farm, now. Is my mother there? Has she come back?"

"Run, Dylan. Don't come back here. They're going to kill you!"

I hear a slap. Jess screams, and somebody says, "Stupid bitch!" then a man's voice is on the phone.

"We havin' a chillin' li'l party with yo mama and your pretty girlfriend, Dylan. I'd hate for you to miss it."

"Eight Ball?" I feel like a gambler who has just had all his markers called in.

"Oh, and don't think 'bout droppin' no dimes to the po-po. Dis here's a private party. Besides, we already got us one pig to carve up."

"How did you find me?" I say, hoping I'm having an alcohol-induced nightmare. Pretending that what is happening isn't really happening.

"We was scopin' the garage. Saw your ho talkin' to Gomez. Followed her to Texas. Lost her for a couple a days, but we finally caught up."

"If you hurt her or my mother, I'm going to kill you."

"See, that's the thing, Dylan. You done wasted my brother. Now it's time for payback. So while you're driving here, you kick around which one of 'em it's gonna be. We'll let the other one live. We ain't no animals, after all. 'Course, we goin' have a little fun with her first. But if we smell any pigs, they both done."

"You bastard!" I say, but he's already hung up.

I get back into the truck and drive. I should call the police. The police know how to handle these things. But what if Ajax and Eight Ball see them coming and kill Jess and my mother before the cops even get to the house?

I wish Wade was here. The truth is, he did cover my back a lot of the time.

But now I'm on my own.

Not totally alone. I do have a gun.

When I get to the farm, I park on the side of the road so Eight Ball and his gang won't see the headlights. When I reach the house, I look inside the window so I can size up the situation. My mother and Jess are sitting in the middle of the living room, tied to kitchen chairs. Mouths covered in duct tape. Ajax and Eight Ball seem to be the only ones with them. They're sitting behind them, though, so I can't get a clear shot. If I go around back, I might be able to take aim at them through the kitchen window.

I round the corner, spot a trail of blood, and nearly let out a yell when I see what's waiting there. Charlotte is lying on the ground, her side slit open, blood pouring out of her gut as well as out of a wound in her leg. She squeals pitifully and I feel sorry for the helpless pig, and for my grandmother, who loves that animal more than she cares for most people. I wonder where she is. Pray she decided to stay the night somewhere in Huntsville. I stick close to the house, edging inch by inch to the kitchen window, afraid even to breathe. Terrified I'll give myself away.

But it's another sound that gives me away. Baby Face whimpers at me from under the back porch. When she sees me, she tries to come to me, but she's dragging one of her back legs behind her. I slip the gun into my back pocket and crouch down low, hoping no one has heard her. See that she is tied to a length of rope. Know I've been set up.

"Nice of you to join us." Spider steps out of the shadows with a Glock he points at my head. I raise my hands, praying he doesn't see the gun in my back pocket. "What you say we go inside for a little reunion?"

We walk into the house and Ajax smiles. "Just in time."

"If you have harmed either one of them . . ."

"Chill, partner," Eight Ball says. "What kind of hosts would we be if we started the party without you? These sure are some damn fine women." He runs his hands across the side of my mother's face, and she tries to pull away from him, but the ropes hold her tight. Then Ajax runs the barrel of his Beretta up and down the buttons of Jess's shirt. He leans in close, and she glares at him in disgust.

I take a step toward him, but Spider jerks me back and pushes his gun into my back. "You move, you die."

Eight Ball holds a Beretta to my mother's head, and she starts to cry softly. "Here's your choice, Dylan. Which ho dies and which ho stays for the party?"

I calculate that I have a gun with five bullets in my back pocket. Consider that by the time I reach for it, Spider could easily blow out my brains with his semiautomatic. I wonder if that would be vengeance enough to satisfy Eight Ball, but I doubt it. I will have to take out Spider first. But then what will Ajax and Eight Ball do? The smart thing would be to shoot me, but the crazed look in Eight Ball's eyes tells me he might not do the smart thing.

"Choose!" Eight Ball yells.

I look at my mother, a thin frail shadow of the beautiful woman she used to be. "I'm so sorry," I tell her. "I wanted to make you proud, but everything is catching up with me."

Eight Ball rips the tape from my mother's mouth. "Any last words?"

"It isn't you, honey. It's me," she says. "It's what I've done. It's catching up to me. I thought I was protecting you, but I was wrong." She looks at Eight Ball. "I don't care anymore. Go ahead. Shoot me. I deserve to die."

"No. It can't end this way. A good man gave his life for us," I tell my mother. "He died so we'd have a chance at a future. We gotta find a way to go on from here." I know this sounds ridicu-

lous, considering the desperateness of the situation, but I mean
every word. When I think about how much my father loved us,
how far he was willing to go, something changes inside of me,
and I feel stronger than I've ever felt.

I think of his words, *If you're breathing, there's still hope*, and I
know that as long as I'm still breathing, I will *never* give up again.

"We're gonna be okay," I tell her.

My mother sits up tall. "I believe you."

"Believe anything you want," says Eight Ball. "But somebody goin' down." He points the gun between my mother's
eyes, but for the first time since that night in the pantry, she
doesn't look afraid.

Something changes in Jess's eyes as well. I follow her
gaze out the kitchen window and that's when I see her—my
grandmother—Levida—wearing the black dress, storming
toward the house and carrying her shotgun.

If only I can stall Eight Ball. "Wait. I'm the one you want.
Let them go."

"Yeah, but their lives are worth more than yours."

"You know I didn't mean to kill Two Tone."

"Yeah, but he's still dead."

"Which one of you good-fer-nothin' bastards shot my pig?"
Levida yells, bursting through the kitchen door. She shoots,
aiming for Eight Ball, but hits the television screen, blowing
glass everywhere.

A piece of it hits Eight Ball in the face, cutting his eye.
He screams in pain and covers his face with his hands.
Meanwhile, Levida takes aim at Ajax, shoots out the window
behind him, but comes so close to hitting him that he drops
his gun and has to scramble across the floor to get it. Spider

momentarily forgets about me and points his weapon at my grandmother.

Shoots.

Grazes her arm.

She falls to her knees, holding her bleeding arm against her body.

I press my .22 against Spider's back, right behind his heart, and pull the trigger. He falls facedown as a pool of blood gathers under him. I grab his semiautomatic. Hear sirens approaching in the distance.

Turn to Ajax, and find him holding his gun and smiling, pointing it at Jess, then my mother, then back at Jess. "Choose!" he orders me.

"Don't do it," I say. "The cops are on their way. Look, I'm putting the gun down." I set Spider's Glock on the coffee table.

The sirens grow closer.

He moves the gun between Jess and my mother. "Which one is gonna get the first bullet?"

I hear car doors open. Close.

"Time's up," Ajax says, pointing the gun at Jess's head.

"No!" I scream. I pick up the Glock and shoot him in the face, just as the cops burst through the door. I feel the bullet from Arnie Golden's service revolver hitting my right shoulder.

Then I drop the gun.

Fall to the floor.

And pray.

EPILOGUE

WHAT HAS HAPPENED SINCE THAT FATEFUL TUESDAY
night is a matter of public record. Eight Ball was extradited
to California on a weapons charge. I was sent to the county
lockup in Austin, where I awaited trial. I hoped to be acquit-
ted of killing Ajax and Spider, given the extenuating circumstances. What actually happened was that the testimonies
of Jess and my mother and grandmother were ripped apart
by the DA, while I was portrayed as a cold-blooded multiple
murderer who killed a boy in California, then fled to Texas as
a fugitive.

According to the district attorney, I had chosen a path
that led me to be in a place where killing Ajax and Spider was
inevitable. Ajax, a young man with no criminal record whatso-
ever, was a poor, unfortunate soul who happened to be in the
wrong place at the wrong time.

And so here I am, a resident of the men's prison in
Huntsville, Texas.

I got a letter from Wade a few months back saying he and

Dorie were expecting a baby and that he'd decided to become a preacher.

Levida visits me every Saturday afternoon and updates me on her two favorite pets—a three-legged hog and a three-legged dog.

My mother and Jess went back to California. My mother sold the house, which I'd deeded to her, and bought a music studio where she teaches voice lessons.

Jess got into Stanford. By day she's a pre-law major, but by night she's lead vocal for a group called the Legal Limit.

They still write every week and come to see me when they can.

Through their letters and my father's book, I finally learned to read. Through the poems and letters I wrote to them, I learned to write.

The horror of this place where I am locked away is indescribable. At night I cover my ears so I won't hear the weeping, begging, and screaming of the voices that echo off the concrete walls. By day I watch the faces of men who have no hope, no love, and no purpose.

But I am not one of them.

I have loved and been loved, thoroughly and deeply by good and decent people who believed in me. Who let me dare to believe in myself.

Despite everything that has happened, I know that I have good inside of me, just like my father had good inside of him.

Parole is still a long way off, but I've been told that Governor Banks can grant me a pardon if he chooses. I think if he really knew what happened, he might. I believe he is a fair man. He offered me mercy once, on a hot Texas summer night, and I wonder if he might search his heart and offer me mercy once again.

The DA never mentioned me pulling a gun on the governor. It wasn't among the charges. Meanwhile, I'm writing my story. But I'm also plotting my escape from this prison cell.

This is my plan.
I will do it with words.
I will write them by day.
I will write them by night.
I will write them on the walls,
the stalls, the halls.
I will write them in big bold ink
on posters I hang on the concrete blocks.
I will write them on little pieces of paper
I stuff into the mattress and the pillow.
I will write them with fingers
bent and cramped from use.
I will write them in blood
if I have to,
but only my own.
And I will keep writing them,
again, and again, and again,
until I fill this prison cell so full of words,
that the bars bend and buckle and burst,
because they cannot contain them.
And then
    I will
        be free.

Acknowledgments

No book could ever be completed without the help, support, and guidance of friends, family members, and experts willing to share their time, experience, and wisdom. I am deeply grateful to the following people:

Those professionals in the legal system and in juvenile justice who shared their experiences and insights—Anthony Galindre, Pete Hackett, Judge Wyatt Heard, and especially Jim Willett, former warden of the Walls Unit, who went out of his way to send me photos of the prison, answer innumerable e-mails regarding a hundred different details, and even gave me a personal tour of the prison museum upon my visit to Huntsville. He has written a wonderful book called *Warden*, telling about his experiences with death row inmates. Some of his vignettes and insights have worked their way into the pages of this book.

Juan Melendez for sharing his harrowing experience of spending seventeen years on death row before being exonerated.

All the other people who graciously provided me with information for my research, including Tom Houts, Michelle Lyons, Christopher Jochens, Jacob Lee Stuyvesant, J.J. Jaeger, and John Marsello.

My agent, Sara Crowe, and my editor, Anica Rissi, whose gentle guidance through the rewriting process helped bring my vision into focus.

Friends and family members willing to read early versions of the manuscript—Kimberley Griffiths Little, Lois Ruby, Pat Marsello, Tom Dean, and Kristen Dean.

Jimmy Santiago Baca for his amazing poetry, his willingness to share how he discovered his great passion for words, and for his continual work with youth at risk.

And finally, to William Butler Yeats, for the poems that continue to inspire us all.

About the Author

CAROLEE DEAN lives in Albuquerque, New Mexico, with her husband, children, and a boxer named Maya. She enjoys long road trips through the desert where she can let her imagination wander and think up stories like this one. She also loves her work as a speech-language pathologist and the fact that it allows her to spend almost every day in high school. Find out more at caroleedean.com.